Paule Marshall grew up in Brooklyn during the Depression and graduated from Brooklyn College in 1953. She is the author of three novels, *Brown Girl, Brownstones* (originally published in 1959 and reissued by The Feminist Press in 1981), *The Chosen Place, The Timeless People* (1969), and *Praisesong for the Widow* (1983), as well as a book of novellas, *Soul Clap Hands and Sing* (1961). She has taught creative writing at Yale, Columbia, the University of Massachusetts/Boston, and the Iowa Writers' Workshop. Paule Marshall has a son and lives in New York City.

"Marshall's characters all ring true with incredible clarity as passionate, deep human beings." — Rita Mae Brown

"When Marshall writes about those she truly loves, she cannot be resisted. She brings (to her characters) an instinctive understanding, a generosity, and a free humor that combine to form a style remarkable for its courage, its color, and its natural control." — The New Yorker

"In short, Paule Marshall can write. . . . By the sheer inventiveness of her detail, she calls our attention away from the message in the background and returns it to the characters on her page." — The New York Times

Reena

and Other Stories

PAULE MARSHALL

Including the Novella "Merle"

and Commentary by the Author

THE FEMINIST
PRESS
Old Westbury
New York

© 1983 by The Feminist Press
All rights reserved. Published 1983
Printed in the United States of America
88 87 86 85 84   6 5 4 3 2

Library of Congress Cataloging in Publication Data
Marshall, Paule, 1929–
    Reena and other stories.
    "Including the novella "Merle" and commentary by
the author."
    Bibliography: p.
    I. Title.
PS3563.A7223A6   1983   813'.54   83-16592
ISBN 0-935312-24-2
This publication is made possible, in part, by public funds
from the New York State Council on the Arts.

Cover design by Lea Smith.
Cover photo credit: Frank Valenti. Models: Denyse Brabham Wyatt
and Maureen Brown. Art created by Schaub Laboratory, Inc.
Text design by Lea Smith.
Typeset by Precision Typographers Inc.
Manufactured by R.R. Donnelley & Sons Co., Crawfordsville, Ind.

A Note from the Publisher

As the publisher of the new edition of Paule Marshall's classic novel, *Brown Girl, Brownstones,* we are pleased to make available again the early short fiction which illustrates the growth of a remarkable writer. This is the first time that these stories, long out of print or difficult to obtain, will appear together in a single volume.

In addition, we are delighted to include Marshall's much acclaimed autobiographical essay, "From the Poets in the Kitchen," which was published in *The New York Times Book Review's* series called "The Making of a Writer." The autobiographical headnotes to each story were written exclusively for this volume.

Perhaps a special word should be said about "Merle," the final long piece in the collection, since connoisseurs of Marshall's work will search their memories in vain for this title. Both something old and something new, "Merle" is a novella excerpted from her 1969 novel, *The Chosen Place, The Timeless People,* and extensively reshaped and rewritten. It stands as an independent story about one of the most memorable women in contemporary fiction.

In memory of my aunt
Branford Catherine Watson
("Bam–Bam")

a West Indian market woman who thought nothing
of walking 14 miles to town and back in a day

CONTENTS

FROM THE POETS
IN THE KITCHEN

1983

Some years ago, when I was teaching a graduate seminar in fiction at Columbia University, a well known male novelist visited my class to speak on his development as a writer. In discussing his formative years, he didn't realize it but he seriously endangered his life by remarking that women writers are luckier than those of his sex because they usually spend so much time as children around their mothers and their mothers' friends in the kitchen.

What did he say that for? The women students immediately forgot about being in awe of him and began readying their attack for the question and answer period later on. Even I bristled. There again was that awful image of women locked away from the world in the kitchen with only each other to talk to, and their daughters locked in with them.

But my guest wasn't really being sexist or trying to be provocative or even spoiling for a fight. What he meant—when he got around to explaining himself more fully—was that, given the way children are (or were) raised in our society, with little girls kept closer to home and their mothers, the woman writer stands a better chance of being exposed, while growing up, to the kind of talk that goes on among women, more often than not in the kitchen; and that this experience gives her an edge over her male counterpart by instilling in her an appreciation for ordinary speech.

It was clear that my guest lecturer attached great importance to this, which is understandable. Common speech and the plain, workaday words that make it up are, after all, the stock in trade of some of the best fiction writers. They are the principal means by which characters in a novel or story reveal themselves and give voice sometimes to profound feelings and complex ideas about themselves and the world. Perhaps the proper measure of a writer's talent is skill in rendering everyday speech—when it is appropriate to the story—as well as the ability to tap, to exploit, the beauty, poetry and wisdom it often contains.

"If you say what's on your mind in the language that comes to you from your parents and your street and friends you'll probably say something beautiful." Grace Paley tells this, she says, to her students at the beginning of every writing course.

It's all a matter of exposure and a training of the ear for the would-be writer in those early years of apprenticeship. And, according to my guest lecturer, this training, the best of it, often takes place in as unglamorous a setting as the kitchen.

He didn't know it, but he was essentially describing my experience as a little girl. I grew up among poets. Now they didn't look like poets—whatever that breed is supposed to look like. Nothing about them suggested that poetry was their calling. They were just a group of ordinary housewives and mothers, my mother included, who dressed in a way (shapeless housedresses, dowdy felt hats and long, dark, solemn coats) that made it impossible for me to imagine they had ever been young.

Nor did they do what poets were supposed to do—spend their days in an attic room writing verses. They never put pen to paper except to write occasionally to their relatives in Barbados. "I take my pen in hand hoping these few lines will find you in health as they leave me fair for the time being," was the way their letters invariably began. Rather, their day was spent "scrubbing floor," as they described the work they did.

Several mornings a week these unknown bards would put an apron and a pair of old house shoes in a shopping bag and take the train or streetcar from our section of Brooklyn out to Flatbush. There, those who didn't have steady jobs would wait on certain designated corners for the white housewives in the neighborhood to come along and bargain with them over pay for a day's work cleaning their houses. This was the ritual even in the winter.

Later, armed with the few dollars they had earned, which in their vocabulary became "a few raw-mouth pennies," they made their way back to our neighborhood, where they would sometimes stop off to have a cup of tea or cocoa together before going home to cook dinner for their husbands and children.

The basement kitchen of the brownstone house where my family lived was the usual gathering place. Once inside the warm safety of its walls the women threw off the drab coats and hats, seated themselves at the large center table, drank their cups of tea or cocoa, and talked. While my sister and I sat at a smaller table over in a corner doing our homework, they talked—endlessly, passionately, poetically, and with impressive range. No subject was beyond them. True, they would indulge in the usual gossip: whose husband was running with whom, whose daughter looked slightly "in the way" (pregnant) under her bridal gown as she walked down the aisle. That sort of thing. But they also tackled the great issues of the time. They were always, for example, discussing the state of the economy. It was the mid and late 30's then, and the aftershock of the Depression, with its soup lines and suicides on Wall Street, was still being felt.

Some people, they declared, didn't know how to deal with adversity. They didn't know that you had to "tie up your belly" (hold in the pain, that is) when things got rough and go on with life. They took their image from the bellyband that is tied around the stomach of a newborn baby to keep the navel pressed in.

They talked politics. Roosevelt was their hero. He had come along and rescued the country with relief and jobs, and in gratitude they christened their sons Franklin and Delano and hoped they would live up to the names.

If F.D.R. was their hero, Marcus Garvey was their God. The name of the fiery, Jamaican-born black nationalist of the 20's was constantly invoked around the table. For he had been their leader when they first came to the United States from the West Indies shortly after World War I. They had contributed to his organization, the United Negro Improvement Association (UNIA), out of their meager salaries, bought shares in his ill-fated Black Star Shipping Line, and at the height of the movement they had marched as members of his "nurses' brigade" in their white uniforms up Seventh Avenue in Harlem during the great Garvey Day parades. Garvey: He lived on through the power of their memories.

And their talk was of war and rumors of wars. They raged against World War II when it broke out in Europe, blaming it on the politicians. "It's these politicians. They're the ones always starting up all this lot of war. But what they care? It's the poor people got to suffer and mothers with their sons." If it was *their* sons, they swore they would keep them out of the

Army by giving them soap to eat each day to make their hearts
sound defective. Hitler? He was for them "the devil incarnate."
Then there was home. They reminisced often and at length
about home. The old country. Barbados—or Bimshire, as they
affectionately called it. The little Caribbean island in the sun
they loved but had to leave. "Poor—poor but sweet" was the
way they remembered it.

And naturally they discussed their adopted home. America
came in for both good and bad marks. They lashed out at it for
the racism they encountered. They took to task some of the
people they worked for, especially those who gave them only a
hard-boiled egg and a few spoonfuls of cottage cheese for lunch.
"As if anybody can scrub floor on an egg and some cheese that
don't have no taste to it!"

Yet although they caught H in "this man country," as they
called America, it was nonetheless a place where "you could at
least see your way to make a dollar." That much they acknowl-
edged. They might even one day accumulate enough dollars,
with both them and their husbands working, to buy the brownstone houses which, like my family, they were only leasing at
that period. This was their consuming ambition: to "buy house"
and to see the children through.

There was no way for me to understand it at the time, but
the talk that filled the kitchen those afternoons was highly functional. It served as therapy, the cheapest kind available to my
mother and her friends. Not only did it help them recover from
the long wait on the corner that morning and the bargaining
over their labor, it restored them to a sense of themselves and
reaffirmed their self-worth. Through language they were able to
overcome the humiliations of the work-day.

But more than therapy, that freewheeling, wide-ranging, ex-
uberant talk functioned as an outlet for the tremendous creative
energy they possessed. They were women in whom the need
for self-expression was strong, and since language was the only
vehicle readily available to them they made of it an art form
that—in keeping with the African tradition in which art and life
are one—was an integral part of their lives.

And their talk was a refuge. They never really ceased being

baffled and overwhelmed by America—its vastness, complexity and power. Its strange customs and laws. At a level beyond words they remained fearful and in awe. Their uneasiness and fear were even reflected in their attitude toward the children they had given birth to in this country. They referred to those like myself, the little Brooklyn-born Bajans (Barbadians), as "these New York children" and complained that they couldn't discipline us properly because of the laws here. "You can't beat these children as you would like, you know, because the authorities in this place will dash you in jail for them. After all, these is New York children." Not only were we different, American, we had, as they saw it, escaped their ultimate authority.

Confronted therefore by a world they could not encompass, which even limited their rights as parents, and at the same time finding themselves permanently separated from the world they had known, they took refuge in language. "Language is the only homeland," Czeslaw Milosz, the emigré Polish writer and Nobel Laureate, has said. This is what it became for the women at the kitchen table.

It served another purpose also, I suspect. My mother and her friends were after all the female counterpart of Ralph Ellison's invisible man. Indeed, you might say they suffered a triple invisibility, being black, female and foreigners. They really didn't count in American society except as a source of cheap labor. But given the kind of women they were, they couldn't tolerate the fact of their invisibility, their powerlessness. And they fought back, using the only weapon at their command: the spoken word.

Those late afternoon conversations on a wide range of topics were a way for them to feel they exercised some measure of control over their lives and the events that shaped them. "Soully-gal, talk yuh talk!" they were always exhorting each other. "In this man world you got to take yuh mouth and make a gun!" They were in control, if only verbally and if only for the two hours or so that they remained in our house.

For me, sitting over in the corner, being seen but not heard, which was the rule for children in those days, it wasn't only what the women talked about—the content—but the way they put things—their style. The insight, irony, wit and humor they brought to their stories and discussions and their poet's inventiveness and daring with language—which of course I could only sense but not define back then.

They had taken the standard English taught them in the primary schools of Barbados and transformed it into an idiom, an instrument that more adequately described them—changing around the syntax and imposing their own rhythm and accent so that the sentences were more pleasing to their ears. They added the few African sounds and words that had survived, such as the derisive suck-teeth sound and the word "yam," meaning to eat. And to make it more vivid, more in keeping with their expressive quality, they brought to bear a raft of metaphors, parables, Biblical quotations, sayings and the like:

"The sea ain' got no back door," they would say, meaning that it wasn't like a house where if there was a fire you could run out the back. Meaning that it was not to be trifled with. And meaning perhaps in a larger sense that man should treat all of nature with caution and respect.

"I has read hell by heart and called every generation blessed!" They sometimes went in for hyperbole.

A woman expecting a baby was never said to be pregnant. They never used that word. Rather, she was "in the way" or, better yet, "tumbling big." "Guess who I butt up on in the market the other day tumbling big again!"

And a woman with a reputation of being too free with her sexual favors was known in their book as a "thoroughfare"— the sense of men like a steady stream of cars moving up and down the road of her life. Or she might be dubbed "a free-bee," which was my favorite of the two. I liked the image it conjured up of a woman scandalous perhaps but independent, who flitted from one flower to another in a garden of male beauties, sampling their nectar, taking her pleasure at will, the roles reversed.

And nothing, no matter how beautiful, was ever described as simply beautiful. It was always "beautiful-ugly": the beautiful-ugly dress, the beautiful-ugly house, the beautiful-ugly car. Why the word "ugly," I used to wonder, when the thing they were referring to was beautiful, and they knew it. Why the antonym, the contradiction, the linking of opposites? It used to puzzle me greatly as a child.

There is the theory in linguistics which states that the idiom of a people, the way they use language, reflects not only the most fundamental views they hold of themselves and the world but their very conception of reality. Perhaps in using the term "beautiful-ugly" to describe nearly everything, my mother and her friends were expressing what they believed to be a fundamental dualism in life: the idea that a thing is at the same time its opposite, and that these opposites, these contradictions make up the whole. But theirs was not a Manichaean brand of dualism that sees matter, flesh, the body, as inherently evil, because they constantly addressed each other as "soully-gal"—soul: spirit; gal: the body, flesh, the visible self. And it was clear from their tone that they gave one as much weight and importance as the other. They had never heard of the mind/body split.

As for God, they summed up His essential attitude in a phrase. "God," they would say, "don' love ugly and He ain' stuck on pretty."

Using everyday speech, the simple commonplace words—but always with imagination and skill—they gave voice to the most complex ideas. Flannery O'Connor would have approved of how they made ordinary language work, as she put it, "double-time," stretching, shading, deepening its meaning. Like Joseph Conrad they were always trying to infuse new life in the "old old words worn thin . . . by . . careless usage." And the goals of their oral art were the same as his: "to make you hear, to make you feel . . . to make you *see*." This was their guiding esthetic.

By the time I was 8 or 9, I graduated from the corner of the kitchen to the neighborhood library, and thus from the spoken to the written word. The Macon Street Branch of the Brooklyn Public Library was an imposing half block long edifice of heavy gray masonry, with glass-paneled doors at the front and two tall metal torches symbolizing the light that comes of learning flanking the wide steps outside.

The inside was just as impressive. More steps—of pale marble with gleaming brass railings at the center and sides—led up to the circulation desk, and a great pendulum clock gazed down from the balcony stacks that faced the entrance. Usually stationed at the top of the steps like the guards outside Buckingham

Palace was the custodian, a stern-faced West Indian type who
for years, until I was old enough to obtain an adult card, would
immediately shoo me with one hand into the Children's Room
and with the other threaten me into silence, a finger to his lips.
You would have thought he was the chief librarian and not just
someone whose job it was to keep the brass polished and the
clock wound. I put him in a story called "Barbados" years later
and had terrible things happen to him at the end.

I sheltered from the storm of adolescence in the Macon Street
library, reading voraciously, indiscriminately, everything from
Jane Austen to Zane Grey, but with a special passion for the
long, full-blown, richly detailed 18th- and 19th-century pica-
resque tales: "Tom Jones," "Great Expectations," "Vanity
Fair."

But although I loved nearly everything I read and would enter
fully into the lives of the characters—indeed, would cease being
myself and become them—I sensed a lack after a time. Something I couldn't quite define was missing. And then one day,
browsing in the poetry section, I came across a book by someone
called Paul Laurence Dunbar, and opening it I found the photograph of a wistful, sad-eyed poet who to my surprise was
black. I turned to a poem at random. "Little brown-baby wif
spa'klin' / eyes / Come to yo' pappy an' set on his knee."
Although I had a little difficulty at first with the words in dialect,
the poem spoke to me as nothing I had read before of the
closeness, the special relationship I had had with my father, who
by then had become an ardent believer in Father Divine and
gone to live in Father's "kingdom" in Harlem. Reading it helped
to ease somewhat the tight knot of sorrow and longing I carried
around in my chest that refused to go away. I read another
poem. "'Lias! 'Lias! Bless de Lawd! / Don' you know de day's
/ erbroad? / Ef you don' get up, you scamp / Dey'll be trouble
in dis camp." I laughed. It reminded me of the way my mother
sometimes yelled at my sister and me to get out of bed in the
mornings.

And another: "Seen my lady home las' night / Jump back,
honey, jump back. / Hel' huh han' an' sque'z it tight . . ."
About love between a black man and a black woman. I had

never seen that written about before and it roused in me all kinds of delicious feelings and hopes.

And I began to search then for books and stories and poems about "The Race" (as it was put back then), about my people. While not abandoning Thackeray, Fielding, Dickens and the others, I started asking the reference librarian, who was white, for books by Negro writers, although I must admit I did so at first with a feeling of shame—the shame I and many others used to experience in those days whenever the word "Negro" or "colored" came up.

No grade school literature teacher of mine had ever mentioned Dunbar or James Weldon Johnson or Langston Hughes. I didn't know that Zora Neale Hurston existed and was busy writing and being published during those years. Nor was I made aware of people like Frederick Douglass and Harriet Tubman—their spirit and example—or the great 19th-century abolitionist and feminist Sojourner Truth. There wasn't even Negro History Week when I attended P.S. 35 on Decatur Street!

What I needed, what all the kids—West Indian and native black American alike—with whom I grew up needed, was an equivalent of the Jewish shul, someplace where we could go after school—the schools that were shortchanging us—and read works by those like ourselves and learn about our history.

It was around that time also that I began harboring the dangerous thought of someday trying to write myself. Perhaps a poem about an apple tree, although I had never seen one. Or the story of a girl who could magically transplant herself to wherever she wanted to be in the world—such as Father Divine's kingdom in Harlem. Dunbar—his dark, eloquent face, his large volume of poems—permitted me to dream that I might someday write, and with something of the power with words my mother and her friends possessed.

When people at readings and writers' conferences ask me who my major influences were, they are sometimes a little disappointed when I don't immediately name the usual literary giants. True, I am indebted to those writers, white and black, whom I read during my formative years and still read for instruction and pleasure. But they were preceded in my life by another set of giants whom I always acknowledge before all others: the group of women around the table long ago. They taught me my first lessons in the narrative art. They trained my ear. They set a standard of excellence. This is why the best of my work must be attributed to them; it stands as testimony to the rich legacy of language and culture they so freely passed on to me in the wordshop of the kitchen.

THE VALLEY BETWEEN

1954

.... my very first published story, written when I could barely crawl, never mind stand up and walk as a writer. I was a mere babe in terms of craft and technique. Yet the need to write "Valley" was strong, because of what I saw happening to my life and the lives of other young women at the time. I had to get my feelings about our situation down on paper, in whatever fashion.

That the characters in the story are white was deliberate. To explain—I did the first two years of my undergraduate work at an all women's, predominantly Jewish, free city college in New York; and practically every day squeals of joy were to be heard in one or another of my classes: somebody else had just gotten engaged. There on a third finger, left hand, would be this outsized diamond, gotten wholesale usually through a relative or family friend who worked or had connections in the diamond center. "I can get it for you wholesale."

Part of me used to envy my classmate her good fortune. No man I married would ever be able to give me a whopper like that. At the same time, those rings always made me feel sad for the bride to be. As bright as most of these young women were, they were doomed to become housewives in Brooklyn or Queens—college having been merely the means to raise their stock in the marriage market. "The Valley Between" was written in part to express my dismay at their future. Cassie, the central character in the story, is the stifled, unfulfilled woman some of them surely became. Her efforts to return to school in the face of her husband's opposition, her desire to realize herself apart from her role as mother and wife anticipated themes that are current in women's literature today. It's been called a '50's story twenty years ahead of its time.

That the characters are white also served to camouflage my own predicament because by the time I wrote "Valley" I was married also—an early, unwise first marriage. I wasn't brave enough back then to deal directly with my unhappiness, or perhaps instinct told me that as a fiction writer I should try to transform the raw stuff of personal experience into art. What-

15

ever, Cassie who couldn't possibly be me with her gray eyes and fair hair was a convenient device behind which to mask my pain.

"Valley." It's a flawed first effort, something from the early days of my apprenticeship. Perhaps I shouldn't include it here. But let it stand.

Cassie tasted the milk, lowered the gas under the pot, and continued to stir slowly. Her short, rather slim body was bent slightly forward at the waist, her eyes focused on nothing. It was pleasurable not to have to think—at least not yet—to be aware only of the warm, sustaining feeling of the brightly lighted kitchen and of the fine rain which blurred the window over the sink. Ellen's voice sounded small and faraway as she began her usual morning sing song:

"Mommy—milk. Mommy—milk."

Cassie poured the warm milk into the chipped pink and white cup marked "Baby." She fingered the relief figures of the dancing boy and girl on its side; the touch brought the image clearly to her mind: she saw their round dimpled faces and the innocent, unwavering smile on their lips, and her first thought was that she had not smiled—really smiled for a long time. On her way to the nursery she took Ellen's juice from the refrigerator and laid Abe's stewed prunes on the table and plugged in the percolator, glancing nervously at the clock.

In the half-light of the nursery, Ellen was sitting in her crib, busily beating on the toy drum which Abe had brought home for her last night and which already had a rent in the skin of the upper part. Ellen had managed to put on her shirt and shorts. Cassie smiled to herself with pride at Ellen's smooth, firm legs and the cherubic curve of her small child's arms.

"Okay, Ellen, time to drink your juice and milk."

Cassie moved her slim fingers over her daughter's soft, brown hair, pushing it back from the forehead, smoothing it gently over her head, letting her fingers linger on the delicately formed neck. Ellen moved blissfully under the caress, her eyes wide and grey-blue over the rim of the cup. Cassie wondered if Ellen would ever remember these mornings when they stood so close in their silent caress. It was unfair that none of the peaceful moments of childhood ever returned to comfort and to make you forget. . . .

"Mommy, what you gonna learn in school today?"

Cassie laughed.

"I'll tell you all about it when I come home. And then you can show me how well you learned your A B C's, all right?"

"I'd much rather go out and play."

"Not today, Ellie, it's raining outside, and you've got a little cold already. Promise me you won't nag Grandma about going out. Just sit in the chair and learn your lesson and play with your dolls."

The sound of the coffee whistle broke across Cassie's voice, startling her.

"Oh, there goes Daddy's coffee—go make him get up. His coffee's boiling."

Cassie went back into the kitchen and pulled out the plug. With quick, jerky movements she hastily placed bread and butter on the table and set two eggs to boil. As she passed through the tastefully furnished living room, she picked up one of Ellen's stray dolls. Almost timidly, she opened the bedroom door; Abe was sitting on the edge of the bed, his feet thrust into a pair of large, loose slippers, sleepily scratching his tousled head and pulling off his rumpled pyjamas.

"Oh, you're up—" Cassie said hesitantly.

"Yeah, that whistle did it. What time?"

"Just seven."

"God, that early? . . .What you doing up so soon?"

Cassie fidgeted with the doll, trying unconsciously to fix its broken head back into the socket of the neck.

"I've got an early class this morning."

Abe didn't bother answering and Cassie began to put away the night-clothes scattered on the chairs. She watched Abe furtively, fearful that if their eyes met they would have to say something decisive and final to each other. She noted vaguely as he moved toward the bathroom in his slow, heavy manner that he was beginning to put on weight.

The water soon ran hoarsely in the basin, then the buzz of the electric razor.

"Is Ellen up?"

She discerned his form, dark and shapeless behind the shut glass door of the bathroom.

"Yes, she's already had her milk. You know she's already mutilated the new drum. Just been having a jam session with herself this morning. Where does she get the energy from?. . ." Cassie stopped, her voice tapering into silence as the shower rasped on, for she knew he couldn't hear her—knew that he hadn't even been listening after the second word.

She went to the kitchen and sat down while Abe said good-morning to Ellen. She noticed now how dreary the day really was and that the white of the kitchen, which had seemed so bright and warm awhile ago, was just a worn, faded yellow. Ellen's shrieks of laughter filled the small apartment, and Cassie smiled—how effortlessly those two loved each other. . . .

Abe came into the kitchen, holding up the tattered drum and laughing.

"That kid is a terror."

He flung it on the table, noticing then that there was only one place set.

"Say, aren't you eating?"

"I've eaten already. I told you, Wednesday's my early day."

"What do you do with yourself if you get there late?" Abe asked, his face turned away from her.

"Oh," she almost laughed with relief, "stand outside the locked door a few minutes and utter a few curses. Then maybe I'll go to the library and read."

"It beats me to figure out why you're killing yourself." Abe sighed heavily, his eyes still averted, "Getting up at all ungodly hours of the morning, running around in all kinds of weather. What for? If we didn't have Ellen, okay, but this nonsense. . . . Look, in the town I come from, a girl gets married and she settles down to take care of her house and kids; she's satisfied with that. Sure, she's got her bridge parties and all that. But not you. What's your rush? Afraid you'll die without having your degrees!"

"I'm not killing myself," Cassie said evenly, trying to keep

the anger and scorn from her voice. "There's nothing wrong
with my finishing school even if I do have Ellen. Your ideas are
a century behind the times. If I could only explain. . . . I have
only two more years; I want to finish them. It's something I
have to do that's important to me. Mother doesn't mind keeping
Ellen. You're the only one that's making a problem out of it."

"But why aren't you satisfied? You got everything. What's
the point of knocking yourself out, leaving Ellen, and trotting
off to school like you were a kid, too. I didn't marry no school
girl. . . ."

"You couldn't understand if I told you," Cassie flung at him
contemptuously. "What's the use. And it's vicious of you to
even imply that I neglect Ellen."

"Well, then what about me? Okay, so you take care of Ellen.
But what about me? Am I supposed to moon around here by
myself evenings while you bury yourself in books? I gotta take
Ellen to the park on Saturdays and the museums so you can
have quiet—to study. You always got your nose buried in a
book even when you're eating. God, you're a woman of twenty-
four. Aren't you tired of school? Didn't you give up all that
when we got married? What am I supposed to do—sit home
and hold hands with myself?"

Abe stabbed viciously at the prunes, splattering the dark, heavy
syrup on the white plastic tablecloth.

"Please stop yelling! Oh, Abe can't you see that two years is
such a little bit of time." And her voice was low and wistful.
"I thought this would have been such a good idea. Both of us
would have had something new in our lives. But it's so different
now that I'm scared. I'm afraid it's not just my going to school
but something much bigger, we're so far apart. . . ."

She couldn't tell him that the past few months had been like
a slow dying for her—for both of them, perhaps; that there was
a wide, untraceable valley between them and that they were the
two proud mountains, unwilling to even look at each other,
incapable of coming together. No, she couldn't tell him this.

"No more, let's not bother talking about it any more." She
felt beaten and worn; her voice was empty and bitter. "Tonight
when we're both calmer, maybe." And she began to walk un-
steadily toward the nursery. Abe yelled after her, "Well, make

up your mind once and for all. I've taken my fill of it." The kitchen door closed on his voice.

"Is Daddy shouting again?"

"It's nothing, Ellen. Come, let me put on your dress and shoes." She turned her face away and swiftly finished dressing her, finding comfort in the soft, warm body as if this were the only friendly thing left in the world. Ellen ran before her into the hall and began climbing the stairs, leaning over to kiss Cassie, and then ran up. Cassie watched until she disappeared into her mother's apartment. Then she hastily pulled on a short coat over her slacks and white turtle-neck sweater. A beret covered her short dark curls and her eyes were very grey and tired as they met in the mirror.

Outside, the day had fully broken, sullen and grey. The delicately hued autumn leaves capered in the wind and the light rain, and clung damply to the sidewalks and porches. The wind moaned softly over the low roofs and Cassie thought of the many times she had walked past these same small, comfortable houses—of how her lifetime was being spent in one compressed, limited place. She took off her beret and let the short, damp gusts blow through her hair.

As she passed Mrs. Lewitt's house, she noticed that the grass was still bright and summer-like; its color greener and sharper because of the beads of moisture shining on the slim, green stalks, clear and jewel-like. She remembered how, on rainy days, she would take this same path to the library—just a girl in a worn rain coat and rubbers which were always too big for her. The library had been her sanctuary, not only against the rainy world, but against all that was incomprehensible and ugly in life. Each day she had found a new world before her. And along with the joy of reading had come, with the years, the desire to learn—to have all the muddled ideas made clear, defined in words and images, and thus made a part of her. It was a never-ending search, giving sustained pleasure, making her life, for that moment at least, meaningful.

Abe, too, in those days which seemed so long ago and dead, had given meaning to her life. She saw him again in his tight sailor suit, slim and graceful, his hair like an Apollo's against the

white cap. He was always ,talking in his queer mid-western
twang, and he used to hold her hand as if it were fragile china.
Somehow, books weren't important then. . . . How happy and
carefree they had been in those early days! And Ellen was their
love merged into something tangible and alive, their idea defined
in flesh.

And when had it started again—at what point had she begun
to feel depressed, aware that something basic to herself was
missing? Aware (and the thought for the first time crystallized
within her) that the girl in the worn rain coat and the oversized
boots was dying, without having been realized and somehow
fulfilled. It was then that she had begun to feel bored, realizing
that her life was routined, secured and warm. Yes, warm, that
was the word. It was the suffocating warmth of the afternoons
in the park, having to listen to the unceasing gossip of the other
mothers. It was the ritual of seven o'clock dinners and having
the same people over to play cards. In desperation, she had
suggested that she would like to return to school, and Abe's
laughter had resounded through the house, hurting her more
than all his present open defiance, making her realize that this
was no longer the laughing sailor. There was a blind spot within
him, with which she couldn't reason. . . .

Cassie walked like a somnambulist toward the bus stop. The
thoughts which she had tried to shut out in the early morning
surged around her like mad Furies, making her oblivious to the
bustling early morning crowd on the bus. Automatically, she
got off at the college and began walking slowly across the campus. The chimes of the library bell broke through her thoughts,
heralding the entrance to her ever-changing world of ideas—a
world whose academic purity had no place for Abe's harsh words
or her own angry answers. And with profound relief she joined
the other jostling students.

"CASSIE, Cassie!"
"Yes, mother. I didn't mean to stay so late. Send Ellen down."
Cassie flung her coat on the hook. "Has she been a . . ."
Her mother opened the upstairs door, her small, bent figure
blocking out the light behind her.

"Cassie, why are you so late? I tried to get in touch with you. Now don't get excited, but Ellen sneaked out . . . in all that rain without a coat. . . ."

Cassie didn't hear much more, and with some part of her which was still rational and aware she whispered, "I stopped, had coffee with some of the girls. . . ." Then, as if she suddenly realized what her mother was saying, she asked, "Ellen, where's Ellen?"

Her mother's voice trailed after her as she ran to the darkened nursery. Ellen's eyes were slightly open; her cheeks were very warm to Cassie's touch.

"I called the doctor right away," her mother continued. "He left some pills for the fever. She'll be all right in a few days."

Cassie said quietly, her hands still on Ellen's face, "I should have been here."

"Now, Cassie, it's not my fault. She could have done the same thing if you had been home with her."

"No, mother, I don't mean that. It's just that now he's won because he'll say it's my fault. He's won . . ." she murmured.

Her mother moved her worn hand over Cassie's hair.

"Stay here and rest. She's sleeping now. I'll cook dinner for you upstairs."

Cassie heard the soft, whispery steps of her mother as she climbed the stairs and the quiet slam of the upstairs door. The sounds came to her as from a great distance—a distance that could not be measured in time or space. The only thing that occupied space was the huddled figure of her child, breathing heavily; time was the fragile second between each breath. Cassie bent over, pulling up the covers around her neck. If she had only come straight home instead of going with them to the restaurant! But it had been so good to talk to someone without being tense. Her head sank on the bar of the crib.

She glanced at the clock, noticing that it was seven just as Abe's key sounded in the lock. She remained there motionless, her lips moving silently.

"Don't let him shout, please, don't let him shout!"

When he came into the kitchen, she was standing in front of Ellen's door, holding the knob behind her.

"What's wrong with you? Where's Ellen? She's sleeping so
early?"

"Well, Abe," Cassie started, her voice pleading and tense, her
fingers tightening around the knob, "don't get excited but Ellen
went out today in the rain and caught a slight cold—nothing
serious—just a little temperature. The doctor came and said she'll
be all right in a few days. Anyway," she said with a short,
nervous laugh, "the rest will do her good."

Abe had whirled around, his eyes staring at her in disbelief as
she spoke. He pushed her roughly out of the way, but she clung
to his sleeve determinedly.

"Don't go in and wake her. It's not that serious. And I won't
let you wake her. I'm going to stay home a few days and take
care of her."

"You're damn right you'll stay home and take care of her.
Either that or you can leave us alone altogether and go live in
your precious school and get lost among your thick books, for
all I care!"

Abe sank down in the chair, flinging his head back against the
wall, his eyes wild and unseeing.

"Christ, what next?" he moaned.

"I'm sorry. I knew you would take it this way. You can't
even see that this isn't my fault. . . ."

"It wouldn't have happened if the kid had been where she
belonged." Abe's anger silenced her. "Your mother's too old
to take care of a young, mischievous kid. She tries her best
because she doesn't want to refuse you. It's unfair for you to
impose upon her—but then you're selfish, anyway. I never knew
when I married you that you could be so self-centered. Nobody
matters but Cassie."

Cassie sat quietly opposite him; her voice, strangely, was strong
and steady as if his words had had no effect on her.

"Yes, I'm selfish and self-centered, just as you are bull-headed
and blind. It's not so much school or even Ellen—it's just us—
two people who should never have met each other. You would
have been much better off with some girl from your home town.
And I—well, that doesn't matter—I should have just finished up
one phase of my life before starting another. I wasn't ready for

the kind of life you have to offer me, and I couldn't give you very much."

Abe averted his eyes, his face wary and guarded.

"Just make up your mind, that's all. I'm through arguing. This," he said, waving in the direction of the nursery, "decides it." Then, shaking his head dully, "I don't know what's gotten into you, you were so different before. . . ."

"And so were you different," she flung at him, a new, hard anger welling up within. "We were both different strangers putting on our best fronts for each other, and we're still strangers now in a worse way, though."

An uneasy stillness fell between them. Abe's eyes still stared at the dark rainy night beyond the window behind Cassie; her gaze bent unwaveringly on him. The minutes fled by. She heard the sounds of the house as the water flowed down a pipe and her mother's footsteps on the floor above. Only when she heard Ellen's slight cough did she speak.

"There's nothing for me to decide. You've done that for me. I'm in the corner now. You'll have your way." Her voice was barely audible, for she was no longer speaking to him. "It's strange, the strong always win somehow. All the cards fall their way—they're the victors even though they're wrong. . . ."

She rose, moved wearily to the sink.

Abe's voice was hesitant and almost soft for the first time in months.

"I didn't mean to brow-beat you, Cassie. I don't want to hurt my own wife. But this way is the best—maybe we can work out something else later on. I'm not a heel."

Cassie cut across him, without turning around. "Stop trying to say that I hate you—I only pity both of us for having lost so much simply because you want me to be happy on your terms. I haven't got the strength to defy you anymore—you and your male strength! Let's not talk."

"Look," he said eagerly, "it'd be like the old days again, you watch! The three of us together all the time. . . ."

He reached for her hand, holding it tentatively. Cassie turned to look at him with vacant, hopeless eyes. She slipped her hand from his, shaking her head sadly, and said very gently,

"Your supper's ready by now, Abe."

BROOKLYN

1952-1961

Sexual harassment? We didn't even think to use the term back in the early fifties when this story takes place. There were no women's groups on campus to which we could take the problem; no notices on the bulletin boards and in the bathrooms with phone numbers to call for help and advice; no sympathetic ear in administration. There was nowhere to turn, no support system of any kind, as I recall. If propositioned, you either cooperated, and were sometimes rewarded with an "A" whether your work deserved it or not; or you refused and ran the risk of getting a "C" or worse; or you dropped the course.

In my case, I turned down the repeated invitations to visit his place in the country, ignored the look in his eyes and the suggestive play of his white wrinkled hands, and in my rage and disgust called him everything but a child of God under my breath. But I didn't bolt. I stayed on in the course; I needed it to graduate. Besides, "old lecher" that he was—"with a love on every wind," to quote Yeats—he was nonetheless an excellent teacher.

Naturally, my refusing him meant that I had to work twice as hard in order to get at least a "B" in the course. I had to see to it that he couldn't possibly justify giving me anything less.

Afterwards, to rid myself of the anger I had held in check over the months, I sat down and started writing "Brooklyn"—really just taking notes for it, because the story didn't assume its present form until some nine years later when it became part of a collection of novellas called SOUL CLAP HANDS AND SING, *which was published in 1961.*

A summer wind, soaring just before it died, blew the dusk and the first scattered lights of downtown Brooklyn against the shut windows of the classroom, but Professor Max Berman—B.A., 1919, M.A., 1921, New York; Docteur de l'Université, 1930, Paris—alone in the room, did not bother to open the windows to the cooling wind. The heat and airlessness of the room, the perspiration inching its way like an ant around his starched collar were discomforts he enjoyed, they obscured his larger discomfort: the anxiety which chafed his heart and tugged his left eyelid so that he seemed to be winking, roguishly, behind his glasses.

To steady his eye and ease his heart, to fill the time until his students arrived and his first class in years began, he reached for his cigarettes. As always he delayed lighting the cigarette so that his need for it would be greater and, thus, the relief and pleasure it would bring, fuller. For some time he fondled it, his fingers shaping soft, voluptuous gestures, his warped old man's hands looking strangely abandoned on the bare desk and limp as if the bones had been crushed, and so white—except for the tobacco burn on the index and third fingers—it seemed his blood no longer traveled that far.

He lit the cigarette finally and as the smoke swelled his lungs, his eyelid stilled and his lined face lifted, the plume of white hair wafting above his narrow brow; his body—short, blunt, the shoulders slightly bent as if in deference to his sixty-three years—settled back in the chair. Delicately Max Berman crossed his legs and, looking down, examined his shoes for dust. (The shoes were of a very soft, fawn-colored leather and somewhat foppishly pointed at the toe. They had been custom made in France and were his one last indulgence. He wore them in memory of his first wife, a French Jewess from Alsace-Lorraine whom he had met in Paris while lingering over his doctorate and married to avoid returning home. She had been gay, mindless and very excitable—but at night, she had also been capable of a profound stillness as she lay in bed waiting for him to turn to her, and this had always awed and delighted him. She had been a gift—and her death in a car accident had been a judgment on him for never having loved her, for never, indeed, having even allowed her to matter.) Fastidiously Max Berman unbuttoned his jacket and straightened his vest, which had a stain two decades old on the pocket. Through the smoke his veined eyes contemplated other, more pleasurable scenes. With his neatly shod foot swinging and his cigarette at a rakish tilt, he might have been an old *boulevardier* taking the sun and an absinthe before the afternoon's assignation.

A young face, the forehead shiny with earnestness, hung at the half-opened door. "Is this French Lit, fifty-four? Camus and Sartre?"

Max Berman winced at the rawness of the voice and the flat "a" in Sartre and said formally, "This is Modern French Literature, number fifty-four, yes, but there is some question as to whether we will take up Messieurs Camus and Sartre this session. They might prove hot work for a summer evening course. We will probably do Gide and Mauriac, who are considerably more temperate. But come in nonetheless. . . ."

He was the gallant, half rising to bow her to a seat. He knew that she would select the one in the front row directly opposite his desk. At the bell her pen would quiver above her blank notebook, ready to commit his first word—indeed, the clearing of his throat—to paper, and her thin buttocks would begin sidling toward the edge of her chair.

His eyelid twitched with solicitude. He wished that he could have drawn the lids over her fitful eyes and pressed a cool hand to her forehead. She reminded him of what he had been several lifetimes ago: a boy with a pale, plump face and harried eyes, running from the occasional taunts at his yarmulke along the shrill streets of Brownsville in Brooklyn, impeded by the heavy satchel of books which he always carried as proof of his scholarship. He had been proud of his brilliance at school and the Yeshiva, but at the same time he had been secretly troubled by it and resentful, for he could never believe that he had come by it naturally or that it belonged to him alone. Rather, it was like a heavy medal his father had hung around his neck—the chain bruising his flesh—and constantly exhorted him to wear proudly and use well.

The girl gave him an eager and ingratiating smile and he looked away. During his thirty years of teaching, a face similar to hers had crowded his vision whenever he had looked up from a desk. Perhaps it was fitting, he thought, and lighted another cigarette from the first, that she should be present as he tried again at life, unaware that behind his rimless glasses and within his ancient suit, he had been gutted.

He thought of those who had taken the last of his substance and smiled tolerantly. "The boys of summer," he called them, his inquisitors, who had flailed him with a single question: "Are you now or have you ever been a member of the Communist party?" Max Berman had never taken their question seriously— perhaps because he had never taken his membership in the party seriously—and he had refused to answer. What had disturbed him, though, even when the investigation was over, was the feeling that he had really been under investigation for some other offense which did matter and of which he was guilty; that behind their accusations and charges had lurked another which had not been political but personal. For had he been disloyal to the government? His denial was a short, hawking laugh. Simply, he had never ceased being religious. When his father's God had become useless and even a little embarrassing, he had sought others: his work for a time, then the party. But he had been middle-aged when he joined and his faith, which had been so full as a boy, had grown thin. He had come, by then, to distrust all pieties, so that when the purges in Russia during the thirties confirmed his distrust, he had withdrawn into a modest cynicism.

But he had been made to answer for that error. Ten years later his inquisitors had flushed him out from the small community college in upstate New York where he had taught his classes from the same neat pack of notes each semester and had led him bound by subpoena to New York and bandied his name at the hearings until he had been dismissed from his job.

He remembered looking back at the pyres of burning autumn leaves on the campus his last day and feeling that another lifetime had ended—for he had always thought of his life as divided into many small lives, each with its own beginning and end. Like a hired mute, he had been present at each dying and kept the wake and wept professionally as the bier was lowered into the ground. Because of this feeling, he told himself that his final death would be anticlimactic.

After his dismissal he had continued living in the small house he had built near the college, alone except for an occasional visit from a colleague, idle but for some tutoring in French, content with the income he received from the property his parents had left him in Brooklyn—until the visits and tutoring had tapered off and a silence had begun to choke the house, like weeds springing up around a deserted place. He had begun to wonder then if he were still alive. He would wake at night from the recurrent dream of the hearings, where he was being accused of an unstated crime, to listen for his heart, his hand fumbling among the bedclothes to press the place. During the day he would pass repeatedly in front of the mirror with the pretext that he might have forgotten to shave that morning or that something had blown into his eye. Above all, he had begun to think of his inquisitors with affection and to long for the sound of their voices. They, at least, had assured him of being alive.

As if seeking them out, he had returned to Brooklyn and to the house in Brownsville where he had lived as a boy and had boldly applied for a teaching post without mentioning the investigation. He had finally been offered the class which would begin in five minutes. It wasn't much: a six-week course in the summer evening session of a college without a rating, where classes were held in a converted factory building, a college whose campus took in the bargain department stores, the five-and-dime emporiums and neon-spangled movie houses of downtown Brooklyn.

Through the smoke from his cigarette, Max Berman's eyes— a waning blue that never seemed to focus on any one thing— drifted over the students who had gathered meanwhile. Imbuing them with his own disinterest, he believed that even before the class began, most of them were longing for its end and already anticipating the soft drinks at the soda fountain downstairs and the synthetic dramas at the nearby movie.

They made him sad. He would have liked to lead them like a Pied Piper back to the safety of their childhoods—all of them: the loud girl with the formidable calves of an athlete who reminded him, uncomfortably, of his second wife (a party member who was always shouting political heresy from some picket line and who had promptly divorced him upon discovering his irreverence); the two sallow-faced young men leaning out the window as if searching for the wind that had died; the slender young woman with crimped black hair who sat very still and apart from the others, her face turned toward the night sky as if to a friend.

Her loneliness interested him. He sensed its depth and his eye paused. He saw then that she was a Negro, a very pale mulatto with skin the color of clear, polished amber and a thin, mild face. She was somewhat older than the others in the room—a schoolteacher from the South, probably, who came north each summer to take courses toward a graduate degree. He felt a fleeting discomfort and irritation: discomfort at the thought that although he had been sinned against as a Jew he still shared in the sin against her and suffered from the same vague guilt, irritation that she recalled his own humiliations: the large ones, such as the fact that despite his brilliance he had been unable to get into a medical school as a young man because of the quota on Jews (not that he had wanted to be a doctor; that had been his father's wish) and had changed his studies from medicine to French; the small ones which had worn him thin: an eye widening imperceptibly as he gave his name, the savage glance which sought the Jewishness in his nose, his chin, in the set of his shoulders, the jokes snuffed into silence at his appearance. . . .

Tired suddenly, his eyelid pulsing, he turned and stared out the window at the gaudy constellation of neon lights. He longed for a drink, a quiet place and then sleep. And to bear him gently into sleep, to stay the terror which bound his heart then reminding him of those oleographs of Christ with the thorns binding his exposed heart—fat drops of blood from one so bloodless—to usher him into sleep, some pleasantly erotic image: a nude in a boudoir scattered with her frilled garments and warmed by her frivolous laugh, with the sun like a voyeur at the half-closed shutters. But this time instead of the usual Rubens nude with thighs like twin portals and a belly like a huge alabaster bowl into which he poured himself, he chose Gauguin's Aita Parari, her languorous form in the straight back chair, her dark, sloping breasts, her eyes like the sun under shadow.

With the image still on his inner eye, he turned to the Negro girl and appraised her through a blind of cigarette smoke. She was still gazing out at the night sky and something about her fixed stare, her hands stiffly arranged in her lap, the nerve fluttering within the curve of her throat, betrayed a vein of tension within the rock of her calm. It was as if she had fled long ago to a remote region within herself, taking with her all that was most valuable and most vulnerable about herself.

She stirred finally, her slight breasts lifting beneath her flowered summer dress as she breathed deeply—and Max Berman thought again of Gauguin's girl with the dark, sloping breasts. What would this girl with the amber-colored skin be like on a couch in a sunlit room, nude in a straight-back chair? And as the question echoed along each nerve and stilled his breathing, it seemed suddenly that life, which had scorned him for so long, held out her hand again—but still a little beyond his reach. Only the girl, he sensed, could bring him close enough to touch it. She alone was the bridge. So that even while he repeated to himself that he was being presumptuous (for she would surely refuse him) and ridiculous (for even if she did not, what could he do—his performance would be a mere scramble and twitch), he vowed at the same time to have her. The challenge eased the tightness around his heart suddenly; it soothed the damaged muscle of his eye and as the bell rang he rose and said briskly, "Ladies and gentlemen, may I have your attention, please. My name is Max Berman. The course is Modern French Literature, number fifty-four. May I suggest that you check your program cards to see whether you are in the right place at the right time."

Her essay on Gide's *The Immoralist* lay on his desk and the note from the administration informing him, first, that his past political activities had been brought to their attention and then dismissing him at the end of the session weighed the inside pocket of his jacket. The two, her paper and the note, were linked in his mind. Her paper reminded him that the vow he had taken was still an empty one, for the term was half over and he had never once spoken to her (as if she understood his intention she was always late and disappeared as soon as the closing bell rang, leaving him trapped in a clamorous circle of students around his .desk), while the note which wrecked his

small attempt to start anew suddenly made that vow more ur-
gent. It gave him the edge of desperation he needed to act finally.
So that as soon as the bell rang, he returned all the papers but
hers, announced that all questions would have to wait until their
next meeting and, waving off the students from his desk, called
above their protests, "Miss Williams, if you have a moment,
I'd like to speak with you briefly about your paper."

She approached his desk like a child who has been cautioned
not to talk to strangers. her fingers touching the backs of the
chair as if for support, her gaze following the departing students
as though she longed to accompany them.

Her slight apprehensiveness pleased him. It suggested a sub-
missiveness which gave him, as he rose uncertainly, a feeling of
certainty and command. Her hesitancy was somehow in keeping
with the color of her skin. She seemed to bring not only herself
but the host of black women whose bodies had been despoiled
to make her. He would not only possess her but them also, he
thought (not really thought, for he scarcely allowed these
thoughts to form before he snuffed them out). Through their
collective suffering, which she contained, his own personal suffering would be eased; he would be pardoned for whatever sin
it was he had committed against life.

"I hope you weren't unduly alarmed when I didn't return
your paper along with the others," he said, and had to look up
as she reached the desk. She was taller close up and her eyes,
which he had thought were black, were a strong, flecked brown
with very small pupils which seemed to shrink now from the
sight of him. "But I found it so interesting I wanted to give it
to you privately."

"I didn't know what to think,' she said, and her voice—he
heard it for the first time for she never recited or answered in
class—was low, cautious, Southern.

"It was, to say the least, refreshing. It not only showed some
original and mature thinking on your part. but it also proved
that you've been listening in class—and after twenty-five years
and more of teaching it's encouraging to find that some students
do listen. If you have a little time I'd like to tell you, more
specifically, what I liked about it. . . ."

Talking easily, reassuring her with his professional tone and a deft gesture with his cigarette, he led her from the room as the next class filed in, his hand cupped at her elbow but not touching it, his manner urbane, courtly, kind. They paused on the landing at the end of the long corridor with the stairs piled in steel tiers above and plunging below them. An intimate silence swept up the stairwell in a warm gust and Max Berman said, "I'm curious. Why did you choose *The Immoralist?*"

She started suspiciously, afraid, it seemed, that her answer might expose and endanger the self she guarded so closely within.

"Well," she said finally, her glance reaching down the stairs to the door marked EXIT at the bottom, "when you said we could use anything by Gide I decided on *The Immoralist*, since it was the first book I read in the original French when I was in undergraduate school. I didn't understand it then because my French was so weak, I guess, but I always thought about it afterward for some odd reason. I was shocked by what I did understand, of course, but something else about it appealed to me, so when you made the assignment I thought I'd try reading it again. I understood it a little better this time. At least I think so. . . ."

"Your paper proves you did."

She smiled absently, intent on some other thought. Then she said cautiously, but with unexpected force, "You see, to me, the book seems to say that the only way you begin to know what you are and how much you are capable of is by daring to try something, by doing something which tests you. . . ."

"Something bold," he said.

"Yes."

"Even sinful."

She paused, questioning this, and then said reluctantly, "Yes, perhaps even sinful."

"The salutary effects of sin, you might say." He gave the little bow.

But she had not heard this; her mind had already leaped ahead. "The only trouble, at least with the character in Gide's book, is that what he finds out about himself is so terrible. He is so unhappy. . . ."

"But at least he knows, poor sinner." And his playful tone went unnoticed.

"Yes," she said with the same startling forcefulness. "And another thing, in finding out what he is, he destroys his wife. It was as if she had to die in order for a person to live and know himself. Perhaps in order for a person to live and know himself somebody else must die. Maybe there's always a balancing out. . . . In a way"—and he had to lean close now to hear her—"I believe this."

Max Berman edged back as he glimpsed something move within her abstracted gaze. It was like a strong and restless seed that had taken root in the darkness there and was straining now toward the light. He had not expected so subtle and complex a force beneath her mild exterior and he found it disturbing and dangerous, but fascinating.

"Well, it's a most interesting interpretation," he said. "I don't know if M. Gide would have agreed, but then he's not around to give his opinion. Tell me, where did you do your undergraduate work?"

"At Howard University."

"And you majored in French?"

"Yes."

"Why, if I may ask?" he said gently.

"Well, my mother was from New Orleans and could still speak a little Creole and I got interested in learning how to speak French through her, I guess. I teach it now at a junior high school in Richmond. Only the beginner courses because I don't have my master's. You know, *je vais, tu vas, il va* and *Frere Jacques*. It's not very inspiring."

"You should do something about that then, my dear Miss Williams. Perhaps it's time for you, like our friend in Gide, to try something new and bold."

"I know," she said, and her pale hand sketched a vague, despairing gesture. "I thought maybe if I got my master's . . . that's why I decided to come north this summer and start taking some courses. . . ."

Max Berman quickly lighted a cigarette to still the flurry inside him, for the moment he had been awaiting had come. He flicked her paper, which he still held. "Well, you've got the makings of a master's thesis right here. If you like I will suggest some ways for you to expand it sometime. A few pointers from an old pro might help."

He had to turn from her astonished and grateful smile—it was like a child's. He said carefully, "The only problem will be to find a place where we can talk quietly. Regrettably, I don't rate an office. . . ."

"Perhaps we could use one of the empty classrooms," she said.

"That would be much too dismal a setting for a pleasant discussion."

He watched the disappointment wilt her smile and when he spoke he made certain that the same disappointment weighed his voice. "Another difficulty is that the term's half over, which gives us little or no time. But let's not give up. Perhaps we can arrange to meet and talk over a weekend. The only hitch there is that I spend weekends at my place in the country. Of course you're perfectly welcome to come up there. It's only about seventy miles from New York, in the heart of what's very appropriately called the Borsch Circuit, even though, thank God, my place is a good distance away from the borsch. That is, it's very quiet and there's never anybody around except with my permission."

She did not move, yet she seemed to start; she made no sound, yet he thought he heard a bewildered cry. And then she did a strange thing, standing there with the breath sucked into the hollow of her throat and her smile, that had opened to him with such trust, dying—her eyes, her hands faltering up begged him to declare himself.

"There's a lake near the house," he said, "so that when you get tired of talking—or better, listening to me talk—you can take a swim, if you like. I would very much enjoy that sight." And as the nerve tugged at his eyelid, he seemed to wink behind his rimless glasses.

Her sudden, blind step back was like a man groping his way through a strange room in the dark, and instinctively Max Berman reached out to break her fall. Her arms, bare to the shoulder because of the heat (he knew the feel of her skin without even touching it—it would be like a rich, fine-textured cloth

which would soothe and hide him in its amber warmth), struck
out once to drive him off and then fell limp at her side, and her
eyes became vivid and convulsive in her numbed face. She
strained toward the stairs and the exit door at the bottom, but
she could not move. Nor could she speak. She did not even cry.
Her eyes remained dry and dull with disbelief. Only her shoulders trembled as though she was silently weeping inside.

It was as though she had never learned the forms and expressions of anger. The outrage of a lifetime, of her history, was
trapped inside her. And she stared at Max Berman with this
mute, paralyzing rage. Not really at him but to his side, as if
she caught sight of others behind him. And remembering how
he had imagined a column of dark women trailing her to his
desk, he sensed that she glimpsed a legion of old men with sere
flesh and lonely eyes flanking him: "old lechers with a love on
every wind. . . ."

"I'm sorry, Miss Williams," he said, and would have wel-
comed her insults, for he would have been able, at least, to distill
from them some passion and a kind of intimacy. It would have
been, in a way, like touching her. "It was only that you are a
very attractive young woman and although I'm no longer
young"—and he gave the tragic little laugh which sought to
dismiss that fact—"I can still appreciate and even desire an attractive woman. But I was wrong. . . ." his self disgust, overwhelming him finally, choked off his voice. "And so very crude.
Forgive me. I can offer no excuse for my behavior other than
my approaching senility."

He could not even manage the little marionette bow this time.
Quickiy he shoved the paper on Gide into her lifeless hand, but
it fell, the pages separating, and as he hurried past her downstairs
and out the door, he heard the pages scattering like dead leaves
on the steps.

She remained away until the night of the final examination,
which was also the last meeting of the class. By that time Max
Berman, believing that she would not return, had almost succeeded in forgetting her. He was no longer even certain of how

she looked, for her face had been absorbed into the single, blurred, featureless face of all the women who had ever refused him. So that she startled him as much as a stranger would have when he entered the room that night and found her alone amid a maze of empty chairs, her face turned toward the window as on the first night and her hands serene in her lap. She turned at his footstep and it was as if she had also forgotten all that had passed between them. She waited until he said, "I'm glad you decided to take the examination. I'm sure you won't have any difficulty with it"; then she gave him a nod that was some-how reminiscent of his little bow and turned again to the win-dow.

He was relieved yet puzzled by her composure. It was as if during her three-week absence she had waged and won a decisive contest with herself and was ready now to act. He was wary suddenly and all during the examination he tried to discover what lay behind her strange calm, studying her bent head amid the shifting heads of the other students, her slim hand guiding the pen across the page, her legs—the long bone visible, it seemed, beneath the flesh. Desire flared and quickly died.

"Excuse me, Professor Berman, will you take up Camus and Sartre next semester, maybe?" The girl who sat in front of his desk was standing over him with her earnest smile and finished examination folder.

"That might prove somewhat difficult, since I won't be here."

"No more?"

"No."

"I mean, not even next summer?"

"I doubt it."

"Gee, I'm sorry. I mean, I enjoyed the course and every-thing."

He bowed his thanks and held his head down until she left. Her compliment, so piteous somehow, brought on the despair he had forced to the dim rear of his mind. He could no longer flee the thought of the exile awaiting him when the class tonight ended. He could either remain in the house in Brooklyn, where the memory of his father's face above the radiance of the Sab-bath candles haunted him from the shadows, reminding him of

the certainty he had lost and never found again, where the
mirrors in his father's room were still shrouded with sheets, as
on the day he lay dying and moaning into his beard that his
only son was a bad Jew; or he could return to the house in the
country, to the silence shrill with loneliness.

The cigarette he was smoking burned his fingers, rousing him,
and he saw over the pile of examination folders on his desk that
the room was empty except for the Negro girl. She had finished—her pen lay aslant the closed folder on her desk—but she
had remained in her seat and she was smiling across the room
at him—a set, artificial smile that was both cold and threatening. It utterly denuded him and he was wildly angry suddenly
that she had seen him give way to despair; he wanted to remind her (he could not stay the thought; it attacked him like
an assailant from a dark turn in his mind) that she was only
black after all. . . . His head dropped and he almost wept with
shame.

The girl stiffened as if she had seen the thought and then the
tiny muscles around her mouth quickly arranged the bland smile.
She came up to his desk, placed her folder on top of the others
and said pleasantly, her eyes like dark, shattered glass that spared
Max Berman his reflection, "I've changed my mind. I think I'd
like to spend a day at your place in the country if your invitation
still holds."

He thought of refusing her, for her voice held neither promise
nor passion, but he could not. Her presence, even if it was only
for a day, would make his return easier. And there was still the
possibility of passion despite her cold manner and the deliberate
smile. He thought of how long it had been since he had had
someone, of how badly he needed the sleep which followed love
and of awakening certain, for the first time in years, of his
existence.

"Of course the invitation still holds. I'm driving up tonight."

"I won't be able to come until Sunday," she said firmly. "Is
there a train then?"

"Yes, in the morning, he said, and gave her the schedule.

"You'll meet me at the station?"

"Of course. You can't miss my car. It's a very shabby but
venerable Chevy."

She smiled stiffy and left, her heels awakening the silence of the empty corridor, the sound reaching back to tap like a warning finger on Max Berman's temple.

The pale sunlight slanting through the windshield lay like a cat on his knees. and the motor of his old Chevy, turning softly under him could have been the humming of its heart. A little distance from the car a log-cabin station house—the logs blackened by the seasons—stood alone against the hills, and the hills, in turn, lifted softly, still green although the summer was ending, into the vague autumn sky.

The morning mist and pale sun, the green that was still somehow new, made it seem that the season was stirring into life even as it died, and this contradiction pained Max Berman at the same time that it pleased him. For it was his own contradiction after all: his desires which remained those of a young man even as he was dying.

He had been parked for some time in the deserted station, yet his hands were still tensed on the steering wheel and his foot hovered near the accelerator. As soon as he had arrived in the station he had wanted to leave. But like the girl that night on the landing, he was too stiff with tension to move. He could only wait, his eyelid twitching with foreboding, regret, curiosity and hope.

Finally and with no warning the train charged through the fiery green, setting off a tremor underground. Max Berman imagined the girl seated at a window in the train, her hands arranged quietly in her lap and her gaze scanning the hills that were so familiar to him, and yet he could not believe that she was really there. Perhaps her plan had been to disappoint him. She might be in New York or on her way back to Richmond now, laughing at the trick she had played on him. He was convinced of this suddenly, so that even when he saw her walking toward him through the blown steam from under the train, he told himself that she was a mirage created by the steam. Only when she sat beside him in the car, bringing with her, it seemed, an essence she had distilled from the morning air and rubbed into her skin, was he certain of her reality.

"I brought my bathing suit but it's much too cold to swim," she said and gave him the deliberate smile.

He did not see it; he only heard her voice, its warm Southern lilt in the chill, its intimacy in the closed car—and an excitement swept him, cold first and then hot, as if the sun had burst in his blood.

"It's the morning air," he said. "By noon it should be like summer again."

"Is that a promise?"

"Yes."

By noon the cold morning mist had lifted above the hills and below, in the lake valley, the sunlight was a sheer gold net spread out on the grass as if to dry, draped on the trees and flung, glinting, over the lake. Max Berman felt it brush his shoulders gently as he sat by the lake waiting for the girl, who had gone up to the house to change into her swimsuit.

He had spent the morning showing her the fields and small wood near his house. During the long walk he had been careful to keep a little apart from her. He would extend a hand as they climbed a rise or when she stepped uncertainly over a rock, but he would not really touch her. He was afraid that at his touch, no matter how slight and casual, her scream would spiral into the morning calm, or worse, his touch would unleash the threatening thing he sensed behind her even smile.

He had talked of her paper and she had listened politely and occasionally even asked a question or made a comment. But all the while detached, distant, drawn within herself as she had been that first night in the classroom. And then halfway down a slope she had paused and, pointing to the canvas tops of her white sneakers, which had become wet and dark from the dew secreted in the grass, she had laughed. The sound, coming so abruptly in the midst of her tense quiet, joined her, it seemed, to the wood and wide fields, to the hills; she shared their simplicity and held within her the same strong current of life. Max Berman had felt privileged suddenly, and humble. He had stopped questioning her smile. He had told himself then that it would not matter even if she stopped and picking up a rock bludgeoned him from behind.

"There's a lake near my home, but it's not like this," the girl said, coming up behind him. "Yours is so dark and serious-looking."

He nodded and followed her gaze out to the lake, where the ripples were long, smooth welts raised by the wind, and across to the other bank, where a group of birches stepped delicately down to the lake and bending over touched the water with their branches as if testing it before they plunged.

The girl came and stood beside him now—and she was like a pale gold naiad, the spirit of the lake, her eyes reflecting its somber autumnal tone and her body as supple as the birches. She walked slowly into the water, unaware, it seemed, of the sudden passion in his gaze, or perhaps uncaring; and as she walked she held out her arms in what seemed a gesture of invocation (and Max Berman remembered his father with the fringed shawl draped on his outstretched arms as he invoked their God each Sabbath with the same gesture); her head was bent as if she listened for a voice beneath the water's murmurous surface. When the ground gave way she still seemed to be walking and listening, her arms outstretched. The water reached her waist, her small breasts, her shoulders. She lifted her head once, breathed deeply and disappeared.

She stayed down for a long time and when her white cap finally broke the water some distance out, Max Berman felt strangely stranded and deprived. He understood suddenly the profound cleavage between them and the absurdity of his hope. The water between them became the years which separated them. Her white cap was the sign of her purity, while the silt darkening the lake was the flotsam of his failures. Above all, their color—her arms a pale, flashing gold in the sunlit water and his bled white and flaccid with the veins like angry blue penciling—marked the final barrier.

He was sad as they climbed toward the house late that afternoon and troubled. A crow cawed derisively in the bracken, heralding the dusk which would not only end their strange day but would also, he felt, unveil her smile, so that he would learn the reason for her coming. And because he was sad, he said wryly, "I think I should tell you that you've been spending the day with something of an outcast."

"Oh," she said and waited.

He told her of the dismissal, punctuating his words with the little hoarse, deprecating laugh and waving aside the pain with his cigarette. She listened, polite but neutral, and because she remained unmoved, he wanted to confess all the more. So that during dinner and afterward when they sat outside on the porch, he told her of the investigation.

"It was very funny once you saw it from the proper perspective, which I did, of course." he said. "l mean here they were accusing me of crimes I couldn't remember committing and asking me for the names of people with whom I had never associated. It was pure farce. But I made a mistake. I should have done something dramatic or something just as farcical. Bared my breast in the public market place or written a tome on my apostasy, naming names. It would have been a far different story then. Instead of my present ignominy I would have been offered a chairmanship at Yale. . . . No? Well, Brandeis then. I would have been draped in honorary degrees. . . ."

"Well, why didn't you confess?" she said impatiently.

"I've often asked myself the same interesting question, but I haven't come up with a satisfactory answer yet. I suspect, though, that I said nothing because none of it really mattered that much."

"What did matter?" she asked sharply.

He sat back, waiting for the witty answer, but none came, because just then the frame upon which his organs were strung seemed to snap and he felt his heart, his lungs, his vital parts fall in a heap within him. Her question had dealt the severing blow, for it was the same question he understood suddenly that the vague forms in his dream asked repeatedly. It had been the plaintive undercurrent to his father's dying moan, the real accusation behind the charges of his inquisitors at the hearing.

For what had mattered? He gazed through his sudden shock at the night squatting on the porch steps, at the hills asleep like gentle beasts in the darkness, at the black screen of the sky where the events of his life passed in a mute, accusing review—and he saw nothing there to which he had given himself or in which he had truly believed since the belief and dedication of his boyhood.

"Did you hear my question?" she asked, and he was glad that he sat within the shadows clinging to the porch screen and could not be seen.

"Yes, I did," he said faintly, and his eyelid twitched. "But I'm afraid it's another one of those I can't answer satisfactorily." And then he struggled for the old flippancy. "You make an excellent examiner, you know. Far better than my inquisitors."

"What will you do now?" her voice and cold smile did not spare him.

He shrugged and the motion, a slow, eloquent lifting of the shoulders, brought with it suddenly the weight and memory of his boyhood. It was the familiar gesture of the women hawkers in Belmont Market, of the men standing outside the temple on Saturday mornings, each of them reflecting his image of God in their forbidding black coats and with the black, tumbling beards in which he had always imagined he could hide as in a forest. All this had mattered, he called loudly to himself, and said aloud to the girl, "Let me see if I can answer this one at least. What *will* I do?" He paused and swung his leg so that his foot in the fastidious French shoe caught the light from the house. "Grow flowers and write my memoirs. How's that? That would be the proper way for a gentleman and scholar to retire. Or hire one of those hefty housekeepers who will bully me and when I die in my sleep draw the sheet over my face and call my lawyer. That's somewhat European, but how's that?"

When she said nothing for a long time, he added soberly. "But that's not a fair question for me any more. I leave all such considerations to the young. To you, for that matter. What will you do, my dear Miss Williams?"

It was as if she had been expecting the question and had been readying her answer all the time that he had been talking. She leaned forward eagerly and with her face and part of her body fully in the light, she said, "I will do something. I don't know what yet, but something."

Max Berman started back a little. The answer was so unlike her vague, resigned "I know" on the landing that night when he had admonished her to try something new.

He edged back into the darkness and she leaned further into

the light, her eyes overwhelming her face and her mouth set in a thin, determined line. "I will do something," she said, bearing down on each word, "because for the first time in my life I feel almost brave."

He glimpsed this new bravery behind her hard gaze and sensed something vital and purposeful, precious, which she had found and guarded like a prize within her center. He wanted it. He would have liked to snatch it and run like a thief. He no longer desired her but it, and starting forward with a sudden envious cry, he caught her arm and drew her close, seeking it.

But he could not get to it. Although she did not pull away her arm, although she made no protest as his face wavered close to hers, he did not really touch her. She held herself and her prize out of his desperate reach and her smile was a knife she pressed to his throat. He saw himself for what he was in her clear, cold gaze: an old man with skin the color and texture of dough that had been kneaded by the years into tragic folds, with faded eyes adrift behind a pair of rimless glasses and the roughened flesh at his throat like a bird's wattles. And as the disgust which he read in her eyes swept him, his hand dropped from her arm. He started to murmur, "Forgive me . . ." when suddenly she caught hold of his wrist, pulling him close again, and he felt the strength which had borne her swiftly through the water earlier hold him now as she said quietly and without passion, "And do you know why, Dr. Berman, I feel almost brave today? Because ever since I can remember my parents were always telling me, 'Stay away from white folks. Just leave them alone. You mind your business and they'll mind theirs. Don't go near them.' And they made sure I didn't. My father, who was the principal of a colored grade school in Richmond, used to drive me to and from school every day. When I needed something from downtown my mother would take me and if the white saleslady asked me anything she would answer. . . .

"And my parents were also always telling me, 'Stay away from niggers,' and that meant anybody darker than we were." She held out her arm in the light and Max Berman saw the skin almost as white as his but for the subtle amber shading. Staring at the arm she said tragically, "I was so confused I never really went near anybody. Even when I went away to college I kept to myself. I didn't marry the man I wanted to because he was dark and I knew my parents would disapprove. . . ." She paused, her wistful gaze searching the darkness for the face of the man she had refused, it seemed, and not finding it she went on sadly. "So after graduation I returned home and started teaching and I was just as confused and frightened and ashamed as always. When my parents died I went on the same way. And I would have gone on like that the rest of my life if it hadn't been for you, Dr. Berman"—and the sarcasm leaped behind her cold smile. "In a way you did me a favor. You let me know how you and most of the people like you—see me."

"My dear Miss Williams, I assure you I was not attracted to you because you were colored. . . ." And he broke off, remembering just how acutely aware of her color he had been.

"I'm not interested in your reasons!" she said brutally. "What matters is what it meant to me. I thought about this these last three weeks and about my parents how wrong they had been, how frightened, and the terrible thing they had done to me . . . and I wasn't confused any longer." Her head lifted, tremulous with her new assurance. "I can do something now! I can begin," she said with her head poised. "Look how I came all the way up here to tell you this to your face. Because how could you harm me? You're so old you're like a cup I could break in my hand." And her hand tightened on his wrist, wrenching the last of his frail life from him, it seemed. Through the quick pain he remembered her saying on the landing that night: "Maybe in order for a person to live someone else must die" and her quiet "I believe this" then. Now her sudden laugh, an infinitely cruel sound in the warm night, confirmed her belief.

Suddenly she was the one who seemed old, indeed ageless. Her touch became mortal and Max Berman saw the darkness that would end his life gathered in her eyes. But even as he sprang back, jerking his arm away, a part of him rushed forward to embrace that darkness, and his cry, wounding the night, held both ecstasy and terror.

"That's all I came for," she said, rising. "You can drive me to the station now."

They drove to the station in silence. Then, just as the girl started from the car, she turned with an ironic, pitiless smile and said, "You know, it's been a nice day, all things considered. It really turned summer again as you said it would. And even though your lake isn't anything like the one near my home, it's almost as nice."

Max Berman bowed to her for the last time, accepting with that gesture his responsibility for her rage, which went deeper than his, and for her anger, which would spur her finally to live. And not only for her, but for all those at last whom he had wronged through his indifference: his father lying in the room of shrouded mirrors, the wives he had never loved, his work which he had never believed in enough and lastly (even though he knew it was too late and he would not be spared), himself.

Too weary to move, he watched the girl cross to the train which would bear her south, her head lifted as though she carried life as lightly there as if it were a hat made of tulle. When the train departed his numbed eyes followed it until its rear light was like a single firefly in the immense night or the last flickering of his life. Then he drove back through the darkness.

BARBADOS

1961

This is another of the novellas from SOUL CLAP HANDS
AND SING. *The four long stories which make up the collection
all have to do with old men. They are—the men—of different
backgrounds and cultures, yet they share a common predicament: their lives have been essentially empty. They have failed
to commit themselves to anyone or anything in a meaningful
way. When confronted with this truth or when their long-
suppressed need for love finally surfaces, they reach out in a
desperate, last-ditch effort to the women in the stories. (While
the women are not major characters, they are nonetheless important as "bringers of the truth," and also because they come
to realize their own strength as a result of the encounter. I saw
this as a second motif.)*

One of the reasons I undertook SOUL *was to see if I could
write convincingly of men. More important, I wanted to use
the relationships between the old men and the young women in
the stories to suggest themes of a political nature. These were of
increasing interest to me at the time.*

*"Barbados" came to me practically ready-made during a year
I spent on Barbados overhauling* BROWN GIRL, BROWNSTONES
*for publication. It was 1958. The owner of the house where I
had rented a room was, like the main character in the story, a
solitary, taciturn old bachelor who had returned home after
having worked most of his life in the United States. (He was
a carbon copy of the stern-faced West Indian custodian of my
neighborhood library when I was a child, and I merged them
into a single character.) The man scarcely said two words to
me the whole time I was there. His house, which served as a
model for the one in the story, called to mind Tara in* GONE
WITH THE WIND. *Large, white, with tall columns at the front,
it was a plantation house for a black man "playing white."
My aging landlord had built it with money he had accumulated
while in the States.*

*There was even a young servant girl, just as in the story,
whom he hired to cook and clean for me. She never said two
words either. (I changed this though when I got around to*

51

*writing about her. She evolves from a silent, submerged, anon-
ymous creature into a young woman with a growing sense of
herself and her rights.)*

*There was scarcely anything for me to invent in other words.
All I did with "Barbados" was to exclude myself from the "big
house" and to provide my two ready-made characters with background, a psychology, and a plot. I never had it so easy.*

Dawn, like the night which had preceded it, came from the
sea. In a white mist tumbling like spume over the fishing boats
leaving the island and the hunched, ghost shapes of the fisher-
men. In a white, wet wind breathing over the villages scattered
amid the tall canes. The cabbage palms roused, their high head-
dresses solemnly saluting the wind, and along the white beach
which ringed the island the casuarina trees began their moaning—a sound of women lamenting their dead within a cave.

The wind, smarting of the sea, threaded a wet skein through
Mr. Watford's five hundred dwarf coconut trees and around his
house at the edge of the grove. The house, Colonial American
in design, seemed created by the mist—as if out of the dawn's
formlessness had come, magically, the solid stone walls, the blind,
broad windows and the portico of fat columns which embraced
the main story. When the mist cleared, the house remained—
pure, proud, a pristine white—disdaining the crude wooden
houses in the village outside its high gate.

It was not the dawn settling around his house which awakened
Mr. Watford, but the call of his Barbary doves from their hutch
in the yard. And it was more the feel of that sound than the
sound itself. His hands had retained, from the many times a day
he held the doves, the feel of their throats swelling with that
murmurous, mournful note. He lay abed now, his hands—as
cracked and calloused as a cane cutter's—filled with the sound,
and against the white sheet which flowed out to the white walls
he appeared profoundly alone, yet secure in loneliness, con-

tained. His face was fleshless and severe, his black skin sucked deep into the hollow of his jaw, while under a high brow, which was like a bastion raised against the world, his eyes were indrawn and pure. It was as if during all his seventy years, Mr. Watford had permitted nothing to sight which could have affected him.

He stood up, and his body, muscular but stripped of flesh, appeared to be absolved from time, still young. Yet each clenched gesture of his arms, of his lean shank as he dressed in a faded shirt and work pants, each vigilant, snapping motion of his head betrayed tension. Ruthlessly he spurred his body to perform like a younger man's. Savagely he denied the accumulated fatigue of the years. Only sometimes when he paused in his grove of coconut trees during the day, his eyes tearing and the breath torn from his lungs, did it seem that if he could find a place hidden from the world and himself he would give way to exhaustion and weep from weariness.

Dressed, he strode through the house, his step tense, his rough hand touching the furniture from Grand Rapids which crowded each room. For some reason, Mr. Watford had never completed the house. Everywhere the walls were raw and unpainted, the furniture unarranged. In the drawing room with its coffered ceiling, he stood before his favorite piece, an old mantel clock which eked out the time. Reluctantly it whirred five and Mr. Watford nodded. His day had begun.

It was no different from all the days which made up the five years since his return to Barbados. Downstairs in the unfinished kitchen, he prepared his morning tea—tea with canned milk and fried bakes—and ate standing at the stove while lizards skittered over the unplastered walls. Then, belching and snuffling the way a child would, he put on a pith helmet, secured his pants legs with bicycle clasps and stepped into the yard. There he fed the doves, holding them so that their sound poured into his hands and laughing gently—but the laugh gave way to an irritable grunt as he saw the mongoose tracks under the hutch. He set the trap again.

The first heat had swept the island like a huge tidal wave when Mr. Watford, with that tense, headlong stride, entered the grove. He had planted the dwarf coconut trees because of their quick yield and because, with their stunted trunks, they always appeared young. Now as he worked, rearranging the complex of pipes which irrigated the land, stripping off the dead leaves, the trees were like cool, moving presences; the stiletto fronds wove a protective dome above him and slowly, as the day soared toward noon, his mind filled with the slivers of sunlight through the trees and the feel of earth in his hands, as it might have been filled with thoughts.

Except for a meal at noon, he remained in the grove until dusk surged up from the sea; then returning to the house, he bathed and dressed in a medical doctor's white uniform, turned on the lights in the parlor and opened the tall doors to the portico. Then the old women of the village on their way to church, the last hawkers caroling, "Fish, flying fish, a penny, my lady," the roistering saga-boys lugging their heavy steel drums to the crossroad where they would rehearse under the street lamp—all passing could glimpse Mr. Watford, stiff in his white uniform and with his head bent heavily over a Boston newspaper. The papers reached him weeks late but he read them anyway, giving a little savage chuckle at the thought that beyond his world that other world went its senseless way. As he read, the night sounds of the village welled into a joyous chorale against the sea's muffled cadence and the hollow, haunting music of the steel band. Soon the moths, lured in by the light, fought to die on the lamp, the beetles crashed drunkenly against the walls and the night—like a woman offering herself to him— became fragrant with the night-blooming cactus.

Even in America Mr. Watford had spent his evenings this way. Coming home from the hospital, where he worked in the boiler room, he would dress in his white uniform and read in the basement of the large rooming house he owned. He had lived closeted like this, detached, because America—despite the money and property he had slowly accumulated—had meant nothing to him. Each morning, walking to the hospital along the rutted Boston streets, through the smoky dawn light, he had known—although it had never been a thought—that his allegiance, his place, lay elsewhere. Neither had the few acquaintances he had made mattered. Nor the women he had occasionally kept as a younger man. After the first months their bodies would grow coarse to his hand and he would begin edging

away. . . . So that he had felt no regret when, the year before
his retirement, he resigned his job, liquidated his properties and,
his fifty-year exile over, returned home.

The clock doled out eight and Mr. Watford folded the newspaper and brushed the burnt moths from the lamp base. His
lips still shaped the last words he had read as he moved through
the rooms, fastening the windows against the night air, which
he had dreaded even as a boy. Something palpable but unseen
was always, he believed, crouched in the night's dim recess,
waiting to snare him. . . . Once in bed in his sealed room, Mr.
Watford fell asleep quickly.

The next day was no different except that Mr. Goodman, the
local shopkeeper, sent the boy for coconuts to sell at the race
track and then came that evening to pay for them and to her-
ald—although Mr. Watford did not know this—the coming of
the girl.

That morning, taking his tea, Mr. Watford heard the careful
tap of the mule's hoofs and looking out saw the wagon jolting
through the dawn and the boy, still lax with sleep, swaying on
the seat. He was perhaps eighteen and the muscles packed tightly
beneath his lustrous black skin gave him a brooding strength.
He came and stood outside the back door, his hands and lowered
head performing the small, subtle rites of deference.

Mr. Watford's pleasure was full, for the gestures were those
given only to a white man in his time. Yet the boy always
nettled him. He sensed a natural arrogance like a pinpoint of
light within his dark stare. The boy's stance exhumed a memory
buried under the years. He remembered, staring at him, the
time when he had worked as a yard boy for a white family, and
had had to assume the same respectful pose while their flat, raw,
Barbadian voices assailed him with orders. He remembered the
muscles in his neck straining as he nodded deeply and a taste
like alum on his tongue as he repeated the "Yes, please," as in
a litany. But, because of their whiteness and wealth, he had
never dared hate them. Instead his rancor, like a boomerang,
had rebounded, glancing past him to strike all the dark ones like
himself, even his mother with her spindled arms and her stomach
sagging with a child who was, invariably, dead at birth. He had
been the only one of ten to live, the only one to escape. But

he had never lost the sense of being pursued by the same dread
presence which had claimed them. He had never lost the fear
that if he lived too fully he would tire and death would quickly
close the gap. His only defense had been a cautious life and
work. He had been almost broken by work at the age of twenty
when his parents died, leaving him enough money for the passage to America. Gladly had he fled the island. But nothing had
mattered after his flight.

The boy's foot stirred the dust. He murmured,"Please, sir,
Mr. Watford, Mr. Goodman at the shop send me to pick the
coconuts."

Mr. Watford's head snapped up. A caustic word flared, but
died as he noticed a political button pinned to the boy's patched
shirt with "Vote for the Barbados People's Party" printed boldly
on it, and below that the motto of the party: "The Old Order
Shall Pass." At this ludicrous touch (for what could this boy,
with his splayed and shigoed feet and blunted mind, understand
about politics?) he became suddenly nervous, angry. The button
and its motto seemed, somehow, directed at him. He said
roughly, "Well, come then. You can't pick any coconuts standing there looking foolish!"—and he led the way to the grove.

The coconuts, he knew, would sell well at the booths in the
center of the track, where the poor were penned in like cattle.
As the heat thickened and the betting grew desperate, they would
clamor: "Man, how you selling the water coconuts?" and hacking off the tops they would pour rum into the water within the
hollow centers, then tilt the coconuts to their heads so that the
rum-sweetened water skimmed their tongues and trickled bright
down their dark chins. Mr. Watford had stood among them at
the track as a young man, as poor as they were, but proud. And
he had always found something unutterably graceful and free in
their gestures, something which had roused contradictory feelings in him: admiration, but just as strong, impatience at their
easy ways, and shame . . .

That night, as he sat in his white uniform reading, he heard
Mr. Goodman's heavy step and went out and stood at the head
of the stairs in a formal, proprietary pose. Mr. Goodman's face
floated up into the light—the loose folds of flesh, the skin slick
with sweat as if oiled, the eyes scribbled with veins and mottled,

bold—as if each blemish there was a sin he proudly displayed or a scar which proved he had met life head-on. His body, unlike Mr. Watford's, was corpulent and, with the trousers caught up around his full crotch, openly concupiscent. He owned the one shop in the village which gave credit and a booth which sold coconuts at the race track, kept a wife and two outside women, drank a rum with each customer at his bar, regularly caned his fourteen children, who still followed him everywhere (even now they were waiting for him in the darkness beyond Mr. Watford's gate) and bet heavily at the races, and when he lost gave a loud hacking laugh which squeezed his body like a pain and left him gasping.

The laugh clutched him now as he flung his pendulous flesh into a chair and wheezed, "Watford, how? Man, I near lose house, shop, shirt and all at races today. I tell you, they got some horses from Trinidad in this meet that's making ours look like they running backwards. Be-Jese, I wouldn't bet on a Bajan horse tomorrow if Christ heself was to give me the tip. Those bitches might look good but they's nothing 'pon a track."

Mr. Watford, his back straight as the pillar he leaned against, his eyes unstained, his gaunt face planed by contempt, gave Mr. Goodman his cold, measured smile, thinking that the man would be dead soon, bloated with rice and rum—and somehow this made his own life more certain.

Sputtering with his amiable laughter, Mr. Goodman paid for the coconuts, but instead of leaving then as he usually did, he lingered, his eyes probing for a glimpse inside the house. Mr. Watford waited, his head snapping warily; then, impatient, he started toward the door and Mr. Goodman said, "I tell you, your coconut trees bearing fast enough even for dwarfs. You's lucky, man."

Ordinarily Mr. Watford would have waved both the man and his remark aside, but repelled more than usual tonight by Mr. Goodman's gross form and immodest laugh, he said—glad of the cold edge his slight American accent gave the words—"What luck got to do with it? I does care the trees properly and they bear, that's all. Luck! People, especially this bunch around here, is always looking to luck when the only answer is a little brains and plenty of hard work. . . ." Suddenly remembering the boy that morning and the political button, he added in loud disgust, "Look that half-foolish boy you does send here to pick the coconuts. Instead of him learning a trade and going to England where he might find work he's walking about with a political button. He and all in politics now! But that's the way with these down in here. They'll do some of everything but work. They don't want work!" He gestured violently, almost dancing in anger. "They too busy spreeing."

The chair creaked as Mr. Goodman sketched a pained and gentle denial. "No, man," he said, "you wrong. Things is different to before. I mean to say, the young people nowadays is different to how we was. They not just sitting back and taking things no more. They not so frighten for the white people as we was. No man. Now take that said same boy, for an example. I don't say he don't like a spree, but he's serious, you see him there. He's a member of this new Barbados People's Party. He wants to see his own color running the government. He wants to be able to make a living right here in Barbados instead of going to any cold England. And he's right!" Mr. Goodman paused at a vehement pitch, then shrugged heavily. "What the young people must do, nuh? They got to look to something. . . ."

"Look to work!" And Mr. Watford thrust out a hand so that the horned knuckles caught the light.

"Yes, that's true—and it's up to we that got little something to give them work," Mr. Goodman said, and a sadness filtered among the dissipations in his eyes. "I mean to say we that got little something got to help out. In a manner of speaking, we's responsible . . ."

"Responsible!" The word circled Mr. Watford's head like a gnat and he wanted to reach up and haul it down, to squash it underfoot.

Mr. Goodman spread his hands; his breathing rumbled with a sigh. "Yes, in a manner of speaking. That's why, Watford man, you got to provide little work for some poor person down in here. Hire a servant at least! 'Cause I gon tell you something . . ." And he hitched forward his chair, his voice dropped to a wheeze. "People talking. Here you come back rich from big America and build a swell house and plant 'nough coconut trees and you still cleaning and cooking and thing like some woman? Man, it don't look good!" His face screwed in emphasis and he sat back. "Now there's this girl, the daughter of a friend that just dead, and she need work bad enough. But I wouldn't like to see she working for these white people 'cause you know how those men will take advantage of she. And she'd make a good servant, man. Quiet and quick so, and nothing a-tall to feed and she can sleep anywhere about the place. And she don't have no boys always around her either. . . ." Still talking, Mr. Goodman eased from his chair and reached the stairs with surprising agility. "You need a servant," he whispered, leaning close to Mr. Watford as he passed. "It don't look good, man. People talking. I gon send she."

Mr. Watford was overcome by nausea. Not only from Mr. Goodman's smell—a stench of salt fish, rum and sweat, but from an outrage which was like a sediment in his stomach. For a long time he stood there almost kecking from disgust, until his clock struck eight, reminding him of the sanctuary within—and suddenly his cold laugh dismissed Mr. Goodman and his proposal. Hurrying in, he locked the doors and windows against the night air and still laughing, he slept.

The next day, coming from the grove to prepare his noon meal, he saw her. She was standing in his driveway, her bare feet like strong dark roots amid the jagged stones, her face tilted toward the sun—and she might have been standing there always waiting for him. She seemed of the sun, of the earth. The folktale of creation might have been true with her: that along a river bank a god had scooped up the earth—rich and black and warmed by the sun—and molded her poised head with its tufted braids and then with a whimsical touch crowned it with a sober brown felt hat which should have been worn by some stout English matron in a London suburb, had sculpted the passionless face and drawn a screen of gossamer across her eyes to hide the void behind. Beneath her bodice her small breasts were smooth at the crest. Below her waist, her hips branched wide, the place prepared for its load of life. But it was the bold and sensual strength of her legs which completely unstrung Mr. Watford. He wanted to grab a hoe and drive her off.

"What it 'tis you want?" he called sharply.

"Mr. Goodman send me."

"Send you for what?" His voice was shrill in the glare.

She moved. Holding a caved-in valise and a pair of white sandals, her head weaving slightly as though she bore a pail of water there or a tray of mangoes, she glided over the stones as if they were smooth ground. Her bland expression did not change, but her eyes, meeting his, held a vague trust. Pausing a few feet away, she curtsied deeply. "I's the new servant."

Only Mr. Watford's cold laugh saved him from anger. As always it raised him to a height where everything below appeared senseless and insignificant—especially his people, whom the girl embodied. From this height, he could even be charitable. And thinking suddenly of how she had waited in the brutal sun since morning without taking shelter under the nearby tamarind tree, he said, not unkindly, "Well, girl, go back and tell Mr. Goodman for me that I don't need no servant."

"I can't go back."

"How you mean can't?" His head gave its angry snap.

"I'll get lashes," she said simply. "My mother say I must work the day and then if you don't wish me, I can come back. But I's not to leave till night falling, if not I get lashes."

He was shaken by her dispassion. So much so that his head dropped from its disdaining angle and his hands twitched with helplessness. Despite anything he might say or do, her fear of the whipping would keep her there until nightfall, the valise and shoes in hand. He felt his day with its order and quiet rhythms threatened by her intrusion—and suddenly waving her off as if she were an evil visitation, he hurried into the kitchen to prepare his meal.

But he paused, confused, in front of the stove, knowing that he could not cook and leave her hungry at the door, nor could he cook and serve her as though he were the servant.

"You know anything about cooking?" he shouted finally.

"Yes, please."

They said nothing more. She entered the room with a firm step and an air almost of familiarity, placed her valise and shoes in a corner and went directly to the larder. For a time Mr. Watford stood by, his muscles flexing with anger and his eyes bounding ahead of her every move, until feeling foolish and frighteningly useless, he went out to feed his doves. The meal was quickly done and as he ate he heard the dry slap of her feet behind him—a pleasant sound—and then silence. When he glanced back she was squatting in the doorway, the sunlight aslant the absurd hat and her face bent to a bowl she held in one palm. She ate slowly, thoughtfully, as if fixing the taste of each spoonful in her mind.

It was then that he decided to let her work the day and at nightfall to pay her a dollar and dismiss her. His decision held when he returned later from the grove and found tea awaiting him, and then through the supper she prepared. Afterward, dressed in his white uniform, he patiently waited out the day's end on the portico, his face setting into a grim mold. Then just as dusk etched the first dark line between the sea and sky, he took out a dollar and went downstairs.

She was not in the kitchen, but the table was set for his morning tea. Muttering at her persistence, he charged down the corridor, which ran the length of the basement, flinging open the doors to the damp, empty rooms on either side, and sending the lizards and the shadows long entrenched there scuttling to safety.

He found her in the small slanted room under the stoop, asleep on an old cot he kept there, her suitcase turned down beside the bed, and the shoes, dress and the ridiculous hat piled on top. A loose night shift muted the outline of her body and hid her legs, so that she appeared suddenly defenseless, innocent, with a child's trust in her curled hand and in her deep breathing. Standing in the doorway, with his own breathing snarled and his eyes averted, Mr. Watford felt like an intruder. She had claimed the room. Quivering with frustration, he slowly turned away, vowing that in the morning he would shove the dollar at her and lead her like a cow out of his house. . . .

Dawn brought rain and a hot wind which set the leaves rattling and swiping at the air like distraught arms. Dressing in the dawn darkness, Mr. Watford again armed himself with the dollar and, with his shoulders at an uncompromising set, plunged downstairs. He descended into the warm smell of bakes and this smell, along with the thought that she had been up before him, made his hand knot with exasperation on the banister. The knot tightened as he saw her, dust swirling at her feet as she swept the corridor, her face bent solemn to the task. Shutting her out with a lifted hand, he shouted, "Don't bother sweeping. Here's a dollar. G'long back."

The broom paused and although she did not raise her head, he sensed her groping through the shadowy maze of her mind toward his voice. Behind the dollar which he waved in her face, her eyes slowly cleared. And, surprisingly, they held no fear. Only anticipation and a tenuous trust. It was as if she expected him to say something kind.

"G'long back!" His angry cry was a plea.

Like a small, starved flame, her trust and expectancy died and she said, almost with reproof, "The rain falling."

To confirm this, the wind set the rain stinging across the windows and he could say nothing, even though the words sputtered at his lips. It was useless. There was nothing inside her to comprehend that she was not wanted. His shoulders sagged under the weight of her ignorance, and with a futile gesture he swung away, the dollar hanging from his hand like a small sword gone limp.

She became as fixed and familiar a part of the house as the stones—and as silent. He paid her five dollars a week, gave her Mondays off and in the evenings, after a time, even allowed her to sit in the alcove off the parlor, while he read with his back to her, taking no more notice of her than he did the moths on the lamp.

But once, after many silent evenings together, he detected a sound apart from the night murmurs of the sea and village and the metallic tuning of the steel band, a low, almost inhuman cry of loneliness which chilled him. Frightened, he turned to find her leaning hesitantly toward him, her eyes dark with urgency, and her face tight with bewilderment and a growing anger. He started, not understanding, and her arm lifted to stay him. Eagerly she bent closer. But as she uttered the low cry again, as her fingers described her wish to talk, he jerked around, afraid that she would be foolish enough to speak and that once she did they would be brought close. He would be forced then to

acknowledge something about her which he refused to grant;
above all, he would be called upon to share a little of himself.
Quickly he returned to his newspaper, rustling it to settle the
air, and after a time he felt her slowly, bitterly, return to her
silence. . . .

Like sand poured in a careful measure from the hand, the
weeks flowed down to August and on the first Monday, August
Bank holiday, Mr. Watford awoke to the sound of the excursion
buses leaving the village for the annual outing, their backfire
pelleting the dawn calm and the ancient motors protesting the
overcrowding. Lying there, listening, he saw with disturbing
clarity his mother dressed for an excursion—the white head tie
wound above her dark face and her head poised like a dancer's
under the heavy outing basket of food. That set of her head
had haunted his years, reappearing in the girl as she walked
toward him the first day. Aching with the memory, yet annoyed
with himself for remembering, he went downstairs.

The girl had already left for the excursion, and although it
was her day off, he felt vaguely betrayed by her eagerness to
leave him. Somehow it suggested ingratitude. It was as if his
doves were suddenly to refuse him their song or his trees their
fruit, despite the care he gave them. Some vital part which
shaped the simple mosaic of his life seemed suddenly missing.
An alien silence curled like coal gas throughout the house. To
escape it he remained in the grove all day and, upon his return
to the house, dressed with more care than usual, putting on a
fresh, starched uniform, and solemnly brushing his hair until it
lay in a smooth bush above his brow. Leaning close to the
mirror, but avoiding his eyes, he cleaned the white rheum at
their corners, and afterward pried loose the dirt under his nails.

Unable to read his papers, he went out on the portico to
escape the unnatural silence in the house, and stood with his
hands clenched on the balustrade and his taut body straining
forward. After a long wait he heard the buses return and voices
in gay shreds upon the wind. Slowly his hands relaxed, as did
his shoulders under the white uniform; for the first time that
day his breathing was regular. She would soon come.

But she did not come and dusk bloomed into night, with a
fragrant heat and a full moon which made the leaves glint as

though touched with frost. The steel band at the crossroads began the lilting songs of sadness and seduction, and suddenly—like shades roused by the night and the music—images of the girl flitted before Mr. Watford's eyes. He saw her lost amid the carousings in the village, despoiled; he imagined someone like Mr. Goodman clasping her lewdly or tumbling her in the cane-brake. His hand rose, trembling, to rid the air of her; he tried to summon his cold laugh. But, somehow, he could not dismiss her as he had always done with everyone else. Instead, he wanted to punish and protect her, to find and lead her back to the house.

As he leaned there, trying not to give way to the desire to go and find her, his fist striking the balustrade to deny his longing, he saw them. The girl first, with the moonlight like a silver patina on her skin, then the boy whom Mr. Goodman sent for the coconuts, whose easy strength and the political button—"The Old Order Shall Pass"—had always mocked and challenged Mr. Watford. They were joined in a tender battle: the boy in a sport shirt riotous with color was reaching for the girl as he leaped and spun, weightless, to the music, while she fended him off with a gesture which was lovely in its promise of surrender. Her protests were little scattered bursts: "But, man, why you don't stop, nuh? . . . But, you know, you getting on like a real-real idiot. . . ."

Each time she chided him he leaped higher and landed closer, until finally he eluded her arm and caught her by the waist. Boldly he pressed a leg between her tightly closed legs until they opened under his pressure. Their bodies cleaved into one whirling form and while he sang she laughed like a wanton with her hat cocked over her ear. Dancing, the stones moiling underfoot, they claimed the night. More than the night. The steel band played for them alone. The trees were their frivolous companions, swaying as they swayed. The moon rode the sky because of them.

Mr. Watford, hidden by a dense shadow, felt the tendons which strung him together suddenly go limp; above all, an obscure belief which, like rare china, he had stored on a high shelf in his mind began to tilt. He sensed the familiar specter which hovered in the night reaching out to embrace him, just as the two in the yard were embracing. Utterly unstrung, incapable of either speech or action, he stumbled into the house, only to meet there an accusing silence from the clock, which had missed its eight o'clock winding, and his newspapers lying like ruined leaves over the floor.

He lay in bed in the white uniform, waiting for sleep to rescue him, his hands seeking the comforting sound of his doves. But sleep eluded him and instead of the doves, their throats tremulous with sound, his scarred hands filled with the shape of a woman he had once kept: her skin, which had been almost bruising in its softness; the buttocks and breasts spread under his hands to inspire both cruelty and tenderness. His hands closed to softly crush those forms, and the searing thrust of passion, which he had not felt for years, stabbed his dry groin. He imagined the two outside, their passion at a pitch by now, lying together behind the tamarind tree, or perhaps—and he sat up sharply—they had been bold enough to bring their lust into the house. Did he not smell their taint on the air? Restored suddenly, he rushed downstairs. As he reached the corridor, a thread of light beckoned him from her room and he dashed furiously toward it, rehearsing the angry words which would jar their bodies apart. He neared the door, glimpsed her through the small opening, and his step faltered; the words collapsed.

She was seated alone on the cot, tenderly holding the absurd felt hat in her lap, one leg tucked under her while the other trailed down. A white sandal, its strap broken, dangled from the foot and gently knocked the floor as she absently swung her leg. Her dress was twisted around her body—and pinned to the bodice, so that it gathered the cloth between her small breasts, was the political button the boy always wore. She was dreamily fingering it, her mouth shaped by a gentle, ironic smile and her eyes strangely acute and critical. What had transpired on the cot had not only, it seemed, twisted the dress around her, tumbled her hat and broken her sandal, but had also defined her and brought the blurred forms of life into focus for her. There was a woman's force in her aspect now, a tragic knowing and acceptance in her bent head, a hint about her of Cassandra watching the future wheel before her eyes.

Before those eyes which looked to another world, Mr. Watford's anger and strength failed him and he held to the wall for support. Unreasonably, he felt that he should assume some hushed and reverent pose, to bow as she had the day she had come. If he had known their names, he would have pleaded forgiveness for the sins he had committed against her and the others all his life, against himself. If he could have borne the thought, he would have confessed that it had been love, terrible in its demand, which he had always fled. And that love had been the reason for his return. If he had been honest he would have whispered—his head bent and a hand shading his eyes— that unlike Mr. Goodman (whom he suddenly envied for his full life) and the boy with his political button (to whom he had lost the girl), he had not been willing to bear the weight of his own responsibility. . . . But all Mr. Watford could admit, clinging there to the wall, was, simply, that he wanted to live—and that the girl held life within her as surely as she held the hat in her hands. If he could prove himself better than the boy, he could win it. Only then, he dimly knew, would he shake off the pursuer which had given him no rest since birth. Hopefully, he staggered forward, his step cautious and contrite, his hands quivering along the wall.

She did not see or hear him as he pushed the door wider. And for some time he stood there, his shoulders hunched in humility, his skin stripped away to reveal each flaw, his whole self offered in one outstretched hand. Still unaware of him, she swung her leg, and the dangling shoe struck a derisive note. Then, just as he had turned away that evening in the parlor when she had uttered her low call, she turned away now, refusing him.

Mr. Watford's body went slack and then stiffened ominously. He knew that he would have to wrest from her the strength needed to sustain him. Slamming the door, he cried, his voice cracked and strangled, "What you and him was doing in here? Tell me! I'll not have you bringing nastiness round here. Tell me!"

She did not start. Perhaps she had been aware of him all along and had expected his outburst. Or perhaps his demented eye and the desperation rising from him like a musk filled her with pity instead of fear. Whatever, her benign smile held and her eyes remained abstracted until his hand reached out to fling her back on the cot. Then, frowning, she stood up, wobbling a little on the broken shoe and holding the political button as if it was a new power which would steady and protect her. With a cruel flick of her arm she struck aside his hand and, in a voice as cruel, halted him. "But you best move and don't come holding on to me, you nasty, pissy old man. That's all you is, despite yuh big house and fancy furnitures and yuh newspapers from America. You ain't people, Mr. Watford, you ain't people!" And with a look and a lift of her head which made her condemnation final, she placed the hat atop her braids, and turning aside picked up the valise which had always lain, packed, beside the cot—as if even on the first day she had known that this night would come and had been prepared against it. . . .

Mr. Watford did not see her leave, for a pain squeezed his heart dry and the driven blood was a bright, blinding cataract over his eyes. But his inner eye was suddenly clear. For the first time it gazed mutely upon the waste and pretense which had spanned his years. Flung there against the door by the girl's small blow, his body slowly crumpled under the weariness he had long denied. He sensed that dark but unsubstantial figure which roamed the nights searching for him wind him in its chill embrace. He struggled against it, his hands clutching the air with the spastic eloquence of a drowning man. He moaned—and the anguished sound reached beyond the room to fill the house. It escaped to the yard, and his doves swelled their throats, moaning with him.

REENA

1962

"Reena" has something of an unusual history in that it's the first and only commissioned story I ever wrote. In an effort perhaps to make up for past neglect, Harper's Magazine *decided to do a special supplement on "The American Female" as they called it for their October '62 issue. They even decided, due probably to the Civil Rights Movement underway at the time, to include an article on black women. They asked me to write it. Since I'd never attempted an article before and thought of myself as strictly a fiction writer, I told them I'd try doing a kind of story-essay. I also informed them that the piece would be confined to the comparatively small group of young black women I knew best: those from an urban, working-class and lower middle-class, West Indian-American background who, like myself, had attended the free New York City colleges during the late forties and fifties. The theme would be our efforts to realize whatever talents we had and to be our own persons in the face of the triple-headed hydra of racism, sexism, and class bias we confronted each day.*

In the story I have the main character, Reena, recount the events of her life to a childhood friend whom she hasn't seen for a number of years. They meet at the wake which follows the funeral of Reena's Aunt Vi, a spinster who like many unmarried women of my mother's generation had spent all of her adult life working as a sleep-in maid for a white family.

Over the course of the night the two friends spend together, Reena touches upon issues that were of major concern to those of us coming of age in the fifties: our struggle, for example, to find meaningful work after graduating college; our relationships with our families, especially our mothers; also, our sometimes troubled relationships with men and the necessity, on our part, of learning to accept the loneliness that was often the price of our accomplishments and independence. The two women speak of politics—in Reena's case, the radical politics of her undergraduate days and her later strong identification with Africa . . . .

As with "The Valley Between," "Reena" anticipated many

71

of the themes that were to come with the flowering of women's literature later on. And perhaps because it was ahead of its time, the story languished from its first publication in Harper's until 1970, when it was reprinted in Toni Cade's landmark anthology THE BLACK WOMAN.

True, "Reena" is a mixed bag technically, a story that reads in part like an essay or an article, and frankly, I've never been really comfortable with it because of that. But it's become a perennial. Women of different backgrounds and of all ages and colors find that it has something to say to them about their lives. They identify with Reena (spelled " 'With two e's!' she would say and imprint those e's on your mind with the indelible black of her eyes and a thin threatening finger that was like a quill.") They love her spirit. There can be nothing more gratifying for a writer.

Like most people with unpleasant childhoods, I am on constant guard against the past—the past being for me the people and places associated with the years I served out my girlhood in Brooklyn. The places no longer matter that much since most of them have vanished. The old grammar school, for instance, P.S. 35 ("Dirty 5's" we called it and with justification) has been replaced by a low, coldly functional arrangement of glass and Permastone which bears its name but has none of the feel of a school about it. The small, grudgingly lighted stores along Fulton Street, the soda parlor that was like a church with its stained-glass panels in the door and marble floor have given way to those impersonal emporiums, the supermarkets. Our house even, a brownstone relic whose halls smelled comfortingly of dust and lemon oil, the somnolent street upon which it stood, the tall, muscular trees which shaded it were leveled years ago to make way for a city housing project—a stark, graceless warren for the poor. So that now whenever I revisit that old section of Brooklyn and see these new and ugly forms, I feel nothing. I might as well be in a strange city.

But it is another matter with the people of my past, the faces that in their darkness were myriad reflections of mine. Whenever I encounter them at the funeral or wake, the wedding or christening—those ceremonies by which the past reaffirms its hold—my guard drops and memories banished to the rear of the mind rush forward to rout the present. I almost become the child again—anxious and angry, disgracefully diffident.

Reena was one of the people from that time, and a main contributor to my sense of ineffectualness then. She had not done this deliberately. It was just that whenever she talked about herself (and this was not as often as most people) she seemed to be talking about me also. She ruthlessly analyzed herself, sparing herself nothing. Her honesty was so absolute it was a kind of cruelty.

She had not changed, I was to discover in meeting her again after a separation of twenty years. Nor had I really. For although the years had altered our positions (she was no longer the lord and I the lackey) and I could even afford to forgive her now, she still had the ability to disturb me profoundly by dredging to the surface those aspects of myself that I kept buried. This time, as I listened to her talk over the stretch of one long night, she made vivid without knowing it what is perhaps the most critical fact of my existence—that definition of me, of her and millions like us, formulated by others to serve out their fantasies, a definition we have to combat at an unconscionable cost to the self and even use, at times, in order to survive; the cause of so much shame and rage as well as, oddly enough, a source of pride: simply, what it has meant, what it means, to be a black woman in America.

We met—Reena and myself—at the funeral of her aunt who had been my godmother and whom I had also called aunt, Aunt Vi, and loved, for she and her house had been, respectively, a source of understanding and a place of calm for me as a child. Reena entered the church where the funeral service was being held as though she, not the minister, were coming to officiate, sat down among the immediate family up front, and turned to inspect those behind her. I saw her face then.

It was a good copy of the original. The familiar mold was there, that is, and the configuration of bone beneath the skin was the same despite the slight fleshiness I had never seen there before; her features had even retained their distinctive touches: the positive set to her mouth, the assertive lift to her nose, the same insistent, unsettling eyes which when she was angry became as black as her skin—and this was total, unnerving, and very beautiful. Yet something had happened to her face. It was different despite its sameness. Aging even while it remained enviably young. Time had sketched in, very lightly, the evidence of the twenty years.

As soon as the funeral service was over, I left, hurrying out of the church into the early November night. The wind, already at its winter strength, brought with it the smell of dead leaves and the image of Aunt Vi there in the church, as dead as the leaves—as well as the thought of Reena, whom I would see later at the wake.

Her real name had been Doreen, a standard for girls among West Indians (her mother, like my parents, was from Barbados), but she had changed it to Reena on her twelfth birthday—"As a present to myself"—and had enforced the change on her family by refusing to answer to the old name. "Reena. With two e's!" she would say and imprint those e's on your mind with the indelible black of her eyes and a thin threatening finger that was like a quill.

She and I had not been friends through our own choice. Rather, our mothers, who had known each other since childhood, had forced the relationship. And from the beginning, I had been at a disadvantage. For Reena, as early as the age of twelve, had had a quality that was unique, superior, and therefore dangerous. She seemed defined, even then, all of a piece, the raw edges of her adolescence smoothed over; indeed, she seemed to have escaped adolescence altogether and made one dazzling leap from childhood into the very arena of adult life. At thirteen, for instance, she was reading Zola, Hauptmann, Steinbeck, while I was still in the thrall of the Little Minister and Lorna Doone. When I could only barely conceive of the world beyond Brooklyn, she was talking of the Civil War in Spain, lynchings in the South, Hitler in Poland—and talking with the outrage and passion of a revolutionary. I would try, I remember, to console myself with the thought that she was really an adult masquerading as a child, which meant that I could not possibly be her match.

For her part, Reena put up with me and was, by turns, patronizing and impatient. I merely served as the audience before whom she rehearsed her ideas and the yardstick by which she measured her worldliness and knowledge.

"Do you realize that this stupid country supplied Japan with the scrap iron to make the weapons she's now using against it?" she had shouted at me once.

I had not known that.

Just as she overwhelmed me, she overwhelmed her family, with the result that despite a half dozen brothers and sisters who consumed quantities of bread and jam whenever they visited us, she behaved like an only child and got away with it. Her father, a gentle man with skin the color of dried tobacco and with the nose Reena had inherited jutting out like a crag from his nondescript face, had come from Georgia and was always making jokes about having married a foreigner—Reena's mother being from the West Indies. When not joking, he seemed slightly bewildered by his large family and so in awe of Reena that he avoided her. Reena's mother, a small, dry, formidably black woman, was less a person to me than the abstract principle of force, power, energy. She was alternately strict and indulgent with Reena and, despite the inconsistency, surprisingly effective.

They lived when I knew them in a cold-water railroad flat above a kosher butcher on Belmont Avenue in Brownsville, some distance from us—and this in itself added to Reena's exotic quality. For it was a place where Sunday became Saturday, with all the stores open and pushcarts piled with vegetables and yard goods lined up along the curb, a crowded place where people hawked and spat freely in the streaming gutters and the men looked as if they had just stepped from the pages of the Old Testament with their profuse beards and long, black, satin coats.

When Reena was fifteen her family moved to Jamaica in Queens and since, in those days, Jamaica was considered too far away for visiting, our families lost contact and I did not see Reena again until we were both in college and then only once and not to speak to. . . .

I had walked some distance and by the time I got to the wake,

which was being held at Aunt Vi's house, it was well under
way. It was a good wake. Aunt Vi would have been pleased.
There was plenty to drink, and more than enough to eat, including some Barbadian favorites: coconut bread, pone made
with the cassava root, and the little crisp codfish cakes that are
so hot with peppers they bring tears to the eyes as you bite into
them.

I had missed the beginning, when everyone had probably sat
around talking about Aunt Vi and recalling the few events that
had distinguished her otherwise undistinguished life. (Someone,
I'm sure, had told of the time she had missed the excursion boat
to Atlantic City and had her her own private picnic—complete
with pigeon peas and rice and fricassee chicken—on the pier at
42nd Street.) By the time I arrived, though, it would have been
indiscreet to mention her name, for by then the wake had become—and this would also have pleased her—a celebration of
life.

I had had two drinks, one right after the other, and was well
into my third when Reena, who must have been upstairs, entered the basement kitchen where I was. She saw me before I
had quite seen her, and with a cry that alerted the entire room
to her presence and charged the air with her special force, she
rushed toward me.

"Hey, I'm the one who was supposed to be the writer, not
you! Do you know, I still can't believe it," she said, stepping
back, her blackness heightened by a white mocking smile. "I
read both your books over and over again and I can't really
believe it. My Little Paulie!"

I did not mind. For there was respect and even wonder behind
the patronizing words and in her eyes. The old imbalance between us had ended and I was suddenly glad to see her.

I told her so and we both began talking at once, but Reena's
voice overpowered mine, so that all I could do after a time was
listen while she discussed my books, and dutifully answer her
questions about my personal life.

"And what about you?" I said, almost brutally, at the first
chance I got. "What've you been up to all this time?"

She got up abruptly. "Good Lord, in here's noisy as hell.
Come on, let's go upstairs."

We got fresh drinks and went up to Aunt Vi's bedroom, where in the soft light from the lamps, the huge Victorian bed and the pink satin bedspread with roses of the same material strewn over its surface looked as if they had never been used. And, in a way, this was true. Aunt Vi had seldom slept in her bed or, for that matter, lived in her house, because in order to pay for it, she had had to work at a sleeping-in job which gave her only Thursdays and every other Sunday off.

Reena sat on the bed, crushing the roses, and I sat on one of the numerous trunks which crowded the room. They contained every dress, coat, hat, and shoe that Aunt Vi had worn since coming to the United States. I again asked Reena what she had been doing over the years.

"Do you want a blow by blow account?" she said. But despite the flippancy, she was suddenly serious. And when she began it was clear that she had written out the narrative in her mind many times. The words came too easily; the events, the incidents had been ordered in time, and the meaning of her behavior and of the people with whom she had been involved had been pains-takingly analyzed. She talked willingly, with desperation almost. And the words by themselves weren't enough. She used her hands to give them form and urgency. I became totally involved with her and all that she said. So much so that as the night wore on I was not certain at times whether it was she or I speaking.

From the time her family moved to Jamaica until she was nineteen or so, Reena's life sounded, from what she told me in the beginning, as ordinary as mine and most of the girls we knew. After high school she had gone on to one of the free city colleges, where she had majored in journalism, worked part time in the school library, and, surprisingly enough, joined a house-plan. (Even I hadn't gone that far.) It was an all-Negro club, since there was a tacit understanding that Negro and white girls did not join each other's houseplans. "Integration, Northern style," she said, shrugging.

It seems that Reena had had a purpose and a plan in joining the group. "I thought," she said with a wry smile, "I could get those girls up off their complacent rumps and out doing some-thing about social issues. . . . I couldn't get them to budge. I remember after the war when a Negro ex-soldier had his eyes

gouged out by a bus driver down South I tried getting them to
demonstrate on campus. I talked until I was hoarse, but to no
avail. They were too busy planning the annual autumn frolic."

Her laugh was bitter but forgiving and it ended in a long,
reflective silence. After which she said quietly, "It wasn't that
they didn't give a damn. It was just, I suppose, that like most
people they didn't want to get involved to the extent that they
might have to stand up and be counted. If it ever came to that.
Then another thing. They thought they were safe, special. After
all, they had grown up in the North, most of them, and so had
escaped the southern-style prejudice; their parents, like mine,
were struggling to put them through college; they could look
forward to being tidy little schoolteachers, social workers, and
lab technicians. Oh, they were safe!" The sarcasm scored her
voice and then abruptly gave way to pity. "Poor things, they
weren't safe, you see, and would never be as long as millions
like themselves in Harlem, on Chicago's South Side, down
South, all over the place, were unsafe. I tried to tell them this—
and they accused me of being oversensitive. They tried not to
listen. But I would have held out and, I'm sure, even brought
some of them around eventually if this other business with a
silly boy hadn't happened at the same time. . . ."

Reena told me then about her first, brief, and apparently innocent affair with a boy she had met at one of the houseplan
parties. It had ended, she said, when the boy's parents had met
her. "That was it," she said and the flat of her hand cut into
the air. "He was forbidden to see me. The reason? He couldn't
bring himself to tell me, but I knew. I was too black.

"Naturally, it wasn't the first time something like that had
happened. In fact, you might say that was the theme of my
childhood. Because I was dark I was always being plastered with
Vaseline so I wouldn't look ashy. Whenever I had my picture
taken they would pile a whitish powder on my face and make
the lights so bright I always came out looking ghostly. My
mother stopped speaking to any number of people because they
said I would have been pretty if I hadn't been so dark. Like
nearly every little black girl, I had my share of dreams of waking
up to find myself with long, blond curls, blue eyes, and skin like

milk. So I should have been prepared. Besides, that boy's parents were really rejecting themselves in rejecting me.

"Take us"—and her hands, opening in front of my face as she suddenly leaned forward, seemed to offer me the whole of black humanity. "We live surrounded by white images, and white in this world is synonymous with the good, light, beauty, success, so that, despite ourselves sometimes, we run after that whiteness and deny our darkness, which has been made into the symbol of all that is evil and inferior. I wasn't a person to that boy's parents, but a symbol of the darkness they were in flight from, so that just as they—that boy, his parents, those silly girls in the houseplan—were running from me, I started running from them. . . ."

It must have been shortly after this happened when I saw Reena at a debate which was being held at my college. She did not see me, since she was one of the speakers and I was merely part of her audience in the crowded auditorium. The topic had something to do with intellectual freedom in the colleges (McCarthyism was coming into vogue then) and aside from a Jewish boy from City College, Reena was the most effective— sharp, provocative, her position the most radical. The others on the panel seemed intimidated not only by the strength and co- gency of her argument but by the sheer impact of her blackness in their white midst.

Her color might have been a weapon she used to dazzle and disarm her opponents. And she had highlighted it with the clothes she was wearing: a white dress patterned with large blocks of primary colors I remember (it looked Mexican) and a pair of intricately wrought silver earrings—long and with many little parts which clashed like muted cymbals over the micro- phone each time she moved her head. She wore her hair cropped short like a boy's and it was not straightened like mine and the other Negro girls' in the audience, but left in its coarse natural state: a small forest under which her face emerged in its intense and startling handsomeness. I remember she left the auditorium in triumph that day, surrounded by a noisy entourage from her college—all of them white.

"We were very serious," she said now, describing the left-wing group she had belonged to then—and there was a defensiveness in her voice which sought to protect them from all censure. "We believed—because we were young, I suppose, and had nothing as yet to risk—that we could do something about the injustices which everyone around us seemed to take for granted. So we picketed and demonstrated and bombarded Washington with our protests, only to have our names added to the Attorney General's list for all our trouble. We were always standing on street corners handing out leaflets or getting people to sign petitions. We always seemed to pick the coldest days to do that." Her smile held long after the words had died.

"I, we all, had such a sense of purpose then," she said softly, and a sadness lay aslant the smile now, darkening it. "We were forever holding meetings, having endless discusssions, arguing, shouting, theorizing. And we had fun. Those parties! There was always somebody with a guitar. We were always singing. . . ."Suddenly, she began singing—and her voice was sure, militant, and faintly self-mocking,

"But the banks are made of marble
With a guard at every door
And the vaults are stuffed with silver
That the workers sweated for . . ."

When she spoke again the words were a sad coda to the song. "Well, as you probably know, things came to an ugly head with McCarthy reigning in Washington, and I was one of the people temporarily suspended from school."

She broke off and we both waited, the ice in our glasses melted and the drinks gone flat.

"At first, I didn't mind," she said finally. "After all, we were right. The fact that they suspended us proved it. Besides, I was in the middle of an affair, a real one this time, and too busy with that to care about anything else."She paused again, frowning.

"He was white," she said quickly and glanced at me as though to surprise either shock or disapproval in my face. "We were very involved. At one point—I think just after we had been suspended and he started working—we even thought of getting

married. Living in New York, moving in the crowd we did, we
might have been able to manage it. But I couldn't. There were
too many complex things going on beneath the surface,"
she said, her voice strained by the hopelessness she must have
felt then, her hands shaping it in the air between us. "Neither
one of us could really escape what our color had come to mean
in this country. Let me explain. Bob was always, for some odd
reason, talking about how much the Negro suffered, and although I would agree with him I would also try to get across
that, you know, like all people we also had fun once in a while,
loved our children, liked making love—that we were human
beings, for God's sake. But he only wanted to hear about the
suffering. It was as if this comforted him and eased his own
suffering—and he did suffer because of any number of things:
his own uncertainty, for one, his difficulties with his family, for
another . . .

"Once, I remember, when his father came into New York,
Bob insisted that I meet him. I don't know why I agreed to go
with him. . . ." She took a deep breath and raised her head very
high. "I'll never forget or forgive the look on that old man's
face when he opened his hotel-room door and saw me. The
horror. I might have been the personification of every evil in
the world. His inability to believe that it was his son standing
there holding my hand. His shock. I'm sure he never fully recovered. I know I never did. Nor can I forget Bob's laugh in
the elevator afterwards, the way he kept repeating: 'Did you see
his face when he saw you? Did you? . . .' He had used me, you
see. I had been the means, the instrument of his revenge.

"And I wasn't any better. I used him. I took every opportunity to treat him shabbily, trying, you see, through him, to
get at that white world which had not only denied me, but had
turned my own against me." Her eyes closed. "I went numb
all over when I understood what we were doing to, and with,
each other. I stayed numb for a long time."

As Reena described the events which followed—the break with
Bob, her gradual withdrawal from the left-wing group ("I had
had it with them too. I got tired of being 'their Negro,' their
pet. Besides, they were just all talk, really. All theories and
abstractions. I doubt that, with all their elaborate plans for the

Negro and for the workers of the world, any of them had ever
been near a factory or up to Harlem")—as she spoke about her
reinstatement in school, her voice suggested the numbness she
had felt then. It only stirred into life again when she talked of
her graduation.

"You should have seen my parents. It was really their day.
My mother was so proud she complained about everything: her
seat, the heat, the speaker; and my father just sat there long
after everybody had left, too awed to move. God, it meant so
much to them. It was as if I had made up for the generations
his people had picked cotton in Georgia and my mother's family
had cut cane in the West Indies. It frightened me."

I asked her after a long wait what she had done after graduating.

"How do you mean, what I did. Looked for a job. Tell me,
have you ever looked for work in this man's city?"

"I know." I said, holding up my hand. "Don't tell me."

We both looked at my raised hand which sought to waive
the discussion, then at each other and suddenly we laughed, a
laugh so loud and violent with pain and outrage it brought tears.

"Girl," Reena said, the tears silver against her blackness. "You
could put me blindfolded right now at the Times Building on
42nd Street and I would be able to find my way to every
newspaper office in town. But tell me, how come white folks is
so *hard*?"

"Just bo'n hard."

We were laughing again and this time I nearly slid off the
trunk and Reena fell back among the satin roses.

"I didn't know there were so many ways of saying 'no' without ever once using the word," she said, the laughter lodged in
her throat, but her eyes had gone hard. "Sometimes I'd find
myself in the elevator, on my way out, and smiling all over
myself because I thought I had gotten the job, before it would
hit me that they had really said no, not yes. Some of those
people in personnel had so perfected their smiles they looked
almost genuine. The ones who used to get me, though, were
those who tried to make the interview into an intimate chat
between friends. They'd put you in a comfortable chair, offer
you a cigarette, and order coffee. How I hated that coffee. They

didn't know it—or maybe they did—but it was like offering me hemlock. . . .

"You think Christ had it tough?" Her laughter rushed against the air which resisted it. "I was crucified five days a week and half-day on Saturday. I became almost paranoid. I began to think there might be something other than color wrong with me which everybody but me could see, some rare disease that had turned me into a monster.

"My parents suffered. And that bothered me most, because I felt I had failed them. My father didn't say anything but I knew because he avoided me more than usual. He was ashamed, I think, that he hadn't been able, as a man and as my father, to prevent this. My mother—well, you know her. In one breath she would try to comfort me by cursing them: 'But Gor blind them,' "—and Reena's voice captured her mother's aggressive accent—" 'if you had come looking for a job mopping down their floors they would o' hire you, the brutes. But mark my words, their time goin' come, cause God don't love ugly and he ain't stuck on pretty . . .' And in the next breath she would curse me, 'Journalism! Journalism! Whoever heard of colored people taking up journalism. You must feel you's white or something so. The people is right to chuck you out their office. . . .' Poor thing, to make up for saying all that she would wash my white gloves every night and cook cereal for me in the morning as if I were a little girl again. Once she went out and bought me a suit she couldn't afford from Lord and Taylor's. I looked like a Smith girl in blackface in it. . . . So guess where I ended up?"

"As a social investigator for the Welfare Department. Where else?"

We were helpless with laughter again.

"You too?"

"No" I said, "I taught, but that was just as bad."

"No," she said, sobering abruptly. "Nothing's as bad as working for Welfare. Do you know what they really mean by a social investigator? A spy. Someone whose dirty job it is to snoop into the corners of the lives of the poor and make their poverty more vivid by taking from them the last shred of privacy. 'Mrs. Jones, is that a new dress you're wearing?' 'Mrs. Brown, this kerosene heater is not listed in the household items. Did you get an authorization for it?' 'Mrs. Smith, is that a telephone I hear ringing under the sofa?' I was utterly demoralized within a month.

"And another thing. I thought I knew about poverty. I mean, I remember, as a child, having to eat soup made with those white beans the government used to give out free for days running, sometimes, because there was nothing else. I had lived in Brownsville, among all the poor Jews and Poles and Irish there. But what I saw in Harlem, where I had my case load, was different somehow. Perhaps because it seemed so final. There didn't seem to be any way to escape from those dark hallways and dingy furnished rooms. . . . All that defeat." Closing her eyes, she finished the stale whiskey and soda in her glass.

"I remember a client of mine, a girl my age with three children already and no father for them and living in the expensive squalor of a rooming house. Her bewilderment. Her resignation. Her anger. She could have pulled herself out of the mess she was in? People say that, you know, including some Negroes. But this girl didn't have a chance. She had been trapped from the day she was born in some small town down South.

"She became my reference. From then on and even now, whenever I hear people and groups coming up with all kinds of solutions to the quote Negro problem, I ask one question. What are they really doing for that girl, to save her or to save the children? . . . The answer isn't very encouraging."

It was some time before she continued, and then she told me that after Welfare she had gone to work for a private social-work agency, in their publicity department, and had started on her master's in journalism at Columbia. She also left home around this time.

"I had to. My mother started putting the pressure on me to get married. The hints, the remarks—and you know my mother was never the subtle type—her anxiety, which made me anxious about getting married after a while. Besides, it was time for me to be on my own."

In contrast to the unmistakably radical character of her late adolescence (her membership in the left-wing group, the affair with Bob, her suspension from college), Reena's life of this pe-

riod sounded ordinary, standard—and she admitted it with a
slightly self-deprecating, apologetic smile. It was similar to that
of any number of unmarried professional Negro women in New
York or Los Angeles or Washington: the job teaching or doing
social work which brought in a fairly decent salary, the small
apartment with kitchenette which they sometimes shared with
a roommate; a car, some of them; membership in various political and social action organizations for the militant few like
Reena; the vacations in Mexico, Europe, the West Indies, and
now Africa; the occasional date. "The interesting men were
invariably married," Reena said and then mentioned having had
one affair during that time. She had found out he was married
and had thought of her only as the perfect mistress. "The bas-
tard," she said, but her smile forgave him.

"Women alone!" she cried, laughing sadly, and her raised
opened arms, the empty glass she held in one hand made eloquent their aloneness. "Alone and lonely, and indulging themselves while they wait. The girls of the houseplan have reached
their majority only to find that all those years they spent accumulating their degrees and finding the well-paying jobs in the
hope that this would raise their stock have, instead, put them
at a disadvantage. For the few eligible men around—those who
are their intellectual and professional peers, whom they can respect (and there are very few of them)—don't necessarily marry
them, but younger women without the degrees and the fat jobs,
who are no threat, or they don't marry at all because they are
either queer or mother-ridden. Or they marry white women.
Now, intellectually I accept this. In fact, some of my best friends
are white women . . ." And again our laughter—that loud, searing burst which we used to cauterize our hurt mounted into the
unaccepting silence of the room. "After all, our goal is a fully
integrated society. And perhaps, as some people believe, the only
solution to the race problem is miscegenation. Besides, a man
should be able to marry whomever he wishes. Emotionally,
though, I am less kind and understanding, and I resent like hell
the reasons some black men give for rejecting us for them."

"We're too middle-class-oriented," I said. "Conservative."

"Right. Even though, thank God, that doesn't apply to me."

"Too threatening . . . castrating . . ."

"Too independent and impatient with them for not being more ambitious . . . contemptuous . . ."

"Sexually inhibited and unimaginative . . ."

"And the old myth of the excessive sexuality of the black woman goes out the window," Reena cried.

"Not supportive, unwilling to submerge our interests for theirs . . ."

"Lacking in the subtle art of getting and keeping a man . . ."

We had recited the accusations in the form and tone of a litany, and in the silence which followed we shared a thin, hopeless smile.

"They condemn us," Reena said softly but with anger, "without taking history into account. We are still, most of us, the black woman who had to be almost frighteningly strong in order for us all to survive. For, after all, she was the one whom they left (and I don't hold this against them; I understand) with the children to raise, who had to *make* it somehow or the other. And we are still, so many of us, living that history.

"You would think that they would understand this, but few do. So it's up to us. We have got to understand them and save them for ourselves. How? By being, on one hand, persons in our own right and, on the other, fully the woman and the wife. . . . Christ, listen to who's talking! I had my chance. And I tried. Very hard. But it wasn't enough."

The festive sounds of the wake had died to a sober murmur beyond the bedroom. The crowd had gone, leaving only Reena and myself upstairs and the last of Aunt Vi's closest friends in the basement below. They were drinking coffee. I smelled it, felt its warmth and intimacy in the empty house, heard the distant tapping of the cups against the saucers and voices muted by grief. The wake had come full circle: they were again mourning Aunt Vi.

And Reena might have been mourning with them, sitting there amid the satin roses, framed by the massive headboard. Her hands lay as if they had been broken in her lap. Her eyes were like those of someone blind or dead. I got up to go and get some coffee for her.

"You met my husband," she said quickly, stopping me.

"Have I?" I said, sitting down again.

"Yes, before we were married even. At an autograph party for you. He was free-lancing—he's a photographer—and one of the Negro magazines had sent him to cover the party."

As she went on to describe him I remembered him vaguely, not his face, but his rather large body stretching and bending with a dancer's fluidity and grace as he took the pictures. I had heard him talking to a group of people about some issue on race relations very much in the news then and had been struck by his vehemence. For the moment I had found this almost odd, since he was so fair skinned he could have passed for white.

They had met, Reena told me now, at a benefit show for a Harlem day nursery given by one of the progressive groups she belonged to, and had married a month afterward. From all that she said they had had a full and exciting life for a long time. Her words were so vivid that I could almost see them: she with her startling blackness and extraordinary force and he with his near-white skin and a militancy which matched hers; both of them moving among the disaffected in New York, their stand on political and social issues equally uncompromising, the line of their allegiance reaching directly to all those trapped in Harlem. And they had lived the meaning of this allegiance, so that even when they could have afforded a life among the black bourgeoisie of St. Albans or Teaneck, they had chosen to live if not in Harlem so close that there was no difference.

"I—we—were so happy I was frightened at times. Not that anything would change between us, but that someone or something in the world outside us would invade our private place and destroy us out of envy. Perhaps this is what did happen. . . ." She shrugged and even tried to smile but she could not manage it. "Something slipped in while we weren't looking and began its deadly work.

"Maybe it started when Dave took a job with a Negro magazine. I'm not sure. Anyway, in no time, he hated it: the routine, unimaginative pictures he had to take and the magazine itself, which dealt only in unrealities: the high-society world of the black bourgeoisie and the spectacular strides Negroes were making in all fields—you know the type. Yet Dave wouldn't leave. It wasn't the money, but a kind of safety which he had never experienced before which kept him there. He would talk about free-lancing again, about storming the gates of the white magazines downtown, of opening his own studio but he never acted on any one of these things. You see, despite his talent— and he was very talented—he had a diffidence that was fatal.

"When I understood this I literally forced him to open the studio—and perhaps I should have been more subtle and indi- rect, but that's not my nature. Besides, I was frightened and desperate to help. Nothing happened for a time. Dave's work was too experimental to be commercial. Gradually, though, his photographs started appearing in the prestige camera magazines and money from various awards and exhibits and an occasional assignment started coming in.

"This wasn't enough somehow. Dave also wanted the big, gaudy commercial success that would dazzle and confound that white world downtown and force it to *see* him. And yet, as I said before, he couldn't bring himself to try—and this contra- diction began to get to him after awhile.

"It was then, I think, that I began to fail him. I didn't know how to help, you see. I had never felt so inadequate before. And this was very strange and disturbing for someone like me. I was being submerged in his problems—and I began fighting against this.

"I started working again (I had stopped after the second baby). And I was lucky because I got back my old job. And unlucky because Dave saw it as my way of pointing up his deficiencies. I couldn't convince him otherwise: that I had to do it for my own sanity. He would accuse me of wanting to see him fail, of trapping him in all kinds of responsiblities. . . . After a time we both got caught up in this thing, an ugliness came between us, and I began to answer his anger with anger and to trade him insult for insult.

"Things fell apart very quickly after that. I couldn't bear the pain of living with him—the insults, our mutual despair, his mocking, the silence. I couldn't subject the children to it any longer. The divorce didn't take long. And thank God, because of the children, we are pleasant when we have to see each other. He's making out very well, I hear."

She said nothing more, but simply bowed her head as though

waiting for me to pass judgment on her. I don't know how long
we remained like this, but when Reena finally raised her head,
the darkness at the window had vanished and dawn was a still,
gray smoke against the pane.

"Do you know," she said, and her eyes were clear and a smile
had won out over pain, "I enjoy being alone. I don't tell people
this because they'll accuse me of either lying or deluding myself.
But I do. Perhaps, as my mother tells me, it's only temporary.
I don't think so, though. I feel I don't ever want to be involved
again. It's not that I've lost interest in men. I go out occasionally,
but it's never anything serious. You see, I have all that I want
for now."

Her children first of all, she told me, and from her description
they sounded intelligent and capable. She was a friend as well
as a mother to them, it seemed. They were planning, the four
of them, to spend the summer touring Canada. "I will feel that
I have done well by them if I give them, if nothing more, a
sense of themselves and their worth and importance as black
people. Everything I do with them, for them, is to this end. I
don't want them ever to be confused about this. They must
have their identifications straight from the beginning. No white
dolls for them!"

Then her job. She was working now as a researcher for a
small progressive news magazine with the promise that once she
completed her master's in journalism (she was working on the
thesis now) she might get a chance to do some minor reporting.
And like most people, she hoped to write someday. "If I can
ever stop talking away my substance," she said laughing.

And she was still active in any number of social action groups.
In another week or so she would be heading a delegation of
mothers down to City Hall "to give the mayor a little hell about
conditions in the schools in Harlem." She had started an organization that was carrying on an almost door-to-door campaign in her neighborhood to expose, as she put it, "the blood
suckers: all those slumlords and storekeepers with their fixed
scales, the finance companies that never tell you the real price
of a thing, the petty salesmen that leech off the poor. . . ." In
May she was taking her two older girls on a nationwide pil-

grimage to Washington to urge for a more rapid implementation of the school desegregation law.

"It's uncanny," she said, and the laugh which accompanied the words was warm, soft with wonder at herself, girlish even, and the air in the room which had refused her laughter before rushed to absorb this now. "Really uncanny. Here I am, practically middle-aged, with three children to raise by myself and with little or no money to do it, and yet I feel, strangely enough, as though life is just beginning—that it's new and fresh with all kinds of possibilities. Maybe it's because I've been through my purgatory and I can't ever be overwhelmed again. I don't know. Anyway, you should see me on evenings after I put the children to bed. I sit alone in the living room (I've repainted it and changed all the furniture since Dave's gone, so that it would at least look different)—I sit there making plans and all of them seem possible. The most important plan right now is Africa. I've already started saving the fare."

I asked her whether she was planning to live there permanently and she said simply, "I want to live and work there. For how long, for a lifetime, I can't say. All I know is that I have to. For myself and for my children. It is important that they see black people who have truly a place and history of their own and who are building for a new and, hopefully, more sensible world. And I must see it, get close to it, because I can never lose the sense of being a displaced person here in America because of my color. Oh, I know I should remain and fight not only for integration (even though, frankly, I question whether I want to be integrated into America as it stands now, with its complacency and materialism, its soullessness) but to help change the country into something better, sounder—if that is still possible. But I have to go to Africa. . . .

"Poor Aunt Vi," she said after a long silence and straightened one of the roses she had crushed. "She never really got to enjoy her bed of roses what with only Thursdays and every other Sunday off. All that hard work. All her life. . . . Our lives have got to make more sense, if only for her."

We got up to leave shortly afterward. Reena was staying on to attend the burial, later in the morning, but I was taking the subway to Manhattan. We parted with the usual promise to get together and exchanged telephone numbers. And Reena did phone a week or so later. I don't remember what we talked about though.

Some months later I invited her to a party I was giving before leaving the country. But she did not come.

TO DA-DUH, IN MEMORIAM

1967

This is the most autobiographical of the stories, a reminiscence largely of a visit I paid to my grandmother (whose nickname was Da-dub) on the island of Barbados when I was nine. Ours was a complex relationship—close, affectionate yet rivalrous. During the year I spent with her a subtle kind of power struggle went on between us. It was as if we both knew, at a level beyond words, that I had come into the world not only to love her and to continue her line but to take her very life in order that I might live.

Years later, when I got around to writing the story, I tried giving the contest I had sensed between us a wider meaning. I wanted the basic theme of youth and old age to suggest rivalries, dichotomies of a cultural and political nature, having to do with the relationship of western civilization and the Third World.

Apart from this story, Da-dub also appears in one form or another in my other work as well. She's the old hairdresser, Mrs. Thompson, in BROWN GIRL, BROWNSTONES, *who offers Selina total, unquestioning love. She's Leesy Walkes and the silent cook, Carrington, "whose great breast . . . had been used it seemed to suckle the world" in* THE CHOSEN PLACE, THE TIMELESS PEOPLE. *She's Aunt Vi in "Reena" and Medford, the old family retainer in "British Guiana" from* SOUL CLAP HANDS AND SING. *And she's Avey Johnson's Great-aunt Cuney in* PRAISESONG FOR THE WIDOW. *Da-dub turns up everywhere.*

She's an ancestor figure, symbolic for me of the long line of black women and men—African and New World—who made my being possible, and whose spirit I believe continues to animate my life and work. I wish to acknowledge and celebrate them. I am, in a word, an unabashed ancestor worshipper.

". . . Oh Nana! all of you is not involved in this evil business
Death,
Nor all of us in life."
—From "At My Grandmother's Grave," by Lebert Bethune

I did not see her at first I remember. For not only was it dark
inside the crowded disembarkation shed in spite of the daylight
flooding in from outside, but standing there waiting for her with
my mother and sister I was still somewhat blinded from the
sheen of tropical sunlight on the water of the bay which we had
just crossed in the landing boat, leaving behind us the ship that
had brought us from New York lying in the offing. Besides,
being only nine years of age at the time and knowing nothing
of islands I was busy attending to the alien sights and sounds of
Barbados, the unfamiliar smells.

I did not see her, but I was alerted to her approach by my
mother's hand which suddenly tightened around mine, and looking up I traced her gaze through the gloom in the shed until I
finally made out the small, purposeful, painfully erect figure of
the old woman headed our way.

Her face was drowned in the shadow of an ugly rolled-brim
brown felt hat, but the details of her slight body and of the
struggle taking place within it were clear enough—an intense,
unrelenting struggle between her back which was beginning to
bend ever so slightly under the weight of her eighty-odd years
and the rest of her which sought to deny those years and hold
that back straight, keep it in line. Moving swiftly toward us (so
swiftly it seemed she did not intend stopping when she reached
us but would sweep past us out the doorway which opened
onto the sea and like Christ walk upon the water!), she was
caught between the sunlight at her end of the building and the
darkness inside—and for a moment she appeared to contain
them both: the light in the long severe old-fashioned white dress
she wore which brought the sense of a past that was still alive
into our bustling present and in the snatch of white at her eye;
the darkness in her black high-top shoes and in her face which
was visible now that she was closer.

It was as stark and fleshless as a death mask, that face. The
maggots might have already done their work, leaving only the

framework of bone beneath the ruined skin and deep wells at the temple and jaw. But her eyes were alive, unnervingly so for one so old, with a sharp light that flicked out of the dim clouded depths like a lizard's tongue to snap up all in her view. Those eyes betrayed a child's curiosity about the world, and I wondered vaguely seeing them, and seeing the way the bodice of her ancient dress had collapsed in on her flat chest (what had happened to her breasts?), whether she might not be some kind of child at the same time that she was a woman, with fourteen children, my mother included, to prove it. Perhaps she was both, both child and woman, darkness and light, past and present, life and death—all the opposites contained and reconciled in her.

"My Da-duh," my mother said formally and stepped forward. The name sounded like thunder fading softly in the distance.

"Child," Da-duh said, and her tone, her quick scrutiny of my mother, the brief embrace in which they appeared to shy from each other rather than touch, wiped out the fifteen years my mother had been away and restored the old relationship. My mother, who was such a formidable figure in my eyes, had suddenly with a word been reduced to my status.

"Yes, God is good," Da-duh said with a nod that was like a tic. "He has spared me to see my child again."

We were led forward then, apologetically because not only did Da-duh prefer boys but she also liked her grandchildren to be "white," that is, fair-skinned; and we had, I was to discover, a number of cousins, the outside children of white estate managers and the like, who qualified. We, though, were as black as she.

My sister being the oldest was presented first. "This one takes after the father," my mother said and waited to be reproved.

Frowning, Da-duh tilted my sister's face toward the light. But her frown soon gave way to a grudging smile, for my sister with her large mild eyes and little broad winged nose, with our father's high-cheeked Barbadian cast to her face, was pretty.

"She's goin' be lucky," Da-duh said and patted her once on the cheek. "Any girl child that takes after the father does be lucky."

She turned then to me. But oddly enough she did not touch me. Instead leaning close, she peered hard at me, and then

quickly drew back. I thought I saw her hand start up as though
to shield her eyes. It was almost as if she saw not only me, a
thin truculent child who it was said took after no one but myself,
but something in me which for some reason she found disturbing, even threatening. We looked silently at each other for a
long time there in the noisy shed, our gaze locked. She was the
first to look away.

"But Adry," she said to my mother and her laugh was cracked,
thin, apprehensive. "Where did you get this one here with this
fierce look?"

"We don't know where she came out of, my Da-duh," my
mother said, laughing also. Even I smiled to myself. After all I
had won the encounter. Da-duh had recognized my small
strength—and this was all I ever asked of the adults in my life
then.

"Come, soul," Da-duh said and took my hand. "You must
be one of those New York terrors you hear so much about."

She led us, me at her side and my sister and mother behind,
out of the shed into the sunlight that was like a bright driving
summer rain and over to a group of people clustered beside a
decrepit lorry. They were our relatives, most of them from St.
Andrews although Da-duh herself lived in St. Thomas, the
women wearing bright print dresses, the colors vivid against their
darkness, the men rusty black suits that encased them like strait-
jackets. Da-duh, holding fast to my hand, became my anchor
as they circled round us like a nervous sea, exclaiming, touching
us with their calloused hands, embracing us shyly. They laughed
in awed bursts: "But look Adry got big-big children!"/ "And
see the nice things they wearing, wrist watch and all!"/ "I tell
you, Adry has done all right for sheself in New York. . . ."

Da-duh, ashamed at their wonder, embarrassed for them, admonished them the while. "But oh Christ," she said, "why you
all got to get on like you never saw people from 'Away' before?
You would think New York is the only place in the world to
hear wunna. That's why I don't like to go anyplace with you
St. Andrews people, you know. You all ain't been colonized."

We were in the back of the lorry finally, packed in among
the barrels of ham, flour, cornmeal and rice and the trunks of
clothes that my mother had brought as gifts. We made our way

slowly through Bridgetown's clogged streets, part of a funereal procession of cars and open-sided buses, bicycles and donkey carts. The dim little limestone shops and offices along the way marched with us, at the same mournful pace, toward the same grave ceremony—as did the people, the women balancing huge baskets on top their heads as if they were no more than hats they wore to shade them from the sun. Looking over the edge of the lorry I watched as their feet slurred the dust. I listened, and their voices, raw and loud and dissonant in the heat, seemed to be grappling with each other high overhead.

Da-duh sat on a trunk in our midst, a monarch amid her court. She still held my hand, but it was different now. I had suddenly become her anchor, for I felt her fear of the lorry with its asthmatic motor (a fear and distrust, I later learned, she held of all machines) beating like a pulse in her rough palm.

As soon as we left Bridgetown behind though, she relaxed, and while the others around us talked she gazed at the canes standing tall on either side of the winding marl road. "C'dear," she said softly to herself after a time. "The canes this side are pretty enough."

They were too much for me. I thought of them as giant weeds that had overrun the island, leaving scarcely any room for the small tottering houses of sunbleached pine we passed or the people, dark streaks as our lorry hurtled by. I suddenly feared that we were journeying, unaware that we were, toward some dangerous place where the canes, grown as high and thick as a forest, would close in on us and run us through with their stiletto blades. I longed then for the familiar: for the street in Brooklyn where I lived, for my father who had refused to accompany us ("Blowing out good money on foolishness," he had said of the trip), for a game of tag with my friends under the chestnut tree outside our aging brownstone house.

"Yes, but wait till you see St. Thomas canes," Da-duh was saying to me. "They's canes father, bo," she gave a proud arrogant nod. "Tomorrow, God willing, I goin' take you out in the ground and show them to you."

True to her word Da-duh took me with her the following day out into the ground. It was a fairly large plot adjoining her weathered board and shingle house and consisting of a small orchard, a good-sized canepiece and behind the canes, where the land sloped abruptly down, a gully. She had purchased it with Panama money sent her by her eldest son, my uncle Joseph, who had died working on the canal. We entered the ground along a trail no wider than her body and as devious and complex as her reasons for showing me her land. Da-duh strode briskly ahead, her slight form filled out this morning by the layers of sacking petticoats she wore under her working dress to protect her against the damp. A fresh white cloth, elaborately arranged around her head, added to her height, and lent her a vain, almost roguish air.

Her pace slowed once we reached the orchard, and glancing back at me occasionally over her shoulder, she pointed out the various trees.

"This here is a breadfruit," she said. "That one yonder is a papaw. Here's a guava. This is a mango. I know you don't have anything like these in New York. Here's a sugar apple." (The fruit looked more like artichokes than apples to me.) "This one bears limes. . . ." She went on for some time, intoning the names of the trees as though they were those of her gods. Finally, turning to me, she said, "I know you don't have anything this nice where you come from." Then, as I hesitated: "I said I know you don't have anything this nice where you come from. . . ."

"No," I said and my world did seem suddenly lacking.

Da-duh nodded and passed on. The orchard ended and we were on the narrow cart road that led through the canepiece, the canes clashing like swords above my cowering head. Again she turned and her thin muscular arms spread wide, her dim gaze embracing the small field of canes, she said—and her voice almost broke under the weight of her pride, "Tell me, have you got anything like these in that place where you were born?"

"No."

"I din' think so. I bet you don't even know that these canes here and the sugar you eat is one and the same thing. That they does throw the canes into some damn machine at the factory and squeeze out all the little life in them to make sugar for you all so in New York to eat. I bet you don't know that."

"I've got two cavities and I'm not allowed to eat a lot of sugar."

But Da-duh didn't hear me. She had turned with an inexplicably angry motion and was making her way rapidly out of the canes and down the slope at the edge of the field which led to the gully below. Following her apprehensively down the incline amid a stand of banana plants whose leaves flapped like elephants ears in the wind, I found myself in the middle of a small tropical wood—a place dense and damp and gloomy and tremulous with the fitful play of light and shadow as the leaves high above moved against the sun that was almost hidden from view. It was a violent place, the tangled foliage fighting each other for a chance at the sunlight, the branches of the trees locked in what seemed an immemorial struggle, one both necessary and inevitable. But despite the violence, it was pleasant, almost peaceful in the gully, and beneath the thick undergrowth the earth smelled like spring.

This time Da-duh didn't even bother to ask her usual question, but simply turned and waited for me to speak.

"No," I said, my head bowed. "We don't have anything like this in New York."

"Ah," she cried, her triumph complete. "I din' think so. Why, I've heard that's a place where you can walk till you near drop and never see a tree."

"We've got a chestnut tree in front of our house," I said.

"Does it bear?" She waited. "I ask you, does it bear?"

"Not anymore," I muttered. "It used to, but not anymore."

She gave the nod that was like a nervous twitch. "You see," she said. "Nothing can bear there." Then, secure behind her scorn, she added, "But tell me, what's this snow like that you hear so much about?"

Looking up, I studied her closely, sensing my chance, and then I told her, describing at length and with as much drama as I could summon not only what snow in the city was like, but what it would be like here, in her perennial summer kingdom.

". . . And you see all these trees you got here," I said. "Well, they'd be bare. No leaves, no fruit, nothing. They'd be covered in snow. You see your canes. They'd be buried under tons of snow. The snow would be higher than your head, higher than your house, and you wouldn't be able to come down into this here gully because it would be snowed under. . . ."

She searched my face for the lie, still scornful but intrigued. "What a thing, huh?" she said finally, whispering it softly to herself.

"And when it snows you couldn't dress like you are now," I said. "Oh no, you'd freeze to death. You'd have to wear a hat and gloves and galoshes and ear muffs so your ears wouldn't freeze and drop off, and a heavy coat. I've got a Shirley Temple coat with fur on the collar. I can dance. You wanna see?"

Before she could answer I began, with a dance called the Truck which was popular back then in the 1930's. My right forefinger waving, I trucked around the nearby trees and around Da-duh's awed and rigid form. After the Truck I did the Suzy-Q, my lean hips swishing, my sneakers sidling zigzag over the ground. "I can sing," I said and did so, starting with "I'm Gonna Sit Right Down and Write Myself a Letter," then without pausing, "Tea For Two," and ending with "I Found a Million Dollar Baby in a Five and Ten Cent Store."

For long moments afterwards Da-duh stared at me as if I were a creature from Mars, an emissary from some world she did not know but which intrigued her and whose power she both felt and feared. Yet something about my performance must have pleased her, because bending down she slowly lifted her long skirt and then, one by one, the layers of petticoats until she came to a drawstring purse dangling at the end of a long strip of cloth tied round her waist. Opening the purse she handed me a penny. "Here," she said half-smiling against her will. "Take this to buy yourself a sweet at the shop up the road. There's nothing to be done with you, soul."

From then on, whenever I wasn't taken to visit relatives, I accompanied Da-duh out into the ground, and alone with her amid the canes or down in the gully I told her about New York. It always began with some slighting remark on her part: "I know they don't have anything this nice where you come from," or "Tell me, I hear those foolish people in New York does do such and such. . . ." But as I answered, recreating my towering world of steel and concrete and machines for her, building the city out of words, I would feel her give way. I came to know the signs of her surrender: the total stillness that would come over her little hard dry form, the probing gaze that like a surgeon's knife sought to cut through my skull to get at the images there, to see if I were lying; above all, her fear, a fear nameless and profound, the same one I had felt beating in the palm of her hand that day in the lorry.

Over the weeks I told her about refrigerators, radios, gas stoves, elevators, trolley cars, wringer washing machines, movies, airplanes, the cyclone at Coney Island, subways, toasters, electric lights: "At night, see, all you have to do is flip this little switch on the wall and all the lights in the house go on. Just like that. Like magic. It's like turning on the sun at night."

"But tell me," she said to me once with a faint mocking smile, "do the white people have all these things too or it's only the people looking like us?"

I laughed. "What d'ya mean," I said. "The white people have even better." Then: "I beat up a white girl in my class last term."

"Beating up white people!" Her tone was incredulous.

"How you mean!" I said, using an expression of hers. "She called me a name."

For some reason Da-duh could not quite get over this and repeated in the same hushed, shocked voice, "Beating up white people now! Oh, the lord, the world's changing up so I can scarce recognize it anymore."

One morning toward the end of our stay, Da-duh led me into a part of the gully that we had never visited before, an area darker and more thickly overgrown than the rest, almost impenetrable. There in a small clearing amid the dense bush, she stopped before an incredibly tall royal palm which rose cleanly out of the ground, and drawing the eye up with it, soared high above the trees around it into the sky. It appeared to be touching the blue dome of sky, to be flaunting its dark crown of fronds right in the blinding white face of the late morning sun.

Da-duh watched me a long time before she spoke, and then she said. very quietly, "All right, now, tell me if you've got anything this tall in that place you're from."

I almost wished, seeing her face, that I could have said no.

"Yes," I said. "We've got buildings hundreds of times this tall in New York. There's one called the Empire State building that's the tallest in the world. My class visited it last year and I went all the way to the top. It's got over a hundred floors. I can't describe how tall it is. Wait a minute. What's the name of that hill I went to visit the other day, where they have the police station?"

"You mean Bissex?"

"Yes, Bissex. Well, the Empire State Building is way taller than that."

"You're lying now!" she shouted, trembling with rage. Her hand lifted to strike me.

"No, I'm not," I said. "It really is, if you don't believe me I'll send you a picture postcard of it soon as I get back home so you can see for yourself. But it's way taller than Bissex."

All the fight went out of her at that. The hand poised to strike me fell limp to her side, and as she stared at me, seeing not me but the building that was taller than the highest hill she knew, the small stubborn light in her eyes (it was the same amber as the flame in the kerosene lamp she lit at dusk) began to fail. Finally, with a vague gesture that even in the midst of her defeat still tried to dismiss me and my world, she turned and started back through the gully, walking slowly, her steps groping and uncertain, as if she were suddenly no longer sure of the way, while I followed triumphant yet strangely saddened behind.

The next morning I found her dressed for our morning walk but stretched out on the Berbice chair in the tiny drawing room where she sometimes napped during the afternoon heat, her face turned to the window beside her. She appeared thinner and suddenly indescribably old.

"My Da-duh," I said.

"Yes, nuh," she said. Her voice was listless and the face she slowly turned my way was, now that I think back on it, like a Benin mask, the features drawn and almost distorted by an ancient abstract sorrow.

"Don't you feel well?" I asked.

"Girl, I don't know."

"My Da-duh, I goin' boil you some bush tea," my aunt, Da-duh's youngest child, who lived with her, called from the shed roof kitchen.

"Who tell you I need bush tea?" she cried, her voice assuming for a moment its old authority. "You can't even rest nowadays without some malicious person looking for you to be dead. Come girl," she motioned me to a place beside her on the old-fashioned lounge chair, "give us a tune."

I sang for her until breakfast at eleven, all my brash irreverent Tin Pan Alley songs, and then just before noon we went out into the ground. But it was a short, dispirited walk. Da-duh didn't even notice that the mangoes were beginning to ripen and would have to be picked before the village boys got to them. And when she paused occasionally and looked out across the canes or up at her trees it wasn't as if she were seeing them but something else. Some huge, monolithic shape had imposed itself, it seemed, between her and the land, obstructing her vision. Returning to the house she slept the entire afternoon on the Berbice chair.

She remained like this until we left, languishing away the mornings on the chair at the window gazing out at the land as if it were already doomed; then, at noon, taking the brief stroll with me through the ground during which she seldom spoke, and afterwards returning home to sleep till almost dusk sometimes.

On the day of our departure she put on the austere, ankle length white dress, the black shoes and brown felt hat (her town clothes she called them), but she did not go with us to town. She saw us off on the road outside her house and in the midst of my mother's tearful protracted farewell, she leaned down and whispered in my ear, "Girl, you're not to forget now to send me the picture of that building, you hear."

By the time I mailed her the large colored picture postcard of the Empire State building she was dead. She died during the famous '37 strike which began shortly after we left. On the day of her death England sent planes flying low over the island in a show of force—so low, according to my aunt's letter, that the downdraft from them shook the ripened mangoes from the trees in Da-duh's orchard. Frightened, everyone in the village fled

into the canes. Except Da-duh. She remained in the house at
the window so my aunt said, watching as the planes came
swooping and screaming like monstrous birds down over the
village, over her house, rattling her trees and flattening the young
canes in her field. It must have seemed to her lying there that
they did not intend pulling out of their dive, but like the hard-
back beetles which hurled themselves with suicidal force against
the walls of the house at night, those menacing silver shapes
would hurl themselves in an ecstasy of self-immolation onto the
land, destroying it utterly.

When the planes finally left and the villagers returned they
found her dead on the Berbice chair at the window.

She died and I lived, but always, to this day even, within the
shadow of her death. For a brief period after I was grown I
went to live alone, like one doing penance, in a loft above a
noisy factory in downtown New York and there painted seas
of sugar-cane and huge swirling Van Gogh suns and palm trees
striding like brightly-plumed Tutsi warriors across a tropical
landscape, while the thunderous tread of the machines downstairs jarred the floor beneath my easel, mocking my efforts.

MERLE

1969, 1983

"Part saint, part revolutionary, part obeah woman"—*obeah meaning juju, mojo, magic, someone who possesses magical powers. That was the way one reviewer described Merle Kinbona, the black woman who is the central figure in* THE CHOSEN PLACE, THE TIMELESS PEOPLE. *It's an apt description, for it suggests the several ways I wanted her to function in the story.*

Merle remains the most alive of my characters. Indeed, it seems to me she has escaped the pages of the novel altogether and is abroad in the world. I envision her striding restlessly up and down the hemisphere from Argentina to Canada, and back and forth across the Atlantic between here and Africa, all the while speaking her mind in the same forthright way as in the book. She can be heard condemning all forms of exploitation, injustice and greed. In El Salvador, Harlem, Haiti, at the Plaza de Mayo in Buenos Aires and amid the favelas of Rio de Janeiro, wherever she goes, she continues to exhort "the Little Fella" as she calls the poor and oppressed to resist, to organize, to rise up against the condition of their lives. Like Gandhi, she considers poverty the greatest violence that can be done a people. I hear her inveighing constantly against the arms race, the Bomb, against a technology run amok: "Everything . . . gone from the face of the earth . . . The silence! You can hear a pin drop the world over. Everybody gone . . ."

On a personal level, she's still trying to come to terms with her life and history as a black woman, still seeking to reconcile all the conflicting elements to form a viable self. And she continues to search, as in the novel, for the kind of work, for a role in life, that will put to use her tremendous energies and talent. Merle. She's the most passionate and political of my heroines. A Third World revolutionary spirit. And I love her.

1

The lower section of the road the woman was traveling, the winding stretch that lay at the very bottom of the hill, had washed away as usual in the rain that had fallen the night before. The woman hadn't been told this, though, and she nearly sent the car she was driving hurtling onto the empty roadbed where it would have been hopelessly mired, for days perhaps, in the thick bog of mud and broken marl.

"Oh, crime, not again!" She braked with such violence both she and her companion, a much older woman seated to her left, went pitching forward almost onto the dashboard. Quickly thrusting her feet into a pair of open-back shoes lying amid the pedals, she slammed out of the car and marched up to where the unnavigable mud slough began just short of her front bumper and stretched out of sight around a bend a good distance ahead.

Visibly annoyed, she stared at the washed-out road as though she would will it into place again, conjure it back. And she might have possessed the powers to do so. For her eyes, as she snatched off her sunglasses, gave the impression of being lighted from within (it was as if she had been endowed with her own small sun), and they were an unusually clear tawny shade of brown, an odd, even eerie, touch in a face that was the color of burnt sugar.

She waited, confident, it seemed, that the road would reappear, one short blunt hand at her hip, the other feeling blindly for her cigarettes in the pockets of her dress.

Standing beside the car, a battered but still regal old Bentley, the woman looked shorter than she was. And she was no longer young. The flesh that had once been firm on her bones was beginning to slacken, and under her bodice there was a weary telltale droop to her breasts. But her legs were still those of a young woman, slender and thoughtfully shaped at the ankle and arch and with a lovely tension to the black skin and muscle beneath.

And she was dressed like a much younger woman, in the open-back shoes and a flared dress of a vivid tribal print, cloth that could have been found draped around a West African market woman. Pendant silver earrings carved in the form of those saints to be found on certain old European churches adorned her ears. Numerous bracelets, also of silver, bound her wrists. These were heavy, crudely made and noisy. They lent a clangorous note to her every move. Even when she was quiet their loud echo lingered. It sounded now above the shrilling of the daytime insects in the cus-cus grass along the road and the Bentley's labored breathing. (She had left the motor running.) She moved always within the ambience of that sound. Like a monk's beads or a captive's chains, it announced her.

"But you know," she said, looking up finally from the empty roadbed, "this whole damn place needs to wash away, never mind the old road." Her swift cutting glance took in first the shabby low-lying hills which ringed her about, whose slopes were green in some places with sugar cane and pitifully bare in others, the soil eroded down to the rock, then the few trees scattered around, mostly breadfruit and long-limbed coconut palms, and finally the one or two small, sun-bleached wooden houses that could be seen clinging like burrs to the mangy slopes. Her gaze reached up to the blue, flawless sky. Briefly, her eyes clashed with the single hot eye of the sun. It returned her a look of monumental indifference, and she hastily put her sunglasses back on.

"Just wash away. The whole bloody show!" But she was almost smiling now, her annoyance giving way to a resigned half-smile which said that in spite of everything she loved the place.

"Mr. Douglin," she called to the bent figure of a man busy trimming the grass up near where the roadbed curved out of sight. The man, dressed in patched and faded denims and wearing a frayed, wide brimmed straw hat, had taken no notice of the car when it drove up, or of the woman, but had continued wielding his cutlass in slow, loving strokes over the grass on the shoulder. He raised up, though, as she called his name, and under the hat brim he was an old, old man, his skin sucked in upon the skeletal frame of his face and his eyes like two cleanly bored holes that had been blasted out of the skull with a gun.

He lifted his cutlass in salute, his manner deferent yet familiar.

"What did you do with Westminster Low Road, please, Mr. Douglin?"

His toothless smile was a raw wound against his blackness. "I sent it so this time." He pointed with his cutlass to a place several hundred yards away, where the level stretch of ground upon which they were standing sloped sharply down into a gully.

"Well, go and get it for me, please, and put it back and know I've got to be at the airport in half an hour's time." Laughing now, she turned and walked back to the car.

Once inside she began rummaging on top of the cluttered dashboard for the cigarettes which she had failed to find in her pockets, all the while damning them along with the vanished road and the heat that had accumulated inside the car while it had been standing, and then the car itself as it resisted her efforts to put it in reverse. Kicking off her shoes, she fought it, her bare feet working the pedals as though they were those of an organ, her hands busy as a juggler's with the gear stick, the choke, the steering wheel, then the matches and cigarettes which she finally unearthed. Each gesture was loud with the ring and clash of her bracelets, and she was still calling to the old man, her head out the window.

"And when are you going to bring the mold for the garden I've been asking you for ever since, Mr. Douglin?"

"I bringing it soon."

"Soon!" She gave an utterly cynical snort. "I know your soon. My bones'll be mold by then. And now the crop's started I know I won't see you. It's the same every crop season. You can't find a soul to do a thing for you. Everybody's cutting canes. Look at the painter I hired the other day. The man walked out on me flat when he heard the crop had started. Left the bucket of paint right in the middle of the dining room now! And the room only half done. And guests coming. The first I've had in months. Bournehills people! Deliver me from them. How are the canes looking?"

"Well, they're not looking so good. They wanted more rain."

"And all the rain we had last night and it's supposed to be the dry season! I tell you, even nature has turned against us in this place."

"And I hear they're talking about closing down Cane Vale

sugar factory." His voice in the sunlit air was like the tolling of a funeral bell.

"Oh, that again!" she cried, and in her renewed anger almost got back out of the car. "They're starting up that old talk again, are they? And what would the small farmers around here do with their canes, tell me? Grind them between their teeth, maybe?" Her voice had risen dangerously, and now, as abruptly, it dropped. "Look, don't start me this morning. Close down what? Hear me good, Mr. Douglin, they can't close a blast!"

With that the car bounded forward, then back, the reverse working at last, and with a wave to Mr. Douglin she swung it around and started back up the hill. She was still talking, her audience now the old woman, nearly as old as Mr. Douglin, beside her on the front seat.

"Did you hear that, Leesy?" she said, her eyes on the road, the outrage still in her voice. "They're starting up the old tune again. But I'm not going to let them upset me this year with that old business. Oh, no. Besides," she said, with a laugh that was clearly forced, "it's as you yourself once said: Whenever they begin the crop season by threatening to close down Cane Vale, it just means that we're going to have a good crop for a change."

The woman Leesy said nothing. She was slight and dry, a mere husk but for her hands, which were as large and work-worn as a cane cutter's. Since she was on her way to town she was wearing what she called her "good clothes": a severe white dress that might have belonged to some nineteenth-century missionary's wife, with a skirt that reached almost to her shoes, a pair of brown Oxfords. A dowdy felt hat, the same earth brown as her face, crowned her head. And she had carefully arranged her hands for the trip to town. The one on her lap was closed tightly around a flowered handkerchief, which contained her money, a few coins, tied in one corner; while the other was gripping the window ledge in profound distrust not only of the other woman's driving, but of the car itself.

She spoke finally, but only after the younger woman had been silent for a time, and the breeze at the open windows had cleared away most of the smoke from her cigarette. And although there

was something of the old man's deference in her voice and
manner, it was tempered, and delicately, infinitely balanced, as
his had been, by the weight of her own authority.

"Every time the least little rain falls these days Westminster
Low Road's got to pick up itself and walk away," she said, the
words as expressionless as her face, as her eyes which were
yellow and clouded with age. The next moment, without her
face changing, her voice rose thin with a kind of triumph. It
was as though some prophecy which she had voiced long ago,
which others had dismissed, was at last coming to pass: "I tell
you," she cried triumphantly, "everything's going down down
to grass. We're seeing the last days now."

The other woman suddenly became more than just silent. Her
entire body seemed to give way momentarily to an exhaustion
she could no longer resist. For an instant her hands went slack
on the steering wheel so that the car, which she was having to
goad up the steep rise, began sliding backward. "Oh, Leesy, it's
true, you know," she whispered in a drained, frightened tone.
"It's true. Everything's going down. Lord, lemme telephone
Lyle."

The one telephone in this part of the island was located in
the police substation, one of a complex of low, white stone
public buildings, consisting of a small local court, a parochial
office (which housed the district's records), and an almshouse,
situated at the top of the hill they were climbing. The hill,
named Westminster because of two tall, uneven peaks which
rose like the spires of a church from its summit, was the highest
in the district and boasted great spurs that reached out in all
directions. From where it stood at the northeastern edge of the
land, it commanded all the lesser hills and valleys lying crowded
between it and a high curving ridge to the west, which on a
clear day could be seen rising like a wall separating this district
from the rest of the island.

Ruthlessly spurring the Bentley up the last stretch of road to
to top, the woman turned in at the almshouse, a long rectangular
building of white coral stone which also served as a local clinic,
hospital, orphanage, old-age home and mental asylum for less
violent cases. She passed one of the mental patients at the gate,

a young man who appeared to be gazing directly at the blinding
noon sun.

"Seifert!" she hailed him.

A huge silk-cotton tree dominated the bare yard, and the
woman pulled up under this. Leaving her companion behind,
she hurried into the almshouse, into a smell of saltfish from the
main meal eaten just an hour ago, disinfectant and despair, calling familiarly to the nurses and patients as she went, to the
orphaned children, telling them all what had happened to the
road at the foot of the hill.

Without breaking her stride she swept out a side door and
on toward the police substation across the way. The heel of her
foot slapped loudly against the open back of her shoe with each
step she took. The hem of her dress flickered about her knees.
Once inside the substation she waved to the officers, who were
idling away yet another hot uneventful day playing dominoes
in the orderly room. Their spotlessly white cockaded hats stood
in a neat row on a nearby shelf. She informed them of the
missing road; unperturbed, they called back that they knew and
word had been sent to the road works department in town.
Then, alone at the sergeant's desk which held the telephone,
she placed her call, her hands once again performing their juggler's act with the old-fashioned telephone (which first had to
be wound), her cigarettes, and matches. Waiting for the operator
to put through the call, she clung to the receiver as though she
believed it could somehow steady and save her.

"Lyle?"—her voice rushed into the mouthpiece—"Are you
there? Merle here. Can you hear me? This miserable telephone!
Listen, love, Westminster Low Road's gone again, down Spring
Gully this time, and it's too late for me to go by M'Lord's Hill
and, as you well know, Drake's can't be trusted after a rain.
Besides which the car's giving trouble. I can hardly get it in
reverse and I'm too damn tired to contend with it because I
was up half the night painting. Did I tell you the painter walked
out on me flat the day he heard the crop was starting? So, love,
do me a favor, yes, and go meet Allen and the others for me . . .
Lyle, are you there? What's wrong? Have you gotten so great
you can't do a favor for an old girl friend? Case! What case?

Look, don't form the fool, man. Have it put off. What case in
Bourne Island could be that important? Somebody steals somebody's chicken and eats the evidence? Somebody sweeps dirt in
their neighbor's yard and they come to blows? That's all the
cases we have about here, so don't try to play Mr. Big with me
because you know what I think about all you legal luminaries
with your duppy nightgowns and musty wigs: leeches, the lot
of you. And as for you lawyers-turned-politicians! . . . All right,
finish for now, but remember, I've had to pay with my sanity
for the right to speak my mind so you know I must talk. Love,
go meet the people for me, yes, and for God's sake, tell Allen
what happened with the road and the old car because he'll be
disappointed that I'm not there to meet him. Tell him I'll def-
initely be down, though, for the reception for them at your
place tonight. I'll rest the car this afternoon and try to finish
painting the dining room. By the way, they're spending tonight
at the Banyan Tree so take them there. I thought they might
as well see the best the island has to offer before they see the
worst. Now, about the reception. See to it that that so-called
expert who's here from England helping you people in government cook up the new development plan comes. I'm sure they'll
want to talk to him. Foreign advisors and experts! They're a
plague on us in the West Indies. And I suppose you'll have to
ask the Honorable Member for Bournehills, even though as far
as I'm concerned we could do without him. And you had best
invite one or two chaps from the Opposition, as hopeless as that
is, so they can at least have their say. And don't forget to tell
your wife, that dear distant cousin of mine, not to make people
wait a half-hour between drinks. And, oh, Christ, man, see to
it that the men don't go off by themselves as usual and leave
the women sitting alone in a corner someplace like they're in
purdah . . ."

Still talking, her voice caught up in what seemed a desperate
downhill race with itself, she began backing toward a window
close by, drawn there by a sound that could have been the low,
unremitting whirr of the heat slowly rising, now that it was past
noon, to a new and ominous high. "Oh, crime, the plane! Lyle,
you've got fifteen, maybe twenty minutes to get to the airport.
Move!"

2

The servant, a white cap perched atop her thick braids, a young, closed black face beneath, appeared almost immediately on the veranda with the tray of drinks as Lyle Hutson summoned her with two sharp handclaps. At the same moment, as if also in response to the same command, the headlights of a car—four feeble unsteady cones of light—appeared in the darkness down the palm-lined driveway. The sound of a motor that seemed about to breathe its last carried to the veranda, and someone in the group around Allen said, "Well, it looks like Merle finally reached."

But Allen already knew. He had instantly recognized those faint wavering lights and the asthmatic sound of the motor. He had been seeing and hearing them all evening, imagining them in his mind's eye and ear all the while he had been moving about the veranda talking. Excusing himself he went over and stood at the top of the steps, feeling relieved, on the one hand, that the long wait was over, but annoyed, on the other, that she had taken so long.

Sweeping past the cars lining the driveway, Merle parked in the middle of the driveway directly in front of the house, and got out.

She was wearing the same shoes, print dress, earrings, and bracelets as earlier in the day; and to this she had added, now that it was evening, a long stole made from the same colorful cloth as her dress. This lay draped offhandedly across her shoulders.

Allen smiled at sight of the dress, his annoyance vanishing. It was the same one she had worn the day he had left over a year ago. It was as though she had put it on to assure him that nothing had changed and she was the same. To confirm this all the more he saw that she was as usual talking to herself as she got out of the car and slammed the door.

"Into the sea," she was saying as she came down the flower-bordered path toward the house. "I'm going to pitch it straight into the sea one of these days, mark my words. It's no use. A car that can't climb an anthill! That creeps along at ten miles an hour! It's not worth the petrol you put in it . . ."

Then suddenly she stopped short, her attention caught by a mass of zinnias in a star-shaped bed near the steps, and with a soft awed cry she gazed at them. And she was utterly still for a moment. Even the saints on her silver earrings who never ceased what seemed an anxious dance were still, as were her many bracelets. Finally, with her off-brown eyes retaining the yellow flame of the flowers she looked up from the bottom step and saw Allen.

"What the heck happened to you?" he said. He was grinning like a schoolboy. "How come you're so late?"

By way of an answer her arms with the stole draped over them opened, her shoulders lifted and her entire body shaped a slow, eloquent shrug. (It was the gesture of a Jew, Saul Amron thought, glancing down at her from where he stood with Lyle Hutson and the others. Prayer shawl and all. Full of that almost indecent love of the dramatic.)

With the gesture she simply offered herself in explanation for her lateness. Then quickly mounting the steps she came up to Allen, took his face between her hands, and brought it down to rest maternally against her cheek for a long silent moment. Stepping back, she said, "Allen-love, hear me. Only God in his infinite mercy has seen me through this day. Everything went wrong. Westminster Low Road ran off in the rain last night. The old car started giving trouble first thing this morning. The painter walked out on me flat and I had to finish doing the dining room myself. Then, this evening before coming down here I thought I'd take a little nap and slept longer than I intended. But you'll forgive me. My dear, you'll be all forgiveness when you see how I've kept up your garden. Did you know that Allen could grow carrots out of stone?" She turned with the question to Saul as he came up.

"No," he said, startled by her abruptness, but recovering quickly. "Although I must say I'm not surprised."

"Well, you should be," she said. "Miracles are hard to come by these days. You should have seen those lovely little loose heads of cabbages he would grow, those carrots no bigger than my thumb"—she held up a stubbed thumb, a resolute brown on one side, beige on the other.

"You ate them, one thing!" Allen cried, pretending an injured tone.

"Ate them! How you mean," she exclaimed. "I loved them. Do you know what it meant to see something live come out of that stony ground? I can still see you out in the yard at the crack of dawn coaxing the damn things up out of that stone and singing like Caruso. Why, I think I even have an old work pants of yours somewhere around the place. I knew you'd be back, you see. So did everyone in Bournehills, for that matter. We're psychic down there, you know. People in the village would stop by the guesthouse and ask, 'Have you heard from Mr. Allen? When did he say he'll be back?' But tell me, how're you keeping?"

And again falling silent she studied his face with the eyes people claimed could read someone's life with a look. And her gaze did appear to penetrate the rimless glasses which served Allen as a kind of psychologist's one-way screen in that he could look out, analytically, upon the world but the world could not look in. Piercing the shield her gaze reached all the way in.

"You've lost all your little color," she said. "You need some sun. Some good strong Bournehills sun. You could do with some, too." She turned again to Saul. "All you white people need a good dose of sun." Then, with a light complex laugh which said she knew how she must appear but didn't care, she held out a hand. "Hello, I'm Merle, the London landlady of the guesthouse where you'll be staying until you find a suitable place in the village. I hope Allen has warned you about me. I'm a talker. Some people act, some think, some feel, but I talk, and if I was to ever stop that'd be the end of me. And worse, I say whatever comes to my mind and the devil with it. But I'm harmless. And I mean well. Ask Allen. He's my good friend . . ."

She appraised Saul with the same close proprietary look she had given Allen. He, too, might have been someone who had once visited the island, then left only to return again after a year's absence, and she was inspecting him to see if he had changed.

"I guess these uppidity folks here have been telling you the worst about my end of the world," she said. "How impossible we are. How much money's been wasted on us. Oh, I know this bunch here in New Bristol. Bournehills, sex, cricket, and politics are all they ever talk about. But don't mind them. You'll like Bournehills, as hopeless as it is. And we'll like you if you're anything like Allen. I'm not exactly clear as to what this big research and development project you have in mind is all about—and don't tell me now because I won't remember a word my head's so turned around from all that's happened today—but I can tell from your face (you've got a decent face) you're not the usual run-of-the-mill advisor or expert.

"Lyle, you rich rascal, come over here." An imperious forefinger ordered Lyle Hutson, who was approaching them through the crowd, to a spot directly in front of her. "What've you brutes been telling this nice gentleman from America about us in Bournehills? You want him to take the next plane out? And who told you to build this house so high up when you know my car's no use anymore. And I see," she said, glancing toward the drawing room, "that most of the ladies are in purdah as usual . . ."

While talking she had lifted her face for his kiss, and despite his laugh as he bent to her, there was something deferential in the way he touched her cheek with his lips. "I see I'm in for your customary tongue-lashing this evening," he said.

" . . . And where's a drink?" She had not paused. "All these servants you've got running about the place and people still can't get a drink. Go fetch one for me, love. You know I can't take this town crowd otherwise. Rum and water," she called after him as he obediently went in search of the servant. "None of that fancy scotch you people on this side of the island drink for style.

"Dear Lyle." Her eyes rested fondly on his retreating back. She spoke only to herself. "With those blasted suits of his from Savile Row and his quotations from *The Aeneid* when he's had in a few grogs. What this place, what the years do to us all, yes.

"Allen"—she turned abruptly back—"did I write you that Glen Hill is gone? Remember it? The little one near Cane Vale factory where we used to find those lovely cashews. Bryce-Parker and his soil conservation team pulled down the last of it some weeks back. To stop the slippage, he says, even though it won't, of course. I can't tell you how it hurt to see that hill go. And do you know that your friend, Delbert, got his leg broken and is running his shop from a bed behind the counter these days? And did I tell you what happened to the television set they gave us free for the social center? My dear, it didn't last the day. All of a sudden the screen just went blank. The whole thing was very mysterious. And yours truly is a working woman again. How's that for news? I didn't last any time at the high school here in town as I wrote you. It seems they didn't approve of my teaching the students West Indian history—their own history now! But I've managed to get another job doing a little social work at the almshouse up Westminster. I got it through Lyle. Who says it doesn't pay to have friends in high places?" Her laugh struck the air a derisive blow. "And Stinger's wife is expecting again. Don't ask me which one this is. All of us in Bournehills lost count long ago. And did I tell you . . ."

The flow of words continued unchecked, the voice rushing pell-mell down the precipitous slope toward its own destruction. And she was talking not only to Allen, who stood like someone transfixed before her, but to Saul as well. He might have known the people, places and events of which she was speaking. And when Lyle Hutson returned with her drink she slipped her arm through his, holding him to her side, forcing him to listen, also.

Saul studied her face; he listened to the desperate voice, and it struck him that this woman who shrugged like a Jew and insisted whenever she glanced his way that he had been here before, had brought all those at the other end of the island, the entire spurned and hopeless lot, with her onto the veranda.

" . . . And naturally, now that the crop's started, word's out that Cane Vale will be closing down soon. The old Damocles' sword is still hanging over our heads." But her laugh as she said this was forced, worried. She turned to Lyle Hutson. "Have you heard anything about it, Lyle?" Then, almost angrily with-drawing her arm from his—"But what's the use of asking you. You probably wouldn't say if you had. After all, you're in league with Kingsley and Sons, even though you might not know it. Judas," she declared, and he laughed, his head flung back. She watched him a moment, scowling, then suddenly broke into

laughter herself. "But never mind, love, you can't help it," she
said. "They put you so. Those English were the biggest obeah
men out when you considered what they did to our minds.
Where's Deanes? Maybe he's heard something. Where's the
Honorable Member for Bournehills, who never comes near the
place except around election time? Deanesie!" she called, looking
around her. "Where're you hiding? He always makes himself
scarce when he knows I'm around. " This in an aside to Saul.
"He's frighten for my tongue. Deanes! Where's the rascal, anyway? And where's your wife?" she asked him, and then didn't
give him time to answer. "I know, inside keeping the wake with
the rest of the ladies. I'll go rescue her. Allen, love, we'll old
talk some more later. Lyle, come help me find Deanesie. Dr.
Amron, I'm going to give you a chance to say something tomorrow."

She was gone, taking Lyle Hutson with her and leaving behind
a silence that continued to hum and jar with her voice and the
scarcely suppressed hysteria behind it.

"Does she go on like that all the time?" Saul asked with an
amazed laugh when she was out of earshot.

"Pretty much," Allen said. He spoke as though he found
nothing wrong with it. "That's just Merle. She never lets you
get in a word if she can help it."

"I see," he said, and turned to watch her as she rapidly made
her way along the crowded veranda. He heard, despite the voices
and laughter, the light slapping of her heel against her shoes.
Her body appeared to waver uncertainly at each step, and seeing
this something in him instinctively reached out to catch her lest
she fall.

Without seeming to pause she managed to give everyone the
same elaborate greeting. Lifting her face she offered them her
dark cheek to be kissed. And she insisted upon the kiss. The
cheek would remain at its high angle until the person bent to
it. It was as if she considered the kiss an obeisance due her, an
acknowledgment on everyone's part of the wide suffering—wide
enough to include an entire history—which her face reflected.

Passing Bryce-Parker, the foreign director of the soil conservation program in Bournehills, she shook a finger in his face,
"All right, Parkey," she cried. "This is the last warning. When

I get up tomorrow I want to see Glen Hill back where it belongs, you hear—or else back to Australia where you come from!" Laughing, she swept ahead, announcing like a town crier to all she passed, "We're still there, everybody. The rain last night only washed away the old road, but the rest of Bournehills is still there . . ."

Inside the large, high-ceilinged drawing room, Harriet Amron sat listening to her hostess, Enid Hutson, who was telling her about Bournehills. It was just moments before Merle would enter.

Enid Hutson, at thirty-eight, had a full, shapely figure, a pretty but blurred face and slow, somnolent eyes that in spite of their slowness still managed to keep a close check on the servants in the room. Although she was perhaps a year or two younger than Harriet she had already assumed the set, complacent air of the older matrons who sat ranged like so many middle-aged wallflowers around the room. The women, holding small glasses of sherry or Coca-Cola, their corseted thighs easing over their chairs, had spent the entire evening inside, with little else to talk about but their children, the latest American fashions, and their servants.

Enid Hutson was a distant relative of Merle's, and shared with her the same maiden name, Vaughan, and the same see-through clear brown eyes. But the resemblance ended there, since Enid was as white as Harriet Amron, except for a mild hint of saffron to her skin. She and Merle had a mutual forebear in the English planter, old Duncan Vaughan, who, long ago, had owned one of the largest sugar estates in Bournehills. The old man was something of a legend on the island. People still talked about how he had sired the last of the forty children he had had from the black women who worked on his estate at the age of seventy-five. He then died, it was said, six months before the child was born, sprawled in his planter's easy chair which he had always slept in instead of a bed, his gout-swollen legs cradled in the chair's canvas sling.

In his will Vaughan, who had never married, had stipulated that the estate be divided among his many offspring, so that his

sons, despite their illegitimacy, had become, most of them, own-
ers of their own small estates. Their children, in turn, had become civil servants, merchants, professionals, and the like who
had scattered throughout the island to establish new branches
of the family. They had sought over the generations to whiten
and legitimatize the line and had succeeded—with the possible
exception of Merle's father's small section of the family, who
had remained in Bournehills and more or less carried on in the
manner of Duncan Vaughan. (Merle's father, Ashton, for instance, a great-grandson of old Vaughan, had had her by a young
weeder on his estate.) But some of the most prominent figures
on Bourne Island were Vaughans and the name was respected
throughout.

Enid was from a branch of the family that for some reason
had remained relatively poor and obscure. Her father had never
risen above the position of senior clerk in the Water Works
Department, and in contrast to Merle, who had attended the
formerly all-white girls' school in town and then gone on to
study in England, Enid had been educated at one of the lesser
secondary schools and had never been out of the island. Thus,
all she had to offer a prospective husband by way of a dowry
was her highly respected family name, her saffron-tinted white
skin and a lush, somewhat sluggish sexuality. And she had
shrewdly waited for someone to whom these things would matter and who could pay the bride price. They had mattered to
Lyle Hutson, even that unresponsive pale yellow body of hers
which he would spend himself at times trying to rouse. And he,
for his part, had been more than able to meet the bride-price
by the time he returned from England and established his law
practice: the huge white stone house overlooking New Bristol,
with its formal gardens and expensive furnishings, the crowd of
servants to the back, the silver-gray Humber out front, the two
children in the island's best schools, and the never-failing invitations to the Prime Minister's and Governor General's homes.
The contract had been well kept, so that when reports of Lyle's
infidelities reached Enid she would give a loud indifferent suck
of her teeth.

"Not me. You'd never get me to live down there," she was
saying to Harriet in a voice that made its slow uninflected way

through everything she said. "Bournehills! Why, that's no place for decent people. I can't believe you're actually thinking of living there. Even if your husband has to stay down there because of his work you should come live in town. Take a house here. But don't stay in Bournehills. You don't know what it's like down in those hills. And those people are another breed altogether. You can't figure them out. They're like they're bewitched or something. To tell the truth, I don't even like to think the place exists. . . ."

Suddenly she broke off, and her body stiffening, she turned toward the door as the sound of Merle's heels, clattering away like small hoofs on the veranda tiles, drew near. With a look of acute dismay, Enid rose to await her.

Merle entered briskly, still calling over her shoulder to those outside. But as she swung round to face the room she stopped short. For an instant something in her visibly faltered at the sight of the women arrayed on the chairs as though they had been left sitting there since their youth.

"Ladies, how?" she said, and despite her wry, mocking tone, there was sympathy, sadness, and genuine affection in the smile she sent round the room. "How goes it? Still dancing attendance on those unfeeling brutes outside?"—she waved toward their husbands outside. "Daphne, how're you keeping? Millicent, love, I can't ever see you unless I take my life in my hands in the old car and come over this way. Lyris, did you hear we nearly got washed away in the rain last night? But we're still there. Is that Doreen? Why, girl, I thought you were still in America on holiday . . . ."

Speaking in the exaggerated island accent she purposely affected, her voice loud in the dismayed, apprehensive silence that had swept the room, she greeted each of them in turn. And as she had done with the men outside she bent her face for the women to kiss, holding it near to their faces until they reluctantly touched her cheek with their lips. "Don't mind the smell, Beryl," she said to a ruddy-skinned woman in a pink dress who shied away as she brought her face close. "It's only turpentine. I had to turn painter today to get the place ready for my guests."

She chided them, "Do you see," she said, "how people come all the way from big America to stay at my guesthouse and I can't get you ladies to come down for even a day. But never mind. I forgive you. All I hope is that you haven't been trying to sabotage my little establishment behind my back by telling the lady from America about the bats and centipedes and the damp, and how when the water is running downstairs you can't get a drop upstairs. I hope you haven't been telling her all that.

"Enid!" she cried, spotting Enid Hutson. "Cousin far removed! The zinnias are lovely."

Her arms opened as though to embrace Enid, she rushed toward her, saying, "You must give me a few to take home with me. We can't grow anything that beautiful in that tired-out Bournehills soil. . . ." Then, coming to a halt just inches away, she dropped her arms with a great clatter of bracelets, and with the cutting yet tender smile, she said, "Oh, love, there's no need to look that way. You won't have to have one of your Merle headaches tonight because I'm going to be on my best behavior out of respect for the lady from America. Where is she hiding, anyway?"

She had glanced quickly across at Harriet upon entering the room, but now she turned and faced her directly, and again she appeared to falter momentarily. She gave what almost seemed a start of recognition. "Why, if you don't put me in mind of someone I knew in England years ago," she said in a wondering, strangely uneasy tone. Then quickly checking herself, she held out her hand. "But you couldn't possibly be anyone else, could you, since you're the professor's wife from America."

Rising, Harriet took the hand thrust at her. "Yes," she said. "That I am. And you must be Mrs. Kinbona."

"Yes," she said, "but don't worry with that Mrs. Kinbona business. That's just a little something left over from my African campaign, the one I lost, and I really shouldn't even be using it anymore. The name's just Merle. And soon it won't even be that. No names. No tags or titles. Just anonymity and silence," she said, speaking so rapidly most of the words were unintelligible. "Ladies, I'm going to steal the professor's wife for a few minutes. It's all right, she'll be perfectly safe. There's a lovely night outside I think she ought to see. No moon, not a star to be seen, but lovely—soft and black and with a cool wind blowing. I would invite you ladies to come along but I know you have to wait until you get word from the gentlemen outside. Oh, don't worry"—this to Harriet with a laugh—"the ladies don't take me on. They're used to me and my gaff. We were all girls together once. Come, my dear."

Talking the while, she led Harriet from the room and through the crowd outside around to a deserted part of the veranda to the left of the house. Drawing over two chairs, she said, "I hope you don't mind. I just thought you might like to be rescued."

"Not at all," said Harriet. "In fact, I'm very grateful. And it is a lovely night."

They stood quietly for a time at the stone balustrade, gazing out into the darkness that was like a black tent raised high above the house. They could smell the mixed fragrances of the flowers in the garden below and, faintly, the rich fecund odor of the soil that fed them, and the smells were those of the night itself, the exhalation of its breath.

"Yes," Merle said, breaking the silence, "it is lovely. This is what we call 'dark night' in Bournehills, meaning no moon, no stars even." Then, taking her seat, she began, "Now about my place. I hope you realized all that talk about the bats and such was mainly for the ladies. They've come to expect that sort of thing from me and I don't like to disappoint them. But the place isn't half bad. Of course, it's not the Banyan Tree Hotel where you're staying now, but at least the sheets are changed twice a week, the food's edible though nothing special, and there's always a drink to be had. There's not much in the way of extras though, unless you count the view of the sea from the house, which is quite breathtaking—although some people find the noise a bit much, and the sea air which is said to cure whatever ails you. But that's all, I'm afraid. Anyway, it should do till you find a place of your own in the village."

"I'm sure we'll be able to manage," Harriet said. "I just hope we won't be taking up too much space. You see we'll probably need one or two extra rooms in which to work."

"Rooms!" she cried. "My dear woman, all I have is rooms! Hardly anyone comes to stay at the place. The local people like the ladies inside feel it's not good enough and the tourists keep to this end of the island and the posh hotels, thank God. Oh,

I have a few odd birds who swear by me, and some of the minor civil servants who can't do better usually spend their holidays there. But most of the time I'm empty, as I am now. In fact, you can rent the whole place if you like and I'll come and live royally in town on the money." At her laugh the medieval saints on her earrings promptly began a stiff dance. "Seriously, I thought I'd let you people have the south wing, which is like a separate house. You could set up shop on the ground floor and live upstairs. Allen I know will want his old room near the garden. And I guess he's told you there's no electricity. But I've got pressure lamps which are almost as good. And there's a kerosene fridge so you can have ice in your drinks. I know you Americans insist on that. Now about the meals . . ."

Harriet's calm remained unshaken throughout the barrage, and giving the woman her carefully drawn, attentive smile, she studied her: the face which struck her as being as dark and impenetrable as the night and the odd way she was dressed. And she was more than aware of the woman studying her, since she did it quite openly. From time to time she would actually turn completely around in her chair and while still recklessly talking stare at her with the unnerving directness of a child. Those eyes probed her face with such intensity Harriet had the impression the woman was searching for someone else, some other face she sensed lurking there.

3

It was odd what happened to their sense of distance on the trip out to Bournehills the next day. The island, which had been nothing more than a tiny blemish on the smooth, tight skin of the sea when Harriet first sighted it from the plane, a place to be covered on foot in less than a day, seemed almost vast now. Perhaps it was because the road they were traveling, a narrow winding corridor cut through the endless cane fields covering the breast of the land, not only appeared to be lengthening as they advanced, but to be taking them deep into the dense green heart of the island, into another time. Or because the canes themselves, bright lances brandishing in the wind and so tall, now that they were ripe, those in the car could not see over them, gave the impression of stretching endlessly away on both sides of the road. The entire world might have been planted in them.

"Humph, they're going to have a good crop over this side of the island," Merle said, casting an envious glance out the Bentley's window. With sudden irritation she sent the car swerving round a sharp turn in the road. Through a break in the high wall of canes they saw that they had been climbing all along without being aware of it. The broad sweep of open country through which they had just traveled, with its neat orderly fields, tiny villages and great sugar mills, with the capitol of New Bristol facing the Caribbean, lay below them in the distance. And now as the cane fields lining the road began to drop back as the land sloped sharply up, they were within view of the sea behind them to the south.

The moment the sea appeared in back, two royal palms rose in the fields on either side of the steep road up ahead. Tall, incredibly straight, their fronds tossing in the wind like the headdress of a Tutsi warrior, the trees crowned the high ridge called Cleaver's which roughly divided the island in two. As Merle spurred the car up to the top, the palms stepped swiftly toward them, growing taller as they advanced. The road ran level for a brief stretch across the narrow spine of the ridge, then took a dangerous swerve and dropped—and the plain, that lovely reassuring pastoral, vanished as if it had never been, the two palm trees stepped majestically out of sight behind, and there, without warning, were the hills.

"Bournehills!" Merle announced, and pulled over to the shoulder. "Bournehills Valley District to be correct. 'Sweet Beulah Land.' Anyone know the hymn? Home, eh, Allen?" She tossed him a fond smile where he sat beside her on the front seat. "Dr. Amron, are you awake back there?" Her gaze sought him in the mirror. "Take a good look, then."

The whole of Bournehills could be seen from this height, all the worn, wrecked hills that appeared to be racing en masse toward the sea at the eastern end of the island. And as usual, because of the thick haze which made the landscape waver and lose shape, the entire place looked almost illusory, unreal, a trick played by the eye.

It looked strangely familiar to Saul. He had gotten out of the car along with Harriet and Allen, leaving Merle behind, and was standing on the sharply inclined shoulder of the road gazing around him—and thinking that he had surely been here before. He was certain he had. Perhaps, it was because the place brought to mind other places up and down the hemisphere where he had worked. It resembled them all, not in physical detail so much but in something he sensed about it. Bournehills, a place he had never seen before, was suddenly the wind-scoured Peruvian Andes. The highlands of Guatemala, Chile. Bolivia, where he had once worked briefly among the tin miners. Honduras, which had proved so fatal. Southern Mexico. And the spent cotton lands of the southern United States through which he had traveled many times as a young graduate student on his way to do field work among the Indians in Chiapas. It was suddenly, to his mind, every place that had been wantonly used, its substance stripped away, and then abandoned. He was shaken and angered by the abandonment he sensed here, the abuse. And he felt this in spite of the occasional field he saw lying like a green scatter rug on a slope. These fields only served to make more eloquent those places which were completely bald, where the depleted soil could no longer even sustain a little scrub or devil grass to disguise what had been done to it. Moreover, these ragged hills, with the night hiding in their folds, even seemed, suddenly, to hold some personal meaning for him, his thoughts becoming complex, circular, wheels within a wheel as he stood there. Bournehills could have been a troubled region within himself to which he had unwittingly returned.

Harriet had come over to stand next to him, and taking her arm he drew it through his and pressed it to his side. He was not only glad all of a sudden that he had finally agreed to letting her accompany him on the trip, he was grateful as well for her calm, her cool touch, her lovely unruffled air, her certainty. He would need them now that he had decided to have a go at life again.

"It's quite some sight," he said.

"Yes, isn't it," she said, a hand shading her eyes, which were slightly overcast. She was remembering her own disturbing impression of Bournehills from the plane yesterday, of its being some unexplored landscape having nothing to do with a physical place as such. It looked even more so close-up.

"Well, I guess you see you've got your work cut out for you," Merle said to Saul when they returned to the car.

"Yes," he said. "Looks like it."

The journey resumed. Merle, tensed over the steering wheel, goaded the balky car up the steep lifts, down the sudden drops and, from time to time on a sudden sharp turn, almost sent it colliding head-on (or so it seemed to the others who were not used to driving on the left side of the road) into an oncoming car or lorry. And all the while her voice kept pace with the spinning wheels below and the noon sun traveling with them overhead. One arm out the window, her bracelets singing a loud, dissonant tune as she pointed and gestured, she called their attention to nearly every tree and stone in the disheartening landscape; she announced the name of every hill they passed—Agincourt, Buckingham, Sussex, Lords, Drake—and she did so proudly, as if despite their near-ruin they were still somehow beautiful to her.

As they penetrated deeper into Bournehills, people began to appear, and Merle waved to them all—to those walking in what appeared slow motion along the roadside who took their time stepping out of the way of the onrushing car, to an occasional woman or child standing before one of the listing sun-bleached shacks, and to the seemingly static forms of the men and women working in the fields. And everywhere they returned her greeting. Pausing in the fields or along the road they would slowly raise their right arms like people about to give evidence in court, the elbows at a sharp ninety-degree angle, the hands held stiff, the fingers straight. It was a strange, solemn greeting encompassing both hail and farewell, and time past and present.

"Westminster Low Road dead ahead," she announced and a few yards farther on brought the car to a halt in the midst of a work gang that was repairing the break in the road.

"Oh, crime," she said, and switched off the motor. Her hands slid to her lap, and a look of unimaginable despair swept her face as she gazed silently out at the men and women working there.

As if unaware of the car parked in their midst they continued at their tasks, the women ferrying over large bucketfuls of crushed stones on their heads from a pile nearby and then sowing them over the prepared roadbed, the men spreading the mixture of stone dust and water used to cement the stones and then sealing down the road with flat, long-handled metal tampers. They went about the work at the same slow, almost dream-like pace as the figures walking along the road or harvesting the fields.

Finally, after some minutes, they paused, and flicking away the perspiration from around their eyes, they turned to those in the car faces that were eloquent of their life upon the ravaged land, that evoked for Saul a host of other faces he had known down the years—Indian, mestizo, black—which had held the same look. They were smiling faintly at Merle, the smiles soft against their blackness, beautifully controlled and knowing: they knew, it was clear, what was coming and were prepared. They said nothing, though, nor did they betray any curiosity about the others with her, but simply stood there under the sun, which had come to a halt when the car stopped, their bare feet rooted in the crushed stones and dust.

"Could you tell me, please, just what it is you're doing?" Merle spoke at last, and her voice was so quiet she would not have been heard but for the silence.

They didn't answer, but the smiles widened slightly, taking on a sly, conspiratorial edge.

"Hyacinth Weekes," she called in the quiet tone to a tall broad-shouldered woman who stood with her filled bucket balanced easily on her head and her thick arms akimbo.

"Yes, please," the woman said, looking off.

"What are you doing?"

"To tell you the truth, Mis-Merle, I couldn't rightly say."

There was a mild stir of laughter like a shy wind moving close along the ground. Their eyes remained turned aside.

"Desmond Vaughan, could you tell me what you're doing?"

The gaunt man in a tattered shirt she addressed was one of the many Vaughans in Bournehills remotely related to her.

"How you mean," the man said, not without a touch of impatience. "I'm here trying to fix up this piece of old road so you'll have someplace to drive that big car of yours."

Amid the suppressed laughter she said in the ominously calm voice, "But Desmond, you know better than me this road's not going to hold. The next good rain and it'll pick up and march off like all the others. You've got to use asphalt or concrete or something so, not just a few chewed-up stones and spit. You know that. And you need a steam roller, not just that flatiron I see in your hand. And there should be gabions at the sides to hold it in place. You know that."

"Is true," he said, unruffled. This might have been a familiar exchange.

"Mr. Innis!" She turned to the supervisor of the crew, a drawn, aloof figure of uncertain age, wearing a threadbare bush jacket and plus fours along with a cork hat to shield him from the sun. He saluted, two black fingers touching his hat brim.

"Where's the asphalt? Where're the gabions?" Her voice was rapidly losing its false calm.

He gave a chiding smile that said she should know better than to ask. "Well, Mis-Merle, we hasn't gotten around yet to those new-fangled things here in Bournehills."

She began shouting then, her voice pitched to the drumming of the heat and the strident hum of the insects hidden every-where. "But what is it with us in this place, will you tell me?" she cried. "Who put us so? Is it that we can't change or we refuse to or what? . . ."

The car leaped forward, the loose stones exploding under its wheels and Mr. Innis and his crew, their hands calmly raised in the solemn stiff-arm greeting that was also farewell, disappeared in the cloud of white dust. Brutally she gunned the Bentley up the steep road to Westminster's summit, her swollen silence replacing the sound of her voice and embarrassing the others in the car to that they kept their gaze out the windows. As they climbed the twisting white marl road, the two peaks which crowned the hill rose like stalagmites before their eyes. The public buildings appeared, a blinding Mediterranean white in the noon glare, with the almshouse, where she worked part-time, dominating the others. And suddenly, her mood changing, she laughed, and putting on her sunglasses, said, "What am I upsetting myself about anyway, will you tell me? Mr. Innis and his old road will be here long after I'm gone. Right, Allen?" She tapped his knee; then, with a wave to the idiot, Seifert, who stood at the almshouse gate staring up into the sun, she sent the car plunging down the precipitous drop into the village of Spiretown, and then out toward the sea at its end.

It was the Atlantic this side of the island, a wild-eyed, marauding sea the color of slate, deep, full of dangerous currents and barrier reefs, and with a sound like that of the combined voices of the drowned raised in a loud unceasing lament—all those, the nine million and more who in their enforced exile, their Diaspora, had gone down between this point and Africa. This sea mourned them. Aggrieved, outraged, unappeased, it hurled itself upon the reefs and then upon the shingle beach, sending up the spume in an angry froth which the wind took and drove in like smoke over the land. Great boulders that had roared down from Westminster centuries ago stood scattered in the surf; these, sculpted into fantastical shapes by the wind and water, might have been gravestones placed there to commemorate those millions of the drowned.

"Talk about a sea, yes," Merle said softly and slowed the car to a crawl. "Have you ever seen anything like it?"

For a time they sat gazing at it in silence. "I had forgotten how loud it is," Allen said, and his hushed tone expressed the awe the others felt.

Moments later they were within sight of the guesthouse, which stood on a slight rise above the beach, with Westminster towering in the distance behind it. Allen, sitting forward eagerly in his seat, called out "Cassia House!" in the relieved and grateful way someone might have said "Home."

The guesthouse appeared to be several buildings, some in limestone, others in wood long weathered by the sun and damp, which had been haphazardly thrown together. The original house, a two-story rocklike structure with thick walls and deeply recessed windows to secure it against hurricanes, had been built as a vacation or bay house by the planter Duncan Vaughan, the common progenitor of Merle, Lyle Hutson's wife, Enid, and the man Desmond Vaughan on the road gang. The various wings and other additions had been built by succeeding generations of Vaughans, including Merle's father. Rambling, rundown, bleak, the house was one with its surroundings, as much a part of the stark landscape of sea and sky as the sea and the dunes and the boulders strewn in the surf. It was one with the hill rising like a sixteenth-century cathedral at its rear.

"Don't look at it too hard, it might collapse," Merle said with a bitter laugh as they swung into the bare front yard. "It's a fright. No plan to it at all. Just thrown together. But then what could you expect of the man who built it, some riffraff out of the gutters of Bristol or Liverpool, who slept on a chair every night of his life and tried to populate the entire island his one. What could you expect of the likes of him?

"And don't look too hard at this old tree either," she said, pulling up under a lone cassia tree. The tree looked as if it had been caught in the eye of a hurricane which had whipped it clean of every leaf, stripped it of its bark, and left it stunned and twisted, near dying or dead.

"It looks about gone, doesn't it?" she said. They had gotten out of the car and were standing gazing up at it. "But it'll surprise you in a few months. When you're just about ready to give up on it and chop it down for firewood, it suddenly breaks out in the biggest yellow blossoms you ever saw. Great clusters of them. And it happens practically overnight. You go to bed one night with the tree looking just as it is and wake the next morning to find it in full bloom. It's something to behold. . . ." Then, with a sad shrug: "But the blossoms don't last any time, I'm afraid. In less than a week's time they're gone and then my lady here"—she slapped the tree affectionately—"is just her old half-dead self again."

"Not a thing's changed, Merle," Allen said gently, as though to comfort her.

She laughed. "Of course not! How could it in this place? Dear, dear Allen," she said fondly, and slipped her arm through his, "Man, I'm glad enough you're back."

4

"What's with your friend, Al?"

"Who? Merle?"

"Yes," he said. "What's her story? How did she come by that white elephant of a house, for example?"

It was evening and the two men were on their way over to the village of Spiretown, where Allen planned to introduce Saul to some of the key people among the small farmers in the district.

"She inherited it," Allen said. He was lighting the path for them with his flashlight and he had armed himself with a stick to drive off the dogs that would converge on them as soon as they reached the first of the houses. "Her father left her both the house and what little land was left from the original estate. She kept the house but sold the land in small plots to people in the village—probably just gave it to them since it's unlikely any of them would've had the money to pay her. But she didn't want it to fall into the hands of the Kingsley group, who own practically the entire district."

"How is it she came into everything?"

"She was the only child, an 'outside' child, it's true, as they say around here, meaning outside the pale of marriage, but the only one, nonetheless. Hers is one of those complicated family histories you still find in places like Bournehills."

He went on to give the circumstances of her birth, describing how, as was often the case in such liaisons, Ashton Vaughan had provided Merle's mother with her own small house and bit of land. And then one day she had been found mysteriously murdered, shot at close range one morning in the house.

"They never found out who did it, but everyone swears that Vaughan's wife, who was a 'high-colored' from town, meaning almost white like Lyle's wife, Enid, either did it herself or hired someone. No one really knows, though. Merle was the only witness they say, but she was only about two at the time and so, of course, couldn't say."

The child Merle had then gone, he said, to live with various members of her mother's family and had been virtually ignored for years by her father. But when his wife died childless, Vaughan had decided to acknowledge her and had brought her, a girl of thirteen, to live with him and had raised her in keeping with his class, sending her to the fashionable girls' school in town and then afterward to England.

"She remained in England for close to fifteen years, I understand," Allen said. "Just what she did there all that time no one but Lyle Hutson really knows and he doesn't ever talk about it. But there're all sorts of stories. She's said to have run around with a pretty offbeat crowd for awhile. She studied history for a time at London U., that much is certain, although she never took her degree. She also married and had a child, but it seems the marriage broke up and her husband, who was from East Africa, took the child with him when he returned home. Why did she permit this? Again, nobody knows except maybe Lyle, because with all the talking she does, she never, but never, talks about any of this. It's known, though, that she had a breakdown right afterward and was very sick for a time. . . ."

He paused, his voice fading into the darkness, then: "She returned here about eight years ago when she heard her father was dying. But she refused to go and see him. She stayed in town until he died, and then the day after the funeral she came back to live in Bournehills."

"She must have been very bitter against him," Saul said.

"She still is," said Allen. "She's always blamed him for what happened to her mother, and she's never forgiven him for having ignored her all those years. And from what I've heard, even when he took her in he didn't pay much attention to her, and most of the time, especially when she was going to school, boarded her with an old woman in town whom she calls her aunt and goes to see faithfully twice a week."

"She's really had a rough time of it."

"Yes," said Allen, "she has. Yet, somehow, it hasn't gotten the better of her. Oh, she's a compulsive talker, sure; and once in awhile she breaks down altogether and just disappears for days in her room. But with all that's happened to her—and there's a lot as I say I don't know about—she hasn't gone under. She's still Merle, herself, and kind of special. . . .

"I had an uncle something like her," he said after a moment. Behind his glasses, shining a dull rose in the glow from the flashlight, his hazel eyes were journeying back over the years. Around them the darkness listened and kept pace. "Everything bad happened to the guy," he said. "At one point he lost everything he owned. Yet he never said die. He could still laugh. I can never help marveling at people like that, who hold their own, remain themselves, no matter what. It's a beautiful quality, that," he said.

"Yes," Saul quietly agreed with him, "it is." Then, "Tell me, how does Mrs. Kinbona get along with the people here?"

"Oh, just great," Allen said. "And that includes everyone, from the lowliest weed picker in the fields to the rector of the big Anglican church in the village, who's a great friend of hers. Everyone thinks she's a little off, of course, but they like her all the same. The small elite in Spiretown, the headmaster of the school and the like are always talking about her behind her back, but they still invite her to their dull teas and socials. She's a Vaughan after all, and her father left her that big house and the land.

"As for the people at the bottom of the heap, the Little Fella, as they're called in Bournehills, she can do no wrong. Because although she was 'raised decent,' as they say, and has lived in England and hobnobs with bigwigs in town like Lyle Hutson, she's never put on airs with them. They know she's on their side and really takes their problems to heart. She feels for us, they say. By the way, she'll be invaluable to us in terms of the project, having access as she does to everyone up and down the line. She's what's called in the books the perfect cultural broker."

"Well, let's hope she sticks around then," Saul said, "because she was saying something at dinner about going back to England."

"Oh, that!" Allen dismissed it. "She's always saying that. But she's not going anywhere. In fact," he said, becoming once more thoughtful, "I don't think she'll ever leave here again, not for any length of time anyway. She's become too much a part of the place. In a way I can't explain, she somehow is Bournehills."

There was a silence broken only by the steady scrape of their shoes on the path and the keening of the sea in the distance.

Then Saul, with a laugh, asked, "And where did she get that fancy wreck of a car?"

Allen also laughed, "That's a story in itself. It belonged to the last English governor before independence. He was a guy, it seems, who believed in living it up big. When he left she somehow managed to get hold of it through Lyle. Knowing Merle, she probably just bought it to get the goat of people in town. I'm sure it's the only Bentley on the island."

"Where'd she get the money for something like that?"

Allen didn't answer immediately, and when he did he sounded boyish, embarrassed. "Well, the rumor goes she returned from England with quite a lot of money that had been given to her by some wealthy woman she had been—how to put it?—involved with, I guess, for years in London. It was more than just friendship I mean. I told you she ran around with a pretty offbeat crowd over there."

"Oh . . ." he said. Then, with an amazed laugh, "Jesus Christ, you friend Merle is a whole damn research project in herself."

He felt Allen stiffen aggressively, ready to defend her against all calumnies. But he relaxed after a moment and said, "Yes, I never thought of it like that, but I guess in a way she is."

5

Saul came to himself to find Merle quietly watching him from the window of the Bentley which she had pulled over to the side of the road. It was over two months now since his arrival in Bournehills and he was getting used to being surprised like this by her.

Often, walking back to the guesthouse from an interview in the village or a visit to the cane fields, he would hear the car in the distance behind him and turning see it swaying, shabby and abused, toward him. She would either be returning from her part-time job at the almshouse or from a visit to the old woman in New Bristol with whom her father had boarded her as a girl. The woman, whom she called aunt, Aunt Tie, had become

partially blind in her old age and Merle went twice a week to
do shopping and other chores for her. She usually spent the
night, sleeping in the room that had been hers years ago, and
returning to Bournehills the following afternoon. Most times
when she stopped for him, the car would be bright with fruit
she had bought at the market in town—mangoes and pawpaws
and sugar apples that looked like small artichokes. The air inside
the Bentley would be heavy with their smells, the sweetness
overwhelming the more familiar odor of the hot, worn leather
upholstery and Merle's special essence, a mix of the strong English cigarettes she smoked, the lightly scented pomade she used
on her hair, the talcum powder she applied in a whitish mask
on her face, and the Limacol lotion with its hint of fresh lime
with which she anointed herself from time to time against the
heat.

Occasionally, his mind would be so filled with all he had
observed he wouldn't hear the Bentley until it had pulled up
alongside him, and startled, he would turn to find her gazing at
him with a speculative smile that had about it the sharp edge of
a knife blade. She invariably made some remark that was in
keeping with the smile, saying perhaps, "Well, how's the in-
vestigating business going? Are you finding out all about us?"
But some days, seeing that he was tired, she would, without a
word, lean across and open the door for him, and grateful, he
would take his place beside her on the sagging front seat.

After a time, without realizing it, he found himself listening
out for the car when walking along the roads, hoping to hear
her behind him.

"What's it?" she said now. "Don't you feel well?"

"It's nothing," he said, "I'm all right. I just stayed out in the
field with Stinger and the others longer than was good for me
and got too much sun. It made me a little dizzy, that's all."

"Are you on your way back to the guesthouse?" she said.

"Yes."

"Then hop in."

He started toward the car, then stopped, knowing that as
badly as he needed the ride, he could not, the way he was feeling
take that endless voice of hers.

She gave a tight smile. "You don't feel like hearing me, is that it? All right, not a word. I promise."

The car was a dim fragrant room filled with her presence. It received him kindly, and resting his head against the seat back he closed his eyes. True to her word, she didn't once speak; and though she drove swiftly, she did so without her usual recklessness. Soon, feeling a brightness on his eyelids he half opened them to see the sandhills rising golden in the late afternoon light at the end of the long pure stretch of road with linked Westminster and the sea.

6

"But if you don't put me in mind of Daphne Pollard," Merle said.

Wearing an ill-fitting bathing suit and with a kerchief tied round her head, she was on her way to take a swim when she met Harriet returning from her customary late afternoon walk. They paused, facing each other, at the bottom of the sandy ledge upon which the guesthouse stood.

"And who's Daphne Pollard?" Harriet spoke absently. Part of her was still sitting on the sun-warmed rocks out at the cliff down the beach watching the slow brilliant demise of the day. She was holding a bunch of the wild flowers she gathered each day.

"The wife of one of the old planters we used to have about here. She's dead now but when she was alive you'd see her walking the beach every evening the same as you wearing her facecloth."

"Her facecloth?"

"Not the one you wash with," she said. "This was a sort of fine linen mask the great ladies used to wear over their faces to protect them from the sun. Miss Daphne used to wear hers pulled all the way down. You never saw what she looked like. And the facecloth still wasn't enough. She would have a servant walking along holding a big parasol over her. That woman was

frightened for the sun, yes! And she was a great collector of
flowers like yourself—what few there are around here. She was
always stopping and picking. You couldn't keep one in the place
for her."

Harriet laughed. She had, very early in their stay, decided
that the only way to deal with Merle was to ignore—very politely but firmly—those things about her which were irritating.
The smile for one with its knife-like edge. The equally sharp,
sad, empty hoot of a laugh for another. The voice that seemed
caught up in some desperate race against both time and itself.
And above all the disconcerting habit the woman had of suddenly leaning close and searching her face as if seeking someone
other than herself there. (She was gazing at her now as if she
spied Daphne Pollard lurking somewhere behind her features.)
All this Harriet ignored, and instead, most of the time, treated
her as though she were an altogether rational, coherent human
being.

"Well," she said with the unperturbed laugh, "I assure you
I'm not Miss Daphne come back to life. After all, I don't go
around wearing a facecloth and nobody trails me with an um-
brella. I'm really not that bad. And," she added, holding up a
few periwinkles in her hand, "I'll put back the flowers if you
like."

Merle gazed hard at her for a moment, then laughed. "Keep
them," she said. "They're nothing but weeds, anyway. Wait
till the cassia blooms and you'll see some real flowers. These
purplish ones are nice, though," she said, and reaching out
touched one of the little mauve open-faced blossoms. Her voice
was suddenly soft. She held the small petal tenderly between
her forefinger and thumb, sampling it the way one would fine
silk. Harriet, hearing the softness in her voice, seeing the gentleness in her touch, sensed in the woman a muted longing for
order, simplicity and repose, and above all, for an end to the
talk.

"Yes," she said, addressing that part of her, "they are nice.
The sandhills are the exact same shade of mauve when the sun's
just about to go down."

"Are they?" Merle cried. "Imagine I've lived here all this time
and never noticed that. Harriet, you should paint. You've got

the eye." She started to leave, then turned back. "By the way,
I saw our rich friend Lyle in town today and he asked for you.
He wanted to know how you were bearing up under the strain
of life in Bournehills. He doesn't seem to feel you'll be able to
stick it."

"I hope you told him I seem to be managing and that the
strain, if there's any, isn't visible yet."

"Yes, I said you were doing all right. More than all right."
It was said with grudging admiration and she began moving
away again. "In fact, I told him you've taken so well to the
place and to Bournehills people, and they to you, it doesn't
seem you've only been here a little over two months. He said
he's coming down soon to see for himself."

7

Several weeks later those at the guesthouse saw the great
Humber flashing silver against Westminster's dun-colored spur
as Lyle Hutson swung the car onto the unpaved road leading
to the house. In minutes' time he made his appearance on the
veranda, tall and impeccable in his Savile Row suit, a dull finish
to his dark-umber skin, his surface smile affixed.

"So tell me, what's the latest over in Babylon?" Merle began
as soon as the greetings were over and she had ordered him a
drink. Saul and Harriet were with them on the veranda. Allen
was over in the village, conducting a survey.

"Big news, man," Lyle said. "The new development plan is
finally ready. It's to be made public Monday."

"Oh?" said Saul.

"Yes, I'm going to send copies to you both."

"So, it's ready, eh," Merle said. "All right, tell us the worst."

He laughed. "Dear Merle, you're a born pessimist. Here
you're ready to condemn the thing before setting eyes on it.
But you won't be able to find fault with this one because, unlike
the last, it's a good solid plan—very sound. You might call it
the Great Leap Forward, Bourne Island style. Waterford—the
'so-called expert from England' as you call him—did a first-rate

job. I know you don't think much of government for bringing
him in, but the chap knows his business."

"What's being stressed in the plan?" Saul asked. He had left
where he had been leaning against the veranda railing across
from where Harriet was seated and gone to stand near Lyle.

"Well," said Lyle, "as Waterford sees it, and I agree, there
are only two ways for us to get into the modern swing of things,
so to speak. One is to bring in far more foreign investors. The
other is to expand our tourist trade. We want, we need more
of those nice fat dollars you Americans spend so freely when
you come down on holiday. Small industry and tourism then,"
he said. "Those two are to take precedence over everything else
for the next five to ten years."

"What about agriculture?" Saul asked. He was frowning.

"How's that?"

"How does it figure in the plan?"

"It figures very high, naturally," Lyle said. After all, we're an
agricultural country—and will be for some time to come. We
haven't forgotten that. Any number of changes and improvements are planned."

"Such as?" Then, as Lyle didn't answer immediately Saul said,
his frown deepening, "I ask because one of the things that trou-
bles me about so many of the development plans one comes
across in places like Bourne Island is that they tend to see industry and tourism as the solution to all problems—while agriculture, which is the base of the economy gets very short shrift
indeed. Don't misunderstand me," he said. "I appreciate the
need to diversify and find other sources of income. And I know
that under the present setup the options are few. But I'm also
convinced that equal if not greater attention has to be given to
agriculture. There has to be, first, a solid land-reform program—
it just doesn't make any sense, for God's sake, for Kingsley and
Sons to own all the goddamn land in Bournehills except for the
little plots belonging to the small farmers; and, second, an all-
out effort to produce as much of your own food as possible.
That above all else." He spoke with passion. "Because a country . . ."

"My dear Doctor," Lyle said, interrupting him, "we're well
aware of what you're saying, and I assure you that all such

matters have been taken into consideration in the new plan. In fact, one of the first things being called for is a full-scale investigation of the entire agricultural picture with an eye to finding ways of increasing food production."

"We had one of those 'full-scale investigations' five years ago, remember?—with the other so called development plan and not a damn thing came of it. We're still importing everything we eat, and it's killing us." It was Merle commenting, in a voice that for her was strangely subdued.

"Because a country," Saul repeated, insisting on making his point, "first has to be able to feed itself before it can think of getting into the modern swing of things as you put it, Lyle. It's as simple—and as difficult as that. Merle's right. It is killing, it's crippling for an island like this to be importing the very basics of life."

"And it wouldn't even be so bad if the food coming in was decent," said Harriet, speaking for the first time. "But that awful rice and bad-smelling salted codfish everyone eats nearly every day."

"Food fit for a slave, my dear Mrs. Amron!" Lyle bent on her his chill, sealed smile. It shone very white against his blackness in the rapidly failing light. "Foisted upon us long ago by our metropolitan masters. And still with us to a depressing degree, I admit. You've named them well. Saltfish, as we call it. The damn, half-rotten rice. The cornmeal that used to be crawling with weevil by the time it reached us when I was a boy. But do you realize that some people up your way made their fortune in the old days selling us these delicacies? Do you know that?"

Then, turning back to Saul, "But you and Merle are right, my dear Doctor. We've got to break the old pattern of depending on the outside for everything we eat. Government knows this. But it also knows it can't be done overnight. We're certain, though, that once we industrialize on a large enough scale we will then have the means to finance the changes needed in agriculture."

"It just doesn't work that neatly, Lyle," he said. "You can't do one without the other."

The latter shrugged. "Everything's a gamble, you Americans

say. And so, even though our approach doesn't seem particularly wise to you, we shall be concentrating our efforts in the years ahead on inducing more of the chaps with money up your way to come down and invest it here. Of course, we have to make it worth their while, so that under the new plan we shall be offering them a number of very attractive incentives."

"Such as?" Merle very quietly asked. She sat drawn deep into her chair, smoking steadily. There was a dangerous calm in her voice.

"Yes," Saul echoed her. "Just how much are you offering them?"

And Lyle, relaxed in his chair, told them. For one, he said, the tax-free period for new businesses was being extended from five to fifteen years, and all customs duties on whatever materials they imported were also being waived for the same period. In addition, the government was planning to build a huge industrial park, so that an investor would find a plant awaiting him—and this for only the most nominal rent. ("How much? Give us the figure," Merle said in the ominously still voice. "Oh, just a token amount, no more than ten or fifteen dollars a year." Lyle's voice remained unruffled.) Finally, under the new plan, each investor would not only be allowed to send all his profits out of the island but could repatriate his capital in full should the business fail.

Saul's sigh was loud and unhappy. "You're certainly giving them a hell of a lot," he said. "Don't get me wrong, I know you have to make it an attractive deal for them, if not they'll take their money elsewhere, but this seems an awfully high price to be paying, given the island's budget, just to bring in a few small plants which, from what I've seen in other places over the years, don't begin to solve the basic problems.

"And why give them such a free hand?" His voice rose. "They should be made to invest in partnership with the government so you'd at least have some say in their operations as well as a share of the profits. It's your country, after all!"

"Whoa there!" Lyle stopped him with a laugh. "All that sounds very suspect, Doctor. I didn't realize we had a rabid socialist in our midst. You've been dissembling all along."

"It doesn't matter how it sounds." He spoke sharply. "All I'm suggesting is that some more equitable arrangement is possible."

"And I assure you it is not possible," Lyle said. His smile had tightened in a small show of impatience. "I see I had best explain our situation to you, even though I must say I thought you knew it by now. But it's clear you don't. The reality, my dear fellow, is that as far as the world goes we are an insignificant green speck in an American lake called the Caribbean. Poor. Totally dependent on a single crop that isn't worth a ha'penny anymore on the world market. Without any resources except perhaps people, and too damn many of them and nowhere to send them now that England has followed the example of your country and barred her door to the nigs. We're somewhat independent, yes. But you and I know that doesn't matter for much. How independent when if England were to cease tomorrow taking our sugar at a preferential price we'd be finished. How when you Americans can plant a missile-tracking station right on our backside and there's nothing we can do about it because the agreement was made long before the present government took office . . ."

He uttered his hollow laugh, stretched languorously in his chair, drank from his glass. "It's indiscreet, I know, to mention such matters," he said, "And I avoid doing so whenever possible. I usually leave such talk to my good friend Merle here and the one or two like her on the island who still cling to the hope of some impossible revolution. But it's obvious, Doctor, you need to be reminded of the realities. You know, very often, people like yourself tend to confuse us with the new, large, potentially wealthy countries in Africa and Asia who have a little something to bargain with, even though at the present they, too, are at the mercy of the giants. We have nothing to bargain with. Therefore the concessions that strike you as excessive. Now as to tourism . . ."

And without pausing he went on to speak of the government's plans for a big promotional campaign in the United States and Canada to sell the island as the newest vacation paradise. "We'll be emphasizing our blue, warm waters, white beaches, palm

trees and happy natives, the usual sort of thing . . ." He ended
with the announcement that one of the big international hotel
chains was interested in having a hotel on the island.

"Of course, we have to agree to them operating a casino in
it," he said. "The church is sure to make a big noise about that,
but they'll come round once we assure them that none of the
unsavory business that often goes along with gambling—American gangsters, prostitution, that sort of thing, will be allowed
to get started. It's something of a risk, I suppose, but we can't
afford to miss out on having one of their hotels here."

There was a long silence, broken only by the unintelligible
comment of the sea on all he had said, and then Merle, as though
musing aloud to herself, said very quietly, "Signed, sealed and
delivered. The whole bloody place. And to the lowest bidder.
Who says the auction block isn't still with us?" The glass she
had been drinking from in hand, she slowly stood up. "Yes,
Lord, you fellas in government are all right," she said. "You're
doing a good job. You're to be congratulated."

"Now, now, Merle . . ." Lyle began.

"Signed, sealed and delivered, I say. The whole place. Is that
what we threw out the white pack who ruled us for years and
put you chaps in office for? For you to give away the island?
For you to literally pay people to come and make money off
us? Fifteen years without having to pay a penny in taxes! All
their profits out of the island! A whole factory for ten dollars a
year! Why, man, Bourne Island comes like a freeness to them.
And with all the concessions, what? We don't see any benefit
as such. It's as Saul said: they don't get at the real problems like
providing enough work for people. Remember the plastic shoe
factory? How many did it employ altogether? How many?" she
shouted down at him in the darkness. "Twenty," she answered
bitterly, "to watch the machines. And over fifty thousand walking the streets of New Bristol every day with nothing to do and
getting desperate. Man, it's a joke."

She swung away in disgust and as quickly spun back. "And
now you're giving away even more. Worse, you're ready to let
in every crook and gambler in the hemisphere just to have some
big hotel. To turn us into another Bermuda with everybody
bowing and scraping for the almighty dollar. Is that all that's

possible for us in these small islands? Is that the only way we can exist? Well, if so, it's no different now than when they were around here selling us for thirty pounds sterling. Not really. Not when you look deep. Consider. Kingsley and Sons still hold the purse strings and are allowed to do as they damn please, never mind you chaps are supposed to be in charge. And the Little Fella is still bleeding his life out in a cane field. Come up to Bournehills some day and see him on those hills. Things are no different. The chains are still on. Oh, Lyle, can't you see that?" she cried and those on the veranda felt the little rush of air, heard the crash of her bracelets as her arms went out to him. "Haven't you fellows in Legco learned anything from all that's gone on in this island over the past four hundred years? Read your history, man!"

Then her voice dropped, and she muttered obscurely to herself, "And then you wonder why Bournehills is the way it is. Why with all the improvements you try out down here it still won't change, get into 'the modern swing of things'? Ha! Bo, you don't know it, but Bournehills is the way it is for a reason—that you people in town are too blind to see. And it will stay so, no matter what, for a reason."

Suddenly, the others forgotten, she bent over him and with her enraged face just inches from his, said, whispering it, "But you know, sometimes I don't recognize you at all. I don't know the person. Tell me, are you the Lyle I once knew in England? The same chap who used to say that things in the West Indies had to be completely turned around in order to favor the Little Fella, that any planning had to be done with him in mind, because it was his country and he had to be made to feel part of it? You used to say that places like Bourne Island needed radical surgery, remember?—that was the expression you always used—the old cancer feeding on us cut away, so we could really build something new. You used to . . ."

"Dear Merle," he said, and the calmness of his voice momentarily silenced her. "Dear, dear Merle. You know what your trouble is?" he waited a moment. Then: "You refuse to grow old. At your age—and I know how old you are, remember—you're still full of all that bogus youthful idealism. And you'll remain the idealist to the end. Which is one of the reasons I love you. You make me feel young again, girl, talking all that socialist nonsense they used to serve up to us at LSE. But hear me, all your high ideals are quite out of order in the present discussion, as is your emotionalism—which has always been your worst fault. I see that I shall have to remind you as I did the doctor of realities of our situation . . ."

"The reality, blast you"—her cry jarred the air—"is that you and others like you have got yours: the big house, the motorcars, the fat jobs, the lot, and it's to hell with the Little Fella. You don't even see him. Do you realize that? Do you know the terrible thing that's happened to us on Bourne Island? It's that we live practically one on top the other because the place is so small and yet we don't see each other, we don't ever touch. Instead of us pulling together when we need each other so much, it's every man for his damn self. That's the reality—and the tragedy of us on this island. But I'm not telling you anything you don't know. You understand it better than I do. You're not just one of those political hacks down in Legco. But you make out you don't. Oh, God, to know, to understand and to act and live as if you don't, man, I wouldn't want to be you for a day . . ."

Suddenly straightening up, she declared with savage vehemence, "Look, don't come around here anymore, you hear. I don't want to see you. Stay in town where you belong. Finish with you!"

Her hand flew out, banishing him; and afraid perhaps that she meant it and was really through with him, Lyle quickly sat up and caught her by the wrist. And though he was laughing, his manner had changed. "Merle, Merle," he said, and his tone had changed also. "What are you upsetting yourself about? You'll just have another one of your attacks. Let's not quarrel, man. You know as well as I do, even though you'd never admit it, that there're no alternatives for us in this place. Not for the time being at any rate. So just relax yourself. Don't think about it so much. Let's remember the old days . . ."

And gazing up at her, he smiled in a tender fashion, some memory stirring in his eyes. "Remember," he said, "that long fire red muffler you used to wear all winter in England? It was twice as long as you were tall. You would wrap it around and around your neck and face until all any one could see were your eyes. You were never without it. People said you wore it as a sign of your politics. You would even put the damn thing on in the house sometimes when it was cold. You even slept in it once, remember? . . ."

"What's all this in aid of?" She tried pulling away.

"Not a thing, girl," he said. His softened gaze remained on her face, his hand around her wrist. And he had forgotten the others on the veranda. For the moment all that existed for him was the memory of that brief period long ago in England when he and Merle had been lovers.

"Not a thing," he repeated. "I know you've forgotten but I often think of the time we spent together in London. That place, yes!" he laughed. "All that blasted damp and fog. That miserable flat you had with the gas heater that never worked when it turned really cold. You used to say the English were the only people who could turn their discomforts into virtues. Remember those parties you used to throw with the money from your rich lady friend in Hampstead who wanted to keep you for herself. They would go on till dawn. Every homesick West Indian student in London would be there. You used to make fishcakes and cook up rice. Man, those were the days."

"You bitch," she said. But the fight had gone out of her. She stood ensnared in the trap of memory he had set for her.

"Remember that long string of a fellow from Trinidad named Richardson? He was with me in the RAF. I used to bring him to your parties sometimes. There was nothing Richy loved more than a fete. But he would refuse to listen to all our talk about the coming socialist revolution in the West Indies. He was always telling us not to be so serious about everything and just go on and enjoy ourselves, that life was nasty, brutish and short. Well, his was, I know. He went down in flames over Germany. I saw it with my own eyes; we were on the same mission. Those Germans shot the plane right out from under him. And remember . . ."

But she had broken free of the hold of his voice, and the hand with the empty glass came up as though to hurl it at him. "What's this in aid of, I ask!" And strangely Lyle looked up at the glass and smiled. Something in his expression, in the way

PAULE MARSHALL

his body strained up in the chair, urged her to throw it. He both sought and required her abuse it seemed—and not only the customary tongue-lashing she dealt him almost every time he visited Bournehills, but this sharp physical blow as well. It was as if this alone could ease the dull ache of some loss and betrayal of which he was never free.

Merle must have understood this because the hand with the glass dropped back to her side and her anger collapsed. And standing there, her gaze bent on him, seeing him both as he was now and as the young man who had once shared her beliefs, her anger, she said in a voice that gently reproved him, "Why would you bring up all that ancient history? Are you looking to lose the only real friend you've got?"

She turned away, only to start at the sight of Saul standing nearby. She had forgotten he was there. Seeing him she involuntarily made as if to step toward him, and he appeared to start toward her. But neither move was completed, and in almost the same moment, she turned and headed toward the door leading inside, moving slow and heavy-footed.

Reaching the doorway she paused and, her back to them, said in a voice that struggled to recapture something of her old spirit, "To hell with all of you. To hell with this place. The first real money I lay my hands on I'm making tracks out of here. Gone! To the other end of the world. Japan or some damn place. You watch." Then, staring numbly down at the empty glass in her hand: "I need a drink and a cigarette. And what's happened to supper? Carrington!" she called, but her voice could scarcely lift above the level of her despair. "Carrington!" she repeated and slowly disappeared into the house calling for the old woman who was the cook.

8

For some time afterward Saul found himself puzzling over the remark about Bournehills Merle had made during the height of her outburst that evening. It had somehow implied that there were other, more profound, even mystical, reasons for the place being as it was. He tried getting her to explain what she had meant, but with no success. First, immediately following her quarrel with Lyle she had sunk into one of the long, numbing depressions that came over her whenever anything happened to upset her—a lingering symptom of the major breakdown she had suffered years ago in England. For several days she had remained shut in her room in the section of the house that was off limits to everyone but Carrington. Then, when she had emerged and he had asked her about the remark, she had looked sharply at him for a moment, then declared almost irritably that she couldn't remember what she had said: "You think I know what I'm saying half the time!" and had refused to discuss it.

But it continued to occupy his thoughts, mainly because it seemed related to something he had come to feel more and more about the district. Although the research was going well, and he and Allen were accumulating an impressive amount of data, he could not rid himself of the feeling that something about the place was eluding him, some meaning it held which could not be gotten at through the usual methods of analysis.

On his way back to Spiretown one day he was overtaken on his way up Westminster Hill by a girl of perhaps twelve carrying a neatly stacked pyramid of mangoes on a tray on her head. She hoped to sell them, she told him, in Canterbury Village on the other side of Westminster. Something in her manner, in her plodding purposeful step, in the small face buried beneath the large tray made her seem as old as she was young. "This blasted old hill," she said, and sold him a dozen mangoes.

They parted company at the almshouse, Saul turning in and the child continuing on. Passing Seifert at the gate, he gave him one of the fruit. And then across the bare sunswept yard where a few of the inmates could be seen milling about, he saw Merle, whom he had been seeking without wanting to admit it to himself. She was seated on a bench beneath the large silk-cotton tree with the children of the almshouse grouped around her. From her gestures and their laughter it was clear she was telling them a story, one of the things she did as part of the rather loosely defined job which Lyle had secured for her.

She looked up, saw him approaching with the mangoes cradled precariously in his arms, saw his clouded face, his dejected walk, and her eyes narrowed, reading him with a look.

"I come bearing small gifts." He hesitated just outside her circle.

She said nothing, but in the same way that she would, when meeting him on the road, sometimes just lean over and without a word open the car door for him, she moved over now on the bench, making room for him. Greeting the children, he sat down; and, again without speaking, she took the mangoes and place them between them on the bench.

She resumed her story, and beside her, already feeling somewhat soothed, Saul listened absently, his gaze on the rapt faces of the children. She was recounting another episode in the life of Spider, the wily hero of the Anancy tales told throughout the islands, who, though small and weak, always managed to outwit the larger and stronger creatures in his world, including man, by his wit and cunning. The children's eyes as they listened were like enormous wells or reservoirs which were storing everything she was saying against some future use.

The story done, she distributed the fruit, and when all the children were gone she turned to him and waited.

"The great man who owns Cane Vale was down today," he said.

"I know. His car passed here not long ago on its way back to town. What happened?"

"Nothing really," he said. "He just took a quick look around. It was me. I just found him and his little visit particularly depressing, mainly because it brought home so clearly what you were saying to Lyle the last time he was down and you two quarreled: how really intact the old order is beneath the shiny new surface he and his friends in town love to point to. Because here was Sir John playing to the hilt the eighteenth-century absentee landlord come out to the colonies to look over his holdings."

"Yes," she said wearily, "the old gentleman's still with us." Then, abruptly she leaned toward him. "Tell me something," she said. "How much good do you think these so-called development schemes and the like, such as the one you have in mind for Bournehills, really do while things remain as they are?"

He looked silently at her for almost a full minute. "You've wanted to ask me that for a long time, haven't you?" he said.

She nodded, causing the design of sunlight and shadow from
the tree to move over her face. "That's right. It didn't just occur
to me."

"You really don't approve of my being here, do you?"

"Not you specifically," she said. "You're better than most.
It's that I don't approve deep down of any white man, even a
decent sort like yourself, coming here from some big muck-a-
muck country like America with all sorts of plans for us, even
if they are meant to help. I guess you could call it the natural
resentment of the have-nots. I'm sure you must have come
across it before. But that's neither here nor there. Answer the
question."

"Yes," he said, "I think projects such as the ones I've done
in various places over the years do some good. They help to a
degree. I wouldn't be here, Merle, if I didn't believe that. But
I know what you're asking. It's a question I've often asked
myself. Whether what I do: setting up a market cooperative
here, a clinic or field canteen there, a leadership-training program
somewhere else, all of them fairly small-scale efforts at improving
things can possibly count for much in the face of what really
needs to be done, the all-out change you and I know is necessary. Whether anything I do matters so long as Sir John and
Kingsley and Sons and their like are still firmly entrenched. Yes,
I've often asked myself that.

"I've even wondered at times whether my kind of work might
not in a way be indirectly serving their ends, since all these
projects, no matter how ambitious, are committed to changing
things gradually and within the old framework. Perhaps whether
I realize it or not I'm really helping to keep the lid on things
for Sir John and his kind, and therefore am as much a part of
the system as they are. I never told you, did I, how the gentleman treated me the first time I met him?"

"No."

"Well, he made it quite clear that no matter what I said about
wanting to help out in Bournehills and liking the people and
the place, he still considered me on his side, part of the establishment."

"He saw a white face, heard you were an American and
couldn't understand how it could be otherwise," she said.

"Yes, that was it." He sighed and leaned forward, his elbows
on his knees and his large hands trailing down. "You know,"
he said, speaking very slowly, his head bent, "although I've
always enjoyed my work and honestly feel that what I do is of
some value, I've also always felt that I should be involved in a
more direct way in helping to bring about the real change. And
I've had my chances . . . ." He hesitated; then, in a shamed sad
voice: "A woman I loved long ago in Peru wanted me to stay
and join the antigovernment movement which was only just
getting started then. But I didn't. And for years I debated with
myself whether I shouldn't return home and do what I could
there, take a stand at the source of so much of the evil I saw
in the countries where I worked. And who knows, maybe that's
what I'll eventually end up doing. I've been thinking about it
lately for some reason—about that and a lot of other things
which also go back years . . . It's odd," he said, gazing out into
the almshouse yard which was deserted now, the inmates having
gone in for their afternoon nap, "but I somehow feel my whole
life coming to a head since I've been here. . . ."

It was the first time he had spoken so openly about himself
and as he turned, his body still bent forward on his knees, to
look at Merle over his shoulder, embarrassment shaded his eyes.
"I hope you don't mind my coming and unburdening myself
like this. It's just that I got so angry watching that little runt
parading around today like some four-star general I had to talk
to someone. No," he said, sitting up abruptly to face her, "not
just someone. You. I knew you'd understand how I felt."

Her gaze was noncommittal. But she sighed, gave the familiar
shrug. "This was your first encounter with the gentleman," she
said, "but how do you think someone like myself feels who's
seen him come and put on his little show every year now for
the past eight years?"

"I know," he said. "I know how difficult it is for you living
here."

"No, you don't," she said. "You don't have a clue."

"And I also know that you think it's impossible for someone
like me,"—with a slight despairing wave of the hand he indicated
his face, pale and near-colorless beneath the thin tan he had

acquired over the months—"especially from where I come, to understand, but I do. I'm really not as hopeless as you believe."

She turned away. In the fretted silence under the tree they could hear the officers over in the police substation slamming the dominoes down on the table in their endless game. Then, her profile to him, Merle said, "No, you have no idea what it's like living here, in a place where you sometimes feel everything came to a dead stop donkeys' years ago and won't ever move again, can't move for some reason; and where some little shriveled-up man in a safari suit still drops in once a year to remind you who's boss. You feel so helpless at times you want to scream like a mad woman or rush out and murder somebody. That's right"—she swung toward him and something in him instinctively recoiled from what he saw in her eyes—"just run out the house one day and throttle the first person you meet. It might even be a friend . . ." Her gaze drifted out to the empty yard, came to rest on the almshouse. "I don't know why I came back to the damn depressing place!"

"Yes," he said, "I often wonder why you did?"

She appeared not to hear him. "God knows I never intended to. I tried to plan things while I was in England so I'd never have to set foot on this island again. But then you know what happens to the best-laid plans, don't you?" She attempted her terse laugh, but couldn't manage it. "They sometimes blow right up in your face. Mine did.

"It's almost, you know, as if I was destined to come back here, so that no matter how hard I tried, there was no avoiding it. Maybe, there are some of us the old place just won't let go." Her voice in the stillness was low, wondering. Saul had never seen her so subdued. He sensed a door within her opening a crack, permitting him a glimpse in.

"Oh, it wasn't so bad when I first got back," she said. "Everything was over for me in England, I had been very sick there, and needed a change. I even thought it might do me good, being back here. It would give me a chance, I told myself, to try and sort out my life and perhaps come to some understanding of myself. Because I don't understand me, you know," she said quietly. "I haven't a clue, for instance, why I lived as I did in

England, all the damn foolish things I did there which caused
me to lose the two most important people in my life."

She paused; he started to press her, but held back, fearful that
if he did the door she had opened partway might close again.
"I hoped I might have been able to sort it out once I was back—
and not only everything that happened those years away, but
when I was a child. I wanted to go all the way back and understand. And I've been trying, really trying, to do just that
these past eight years. To come to some understanding! To have
it make some sense!" She spoke with intensity. Then, in a spent,
flat voice, "I needn't tell you I haven't made much progress."

She fell silent, and in her partly averted face Saul could see
how the lonely eight-year search for coherence and vision had
exhausted her. But he saw other things as well: the blunt strength
to the bones beneath the dark skin, the warmth her eyes gave
off as if from some inextinguishable light within, the chin as
smoothly rounded as a girl's.

"Does it ever make any sense?" he said, and he was speaking
of his own life as well, "I suspect not. One thing, Merle, you've
got to stop living like this, shut away like this. I know I have
no right to be giving advice, but you've got to do something
more with yourself than this"—he indicated the bare almshouse
yard. "Not that it isn't a good thing, coming up here and reading
to the kids, letting them know they haven't been completely
deserted by the world, but it just isn't enough for someone like
you. Nor is the guesthouse. You need something more, a real
job that will make use of all you have to offer."

She turned to face him, and he quickly lowered his gaze,
unable to take the wide false smile she trained on him. "You
mean you've been here all these months and haven't heard about
me?" she said. "I can't hold a job. Hasn't anybody told you
that yet? Not any halfway decent job. Everybody around here
knows that. Take the last one I had. The headmaster at the
school where I was teaching didn't approve of my version of
history. Worse, he accused me of trying to incite the students.
To what he never said. Well, we had words and he won, naturally. I was fired in double-quick time. The thing had me upset
for weeks. Maybe you heard about it. It happened just shortly
before you people came."

"Yes," he said. "You mentioned it the night we met."

"So I did. I'd forgotten. And that's how it's been all along, both here and in England. I couldn't hold on to the few jobs I had there either. In fact, I would say nothing I've tried my hand at has ever turned out well. I must not have lived right in my youth. Why, I couldn't even get through the course in history I went there to study. And I can't even run a simple guesthouse so that it halfway pays. Me!" She laughed her sad, sharp hoot. "I'm about as much use as those old people you see dragging around this yard. As half-alive as them. No, less so. At least they shuffle around trying to keep the circulation going, but I've stopped dead in my tracks. Paralyzed. People in Bournehills would say somebody's worked obeah on me and put me this way, what you'd call a spell. And they'd be right, because in a way"—her voice again took on the awed, almost frightened note—"I am like someone bewitched, turned foolish. It's like my very will's gone. And nothing short of a miracle will bring it back I know. Something has to happen—I don't know what, but something to bring me back to myself. Something that's been up has to come down," she cried fiercely; there was a harshness in her eyes, "before I can get moving again!"

Her talk, her odd look made him uneasy, and he said, "Maybe it might be a good thing, Merle, for you to get away from Bourne Island as you keep saying you'd like to do. Perhaps you'd find it easier to make a new start somewhere else . . ."

Her eyes cleared; she once again gave him the false, brilliant smile. "You're a hundred per cent right," she said. "Now where shall I go? You suggest a place."

"Well, there's no end of places," he said. "Perhaps another one of the islands or Europe or Africa . . . I understand from Allen"—and he spoke with great caution—"that your husband and little girl live in East Africa, and although I don't know what the situation is with your marriage, you might like to . . ."

But he got no further, for with a look that had to do with the sudden hardening of the sunlight her eyes contained she silenced him. He felt the door that had opened a fraction slam shut in his face.

"I'm sorry," he said. "I know you never talk about them, but I just thought . . ."

She rose abruptly, jolting the bench as she did. "Well, this has been a very pleasant little chat," she said, "but government isn't paying me to sit around all day running my mouth. Besides, I've work to do inside before I leave. It's not much of a job, as you say, but I can't afford to lose it. After all, there's no telling when you people will find a place of your own in the village and I'll be left with a houseful of empty rooms again."

He stood up. "Forgive me," he said. "I didn't mean to upset you."

But she was already moving swiftly toward the entrance to the almshouse, and before he finished his apology she had disappeared inside.

9

He tried again some weeks later to get her to talk about herself. It was a Sunday morning and he was returning to the guesthouse after having attended the weekly butchering of a pig (or sometimes it was a cow) which supplied the village with what little meat there was.

Merle on her way from church drew up alongside him.

He didn't hear the car at first. He was more than a little drunk, having indulged freely in the rum drinking that was an important part of the "pigsticking" as it was called in Bournehills. Then, too, he was thinking of a group of children who had passed him only minutes ago. They had been out at the beach gathering broom sage and sand to be used to clean the floors at home. Coming toward him along the road they had appeared to be walking out of the sun directly behind them as if out of the mouth of a giant cornucopia. As he turned, his mind still filled with their small faces, and saw Merle in the fussy hat she wore to church, which didn't become her, it seemed to him that her dark face mirrored not only the faces of the children but the men and women he had just left at the pigsticking. She appeared to contain them all. So that for a moment, perhaps because he was drunker than he realized, he didn't see her simply as Merle, but some larger figure in whose person was summed up both Bournehills and its people. And it suddenly occurred

to him that perhaps he would have to come to know and understand her, really know her, before he could ever hope to
know and understand Bournehills; that she was, in the old Biblical sense, the way.

" 'Woe unto them that rise up early in the morning to follow
strong drink,' " she called from the window, her chiding smile
taking in his slightly wavering stance and bloodshot eyes.

He laughed, and going over, bent down to the window beside
her, his folded arms on the ledge, his face close to hers. "How
are you? Did you pray for me this morning?"

"Heathen," she said. "If I thought for a moment prayer did
any good I'd have prayed for myself."

"Then why are you so faithful?" he cried, indicating the prayer
book lying on top of her gloves and purse beside her on the seat.

"Because I like the way old Mr. Dodds plays the organ, that's
why." Her tone was defiant. "And the way the sun when it
rises lights up the rose window over the altar. And the smell of
the incense. And the way the rector rushes through the service
so you can't make out a word he's saying to save your soul.
That's why. Does that answer you?"

He shook his head, saying no. His eyes on her face demanded
that she give the real reason, that she tell what she was seeking.
She refused, turning irritably aside to escape his gaze. But after
a time, as he continued to press her with his silence, she reached
up, took off the unbecoming hat, and said, "I don't know why
I go and sit up every Sunday in the damn drafty place. It doesn't
help. Maybe, although I know better, I somehow believe that
if I go there often enough and sit looking at that rose window
and listening to the mumbo jumbo, a miracle will happen and
I'll be able to do the one thing I must do if I'm ever to get my
life moving again."

"And what's that?" Then, as she maintained a stubborn silence: "Tell me."

She turned to face him fully at the car window. Her eyes,
filled with their special light, were very still and clear. He had
the impression he could see all the way into her.

"What you started to say that day up at the almshouse before
I cut you off. Go see my child. Just forget about everything that
happened and what an unfit mother I am and go see her."

She quickly held up a hand, forbidding him to question her
further. "You know I won't talk about it, so don't ask," she
said. The hand remained raised, holding him to silence; finally,
she lowered it and, her mood changing, looked him up and
down with a playful smile. "Come on, you'd better ride the
rest of the way home because to tell the truth you don't look
any too steady on your feet."

"You wouldn't be steady either," he said, "if you had had
six shots of rum on an empty stomach at five thirty in the
morning."

"You're getting to be as big a rumhead as your pals in the
village. I hope you know that," she said when he was seated in
the Bentley and they were underway.

"It's all part of the research, Ma'am," he said. "All done in
the interest of science." He held up a paper bag of meat. It had
begun to soak through. "I almost forgot. For you from the
butcher with his compliments. Five pounds of freshly slaugh-
tered pig."

"How much of the five pounds is fat?"

"A good three and a half I'd say."

She laughed, a warm burst totally unlike her usual sad hoot.
Bringing the car to a halt, she sat around in her seat and stared
quietly at him for a long time. Outside, Westminster's great
spur towered above them to the right; to the left lay the low
dunes overrun with sea grape and sedge; beyond these the perennially grieving sea.

"You know something?" she said.

"What?"

"Sometimes you come close to being what we call in Bournehills real people. Yes," she said quickly as though afraid he
would deny it. "You almost come like one of us at times. Maybe
it's the techniques you have to learn in your business on how
to get in with people. But I don't think so. Or perhaps it's
because you're a Jew and that's given you a deeper understanding. After all, your people have caught hell far longer than mine.
But I doubt it. Because I got to meet quite a few Jews in London:
the East End was overrun with them in my time; people were
saying they were taking over England"—he found himself laughing despite his sudden discomfort at that familiar old saw—"and

although one or two of them became my very close friends, most of them were as bad as the English and had no use for black people. Some of them, in fact, behaved worse toward us than the English. You would have thought they would have been more sympathetic, having gone through so much themselves. But it seems suffering doesn't make people any better or wiser or more understanding. They used to say it did, that it was—how did they put it? an ennobling experience. Ha! I haven't seen much evidence of that, my dear. It's a sad thing to say—and let's hope those like myself do better when it's our turn up—but there you are.

"So, it's not that with you," she went on, the voice tumbling down its endless decline. "It's . . . how to say it . . ." She paused, and again inspected him: his eyes which gave evidence of the morning's dissipation, the high smooth forehead, the nose rising like a declaration of something or other out of the rueful face, and the uncertain expression there which said he didn't quite know how to take her comments on the Jews, whether to be annoyed, defensive or simply to accept the harsh truth of much of what she had said.

Then, suddenly she smiled—and in such a way none of it mattered.

"It's just you," she said, her voice intimate in the standing car. "It's what I saw in your face that first night at Lyle's. I can read people's faces, you know. I would have made a good obeah woman. It's that, like me, you've been through a lot, and you're only now coming to yourself. And that you're trying, really trying, poor fellow, to do your best here in Bournehills."

He laughed at her "poor fellow" but he was deeply moved— and grateful—for he remembered the premonition of defeat and eventual exile home that assailed him from time to time.

"Dear Merle," he said, and thinking of how her face before had embodied the whole of Bournehills, he reached across and touched the place on her ear where the continuous weight of her earring had pulled the lobe down slightly over the years. "I love you for that," he said.

She looked at him hard for a moment; then with a laugh, lightly struck away his hand. "Damn nonsense," she said.

10

"I hear your husband's a scientist. What's his field?" he asked as he set his glass of rum and water down amid the ringed imprints of other glasses on the scarred table. They had been sitting there for some time talking of other things before he asked the question.

It was carnival Tuesday night some months later. The whole of Bournehills practically had come to New Bristol for the two-day celebration that preceded Ash Wednesday and Lent. Harriet, unable to take anymore of the jump-up in the streets—the noise, the crush, the dark tidal wave of faces, had gone to spend the last night of the fete with Lyle Hutson's wife, Enid. Allen who also found carnival overwhelming was on his way back to Bournehills now that it was over. But Saul and Merle, reluctant to see the festivities end, had joined other holdouts like themselves over at a nightclub on the bay where the last of the celebration would go on till dawn. Merle was then due to go to a breakfast party being given by one of her few friends in town.

"I said I hear your husband's . . ."

"You don't intend giving up, do you," she said, cutting him off with a laugh. She was in a gay mood, in keeping with the high mood of the crowd dancing just beyond their table, which was out on the balcony of the nightclub overlooking the water. "You mean to get in my business if it's the last thing you do. But you're wasting your time because you'll never put me through one of your interviews. Oh, no, there'll be no data out of me tonight." She was smiling though. She hadn't cut him off with the harsh look as at the almshouse that time.

"I'm not working tonight," he said quietly. "In fact, I'm never working with you. I'm just trying to be your friend."

The silence which followed was filled with his insistence that she talk. Her smile died, taking her gaiety with it, and she swung away her face as if spurning his offer of friendship. And it remained turned away for the longest time, while across the table Saul kept up his silent demand.

Until finally, speaking more to herself than to him, her gaze turned inward, she said, "That was one beautiful black man, yes!"

Another long pause. It seemed that was all there would be. Then: "Oh, not that he didn't have his faults. He was a man once he made up his mind about something there was no changing it, and he had no patience with weakness of any sort. He could be hard, in other words. But still beautiful, you know. He was one of those people who are absolutely clear in their minds about so many of the things that leave most of us— especially when we're young—muddled and confused; you know, for example, exactly what they want to do with their lives. They've set a goal for themselves and they mean to reach it—and no nonsense about it. Ketu was like that. He knew, more than any man I'd ever met, what he was about.

"Take the field he was in," she said. "He had already done a degree in economics when I met him, but he had decided to stay on in England and specialize in agricultural economics because he believed, as you and I do, that the main job in these poor agricultural countries has to be on finding ways of improving the lot of the Little Fella out on the land. He used to talk about that all the time. It's the same thing we used to go on about at those parties of mine, but he was the first African, or West Indian for that matter, I'd ever met who was actually studying anything directly related to it. Most of the chaps in those days were doing either medicine or law. We needed the doctors, of course, but we could have done without all those lawyers cluttering up the place. They were only out for themselves.

"Ketu was altogether different. He knew the work that had to be done if the independence all of us were so busy demading at the time was to have any meaning. He was one of those rare, truly committed people. And because he was, he hadn't been taken in, like so many of us poor little colonials come to big England to study, by the so-called glamor of the West. There was no turning his head, in other words. He had come for certain specific technical information and he wasn't interested in anything else they had to offer, either, as he once put it, their gods, their ways or their women.

"I wouldn't even try to tell you what it meant for me to meet someone like him." Her voice was so muted it scarcely carried across the table. She had finally turned her face back to Saul. "I can only tell you what I was able to do as a result and then maybe you'll understand. First, I was finally able to break completely with this Englishwoman I had been involved with for years. I'm sure you've heard talk of that. To free myself of her money and my dependency. I moved up to Leeds to be near Ketu, found a part-time job and started reading history again at the university. And after awhile we were married."

Quietly, the words by virtue of their very stillness holding their own against the noise around them, she said. "We had only the two years together, scarcely any time worth speaking of, but in a way you know they made up for all the others before—and since. There's no describing them. Let's just say I became a different person with him. Softer, for one. And I didn't talk near as much," she said. "You wouldn't have recognized the old fire-eater." A hint of her old smile—but this time tempered by the softness—flashed and was gone.

"But I should have told him about myself!" It was a sudden outcry. "About the way I had lived all those years and about the damn woman! I should have taken my chances and told him. Maybe he would have understood. But I didn't have the nerve. All talk but no real nerve. Besides, I didn't see any point in it. The old life was behind me. I had seen the last of that woman and her money. Or so I thought. But she fooled me. She let me know, in no uncertain terms, there's no doing away with the past that easily."

"What happened?" He spoke after she had been silent for a time.

"The bloody checks she used to send me started coming again, that's what! She had somehow managed to track me down all the way to Leeds and the blasted money started coming again. And she had chosen her time well, the bitch. Because I was pregnant and was going to have to leave off working soon. I held out for a while and sent the first two or three flying back to her without so much as opening the envelope. But then when the baby came we were really hard up, and I started cashing them. . . .

"I know," she said, her head bowed to avoid his gaze. "You don't have to say it. I should never have done it, bills or no bills."

"I'm not saying that, Merle."

She didn't hear him, nor had she really been speaking to him. "But I couldn't see turning away money when we needed it so badly. I told Ketu the money was from my father, that he had had a change of heart when I wrote him about the baby and wanted to help. And I told myself I would start sending the checks back as soon as the baby was old enough to be put in a creche and I could go back to work. And I did once I started working again. But it was no use.

"She had no intention of letting me off that easily. Like the country that had spawned her, she couldn't tolerate people she considered her inferiors turning their backs on her. She had to feel she had the power of life and death over them. So she simply went to my husband with everything. Right out to the university! And she brought along the canceled checks—all of them, including the ones I had said were from my father. There was no lack of evidence.

"If you had seen that man's face when he came home that day," she whispered. "The look on it . . . I'll carry that look with me to the grave.

"I couldn't even make out at first what he was saying he was speaking in such a jumbled-up way. He could scarcely get his words out. But finally he said her name and I knew."

Long moments passed, and then her hand sketched a vague gesture of futility. "I tried explaining, of course, over and over again. But it was no use. He couldn't understand any of it. If it had been a man, he might have felt different. But carrying on with some woman! Taking money from her! And then there were the lies I had told him about the checks. There was no explaining them away. Nor was there any forgiving them—not for someone like him. . . .

"Oh, he tried to see my side of it. He really did. At times we both made as though it had never happened and our life together was the same. But that didn't work. Nothing helped. Something in him had turned from me and he just couldn't feel anything for me anymore. I can't tell you what a hell those last

few months were. Every little disagreement ended with us going
over the same old ground. And it wasn't only what he said then,
but the way he would look at me. . . ." A shiver passed over
her, and she shrank back in her seat seeing that look. "As
though," she whispered, "I stood for the worst that could happen to those of us who had come to England and allowed
ourselves to be corrupted. I wasn't Merle to him any longer, a
person, his wife, the mother of his child, but the very thing he
had tried to avoid all his years there.

"It got so," the crushed voice went on, "that he wouldn't look at
me, wouldn't so much as let his eye catch mine. And days
would go by without his speaking. After a time he began acting
as though he didn't even want me to touch my own child.
Sometimes when I was feeding or changing her he would jump
up and take her from me like he was afraid I was somehow
contaminating her with my touch. And at night when I tried
touching him he would turn his back. I would beg him. Me,
who never begged a soul for a thing in my life! And he would
pretend not to hear. He stopped sleeping with me altogether
after awhile.

"Do you know what living like that can do to you?" she
quietly asked. "Loving someone who's lost all feeling for you?
Have you any idea what it's like? No," she said with a bitter
shake of her head that envied him his ignorance, "you don't
have a clue. It can make you give up, so that you don't care
about anything anymore, including your own child. It can make
you want to prove you're as terrible as the person says you are.

"That's what it did to me. I got so I didn't give a damn about
anything. I began staying out, neglecting the child, doing all
sorts of crazy things—just trying to prove, I suppose, that I was
as rotten as he believed. Sometimes when the silence in that flat
became more than I could bear I would take the bloody train
to London and hang around with the old crowd for a day or
two. And when he threatened to have done with me altogether
and leave, taking the baby with him, I told him I didn't care,
he could do what he damn well pleased. . . .

"So I wasn't surprised when I came back one day from one
of my little trips to London and found them gone." She spoke
in a detached, almost indifferent manner, but her voice was

beginning to waver and break behind the words. "No, I wasn't in the least surprised. I had been expecting it, in fact. He had finished his course by then and had just been offered a post teaching agriculture at Makerere in Uganda, and he was eager to leave. And he was perfectly right to go without me, and to take his child. I certainly wasn't someone for him to take any place as his wife or to have raise his child. He did right. I was the one mistake he had made all his years in England and he was leaving it behind. You couldn't blame the man for that, could you?

"And yet," she said, trying to steady her voice against the tremor that was overtaking it, "even though I had been expecting it and knew in my heart he had done the best thing, the sight of the flat that day was too much. I had been slowly going out of my mind for months, I guess, from the way I'd been acting, but that really set me off. I was sick for a long time, just limp, like someone dead. And I might well have ended up in the madhouse had not some good friends in London who had money taken me in and arranged for me to see a psychiatrist they knew on Harley Street. And talking to him helped. He was a good Juju man—expensive but good. I slowly came round. But there was nothing to keep me in England once I was better, so when Lyle wrote saying that Ashton Vaughan was dying I decided to come on back. I thought being here might be a change for the better. I'd get a job, try to make a new life for myself, and maybe in that way get over it a little. But there's no getting over it. And time's been no help. These eight years I've been back here have been like a day.

"*Oh!*" An old wound might have suddenly opened, sending the pain like a knife through her. "If only you had seen the flat that day! It didn't look as if they had gone. Everything was still there—all the furniture, his desk, the pull-out sofa we slept on, and in the other room the baby's crib next to the dresser where I kept her things, with the drawers closed as if her clothes were still inside. Everything in place, but empty. I've never been in a place that felt more empty. And yet I couldn't believe they were gone. I kept telling myself he had only taken her out somewhere and they would soon be back. All I had to do was wait. And I did. I must have stood for hours in the middle of that room waiting for them, unable to move. And in a way, you know," she said, her voice breaking finally and the tears gathering, slipping quietly in like mourners taking their places around a bier, "I'm still there. I'm still standing in the middle of that two room flat in Leeds waiting for them to come back. . . .

"*Brute!*"

The word dealt the air a savage blow, and for an instant, as her enraged and anguished face with its tear-filled eyes came lunging across at him, Saul almost thought she meant him, that he was the one accused, and instinctively drew back. "Brute! How could he have just walked out like that? Without a word. With not so much as a note. Just gone. You come home one day and find the bloody flat empty. Everything tidy and in place, but empty. And to take the child with him! How could he have just run off with her like that? What right had he? She was as much mine as his. I was still her mother, no matter what I had done or how I had lived, and that gave me some say in what was to happen to her. And never a word from him all these years. He's never once answered my letters. . . . All right," she cried, "it's true: I did him a great wrong and it wasn't in him to forgive me; he wanted nothing more to do with me and he left, but oh, Lord, have some human feeling and write every once in a while and let me know how my child's getting along, how she's growing. But nothing. Not a word all this time. Oh, the brute! . . ."

Her eyes glazed by the tears, her voice a suppressed shout, her face convulsed, she cursed him: the old wound giving off its venom. Caught by the fury in her voice several people dancing nearby glanced over, and seeing the angry face thrust close to Saul's across the table, quickly drew aside, thinking they were quarreling.

" . . . And what right had he to judge me, anyway? . . ." The contorted face rushed closer, the low-pitched shout seemed louder than the din around them. "Was he God? . . . Or was I the only person who ever lied to someone they loved or tried to cover up their past? I only did it because I didn't want to risk losing him. I couldn't bear to have him know what a botch I had made of everything before meeting him. I wanted him to think well of me. Is that so terrible? Does that make me the worst person in the world? Oh, damn him! Damn him! Damn him! Damn him for not understanding. Damn him for not giving me a chance. Damn him for leaving me standing there all this time waiting for them to come back!''

In the silence filled with the echo of her enraged voice, Saul saw her as she must have looked that day standing rooted to the one spot in the apartment: her dazed and stricken face, the eyes that refused to accept the meaning of the emptiness she sensed there, and then all of her slowly giving way to the paralysis, grief and collapse that had left her, as she said, like someone dead for long afterwards. Not knowing what to say, he placed a hand lightly on hers, and found it lifeless, almost cold. Her private sun had gone into eclipse behind the film of unshed tears. And the faint lovely lines from the wings of her flared nose to her mouth that in arching wide, shaped her smile, had become deep tell-tale lines of age.

They remained like this for some time: Merle, her anger exhausted, staring with the dulled eyes and drawn, aging face into the other time, still waiting; Saul, his hand on hers, watching her from under his eyelids that were too heavy suddenly for him to lift, and feeling helpless to do or say anything that might ease her. For a moment he found himself almost regretting that she had spoken. It was strange, but as much as he had hoped she would one day talk about herself, he could not help experiencing a fleeting regret and even something akin to resentment. Perhaps because he knew that in loving her some measure of her sorrow and loss would be added to his own and he would carry it with him long after he had left Bourne Island and her face had dimmed in his memory. It would be yet another stone for him to roll before him up the hill.

Around them the postcarnival din continued to affront the silence of the sleeping town outside the nightclub, but the noise had dropped from its almost frightening high and people were beginning to leave. Their costumes soiled and torn, the heavy carnival make-up smeared and mixed in with their perspiration so that their faces, a melange of black, white, yellow and brown, appeared to be dissolving in a wash of color, they filed slowly out of the club. Beyond the balcony the sea had swallowed the

moon which had greeted Saul and Merle when they first entered
and the sea and sky had merged, becoming one in the darkness
that would not last the hour. For it would soon be dawn, Ash
Wednesday morning.

As if she sensed the morning stirring to life behind the screen
of night, Merle roused, her mind traveling the distance from the
tiny flat in Leeds back to the balcony and the ring-scarred table
at which they were sitting. And glancing inside where a few
people were still doing the reckless jump-up, she closed her eyes.
With the tears which she could not, even after all these years,
bring herself to shed standing in them, she closed them. And in
a way Saul understood only too well, that said she had seen
enough of the world and had no wish to look upon it anymore.

"Oh, Merle!" he said.

"Yes," she nodded, her lids drawn shut, "say it like that. I
need to hear it said that way."

Opening her eyes she gave him a wan smile and gently with-
drew her hand from under his. Her gaze wandered out to the
unseen water where the dawn waited, then slowly, after many
minutes, drifted back to the scene inside the club, and she said
with sudden irritability, "I don't feel to go to any damn breakfast do this morning, you know. I've had my fill of carnival and
people jumping up as if there's something to be all that happy
about."

"Stay with me, then," he said quietly, his eyes on her face,
which was turned from him, watching the departing revelers.
"We'll find someplace other than this to go. I know I don't
have a right in the world to ask, but stay with me, Merle, for
what's left of tonight." And strangely he was the one who
sounded in greater need of comforting.

She slowly turned back and, for a long time, while the crowd
around them continued to thin, they gazed almost impassively
at each other across the table, her eyes narrowed because of the
smoke from her cigarette, which she once jokingly claimed was
her protection against people like him, who were always collecting data. Finally she smiled, a sad fond smile that had something of the edge he had come to love to it. She lightly shrugged,
saying with the gesture that she had done with love long ago.

"On one condition," she said.

"What's that?"

"That you don't make too much of it, meaning it goes no further than tonight."

He held back, then reluctantly nodded. "I don't know if that's altogether possible," he said, "but I'll try."

Downstairs, the brisk wind off the sea had driven the debris of carnival, the streamers, confetti and torn bits of colored crepe paper, neatly up against the side of the building, so that the street looked as if it had been swept clean when they emerged. The dew, falling like a light spring rain, had borne the dust churned up over the two days down with it and packed it tightly once again between the cobblestones. The last of the carnival echoes that had lingered long after the midnight curfew had also died, and the old town, straining gently at its mooring on the bay, had recovered much of its accustomed tone; its ancient calm had been restored. The two of them sensed this as they moved through its close winding streets, past the shuttered houses and shops that would soon open to the day. By the time they reached the house where Merle had boarded as a schoolgirl, and where she still slept whenever she stayed in town, the sky was the color of the ashes that would be placed on the foreheads of the faithful later in the morning.

11

The cassia was in bloom. Great clusters of yellow blossoms hung like Christmas ornaments on the old tree in the guesthouse yard, their bright weight bearing the lower branches down almost to the ground, their fragrance scenting the salt air and the light from them softening the harsh landscape of sandhill and sea. And it had all happened overnight, as Merle had said it would. Yesterday the tree had looked its usual self: leafless, stripped of its bark even, dead to all appearances. No one had thought to notice the small, tightly closed buds, mere nodules, that had quietly sprouted over the last week. And then during the night, under cover of the darkness, the buds had opened, the flowers unfolding, exploding full-bloom while those in the house and in the village slept.

"Talk about miracles!" Merle exclaimed softly. Wearing a long, somewhat faded maroon-colored kimono, she stood gazing up at the blossom-laden tree with a look of such wonder it was as if she was seeing it for the first time. Behind her was gathered a small, equally awed crowd of onlookers: Allen, who had discovered the tree when he came out earlier to tend his garden and had summoned her, the usual group of children with the basins of sand and bundles of broom sage on their heads, and Carrington the cook. She stood off by herself in the pitted yard, a tall, large-boned figure, her vast bosom contained within the bib of her apron.

Saul and Harriet, though, weren't there. They no longer lived at the guesthouse. Shortly after carnival they had found a place of their own in the village. But Merle had sent one of the children to call them so they might see the tree.

"I can't get over it, you know, no matter how often I see it," she was saying. "You're about ready to give up on the blasted thing and make firewood out of it and then, lo and behold, you wake up one morning and find all this waiting for you. All this in the space of one night now! It's enough to make you think some magician came along while you were sleeping and seeing how naked and sorry-looking the old tree was, took pity on it and touched it and it bloomed. Just so! At his touch. And the flowers this year are the largest yet. I tell you, it's enough to restore your faith in something or the other."

As she held forth, they heard Saul's car approaching, and turning saw it jolting over the unpaved road between the sand-hills and Westminster's tall spur. Minutes later he was pulling up in the yard and walking toward them, followed by Harriet and the child who had been sent to call them. He bent down as he passed under the tree to avoid the blossoms.

"Behold the bridegroom!" Merle laughingly hailed him.

He raised up, laughed. "You're awfully cheerful this morning."

"And who wouldn't be? Just take a look at our old friend here. Didn't I tell you she would surprise you one of these days? I'm sure, though, you never expected it would be anything like this."

"No," he said, "you're wrong. I fully expected to be overwhelmed." He hadn't as yet really looked at the tree.

"True!" she laughed, and in the next moment swung toward
Harriet, "And what do you think of the old girl this morning,
Harriet?"

Harriet didn't answer immediately. Instead she stood for a
time gazing thoughtfully at the cassia. It was almost as if she
was waiting for the sound of Merle's voice to die and the air
to clear before speaking. And she appeared strangely abstracted,
remote: there yet not there.

"I must say I'm rather overwhelmed also," she said finally,
keeping her eyes on the tree. "I would never have imagined it
had this much life in it. It is lovely." Then, turning to Merle,
she added, "It's a pity, isn't it, all this finery can't last?"

"No," Merle said promptly. "It's only right they go their
way. Let them fall. Otherwise we'd start taking them for granted
and not even notice them after awhile. Besides, it gives us something to look forward to each year. You're right though. By
this and next week all this lovely gold will be gone and my lady
here will be her usual naked, half-dead self again. But what to
do, yes? That's all in life, as the old people say."

12

Merle met him on the veranda of Aunt Tie's large, faded
yellow house. She had heard the car pull up behind her Bentley
parked out front and had come to stand in the archway hung
with bougainvillaea that stood above the steps. Silent, refusing
to return his wave, she watched with expressionless eyes as he
made his way toward her up the path.

"I know you're avoiding me," he said. "But I've come anyway."

He had paused uncertainly two steps below her so that their
eyes were on the same level, and for a time she silently inspected
his dejected face and shadowed eyes. Then, and it was said with
surprising gentleness, "It's not you. Or it's not only you, I
should say."

"What's the rest of it?" he said, coming up to stand next to
her. "What else besides me has you spending all your time in
town these days? Tell me," he insisted. "I miss not being able
to catch a glimpse of you, if nothing more, when I go over to
the guesthouse."

"Kingsley and Sons," she said flatly and went and sat down.
"It's this decision they made shortly after carnival to delay grinding the smallholders' canes until the entire estate crop is done.
They've never done anything like it before. And they picked
right after carnival, as if to punish people for going into town
and having a little fun. I can't bear to see how worried everybody in Bournehills is and how helpless they look. . . ."

He dropped with a sigh into the chair beside hers. "I know,"
he said. "It has me worried too."

"And it's not, you know, that the few miserable canes they
grow bring in any money to speak of," she said. "It's more the
principle of the thing. It's important to Bournehills people that
they have their own little crop which they can take over to
Cane Vale and sell. It makes them feel they're somebody, too.
And it wouldn't even be so bad if you knew what Sir John and
those people at Kingsley were up to, what was behind the whole
business of having them wait. But nothing—" her voice dropped.
"You don't have a clue."

"Yes, that is the worst of it—the not knowing," he said.

Hearing their voices on the veranda, Aunt Tie had come to
the door, and he went over to greet her. She was a small,
stooped woman, her hands misshapen by arthritis, and with a
face that was not only the exact color of an unblanched almond
but had the same striated shriveled look to it. She insisted on
wearing sunglasses even in the house to protect her failing eye-
sight. And she almost never came out on the veranda anymore
in spite of the deep shade offered by the bougainvillaea. The
light there was too strong, she said. Her sole interest was listening to the death announcements broadcast over the radio for
the names of friends she could no longer visit.

Merle, whom the old woman treated as if she were still a
schoolgirl, scolding and indulging her by turns, called for Aunt
Tie to join them on the veranda, teasing her. The old woman,

appealing to Saul to "teach that girl to respect her elders," hastened back into the dim heart of the house. Minutes later she sent out the servant with a pitcher of cold ginger beer for them.

"Dear Aunt Tie," Merle said. "She was Mother and Father to me."

"Didn't you and your father ever get along?"

"Father? What father?" The bitterness she held against Ashton Vaughan erupted instantly. "Ashton Vaughan was somebody to call father? A man who for years made out he didn't recognize his own child when he passed her on the road? And who when he did finally decide to admit she was his and take her to live with him scarcely spoke to her, and as soon as he could packed her off to some fancy school in town, where the half-white children there made her life miserable because she was black and her mother had been a common laborer who had had her without benefit of clergy at sixteen.

"Can you," she continued, her voice rising, "call someone a father who never said a word when the child's mother, who was supposed to be his favorite out of all the women he kept at the time, was murdered in cold blood? That's right. Just shot down in the house one day with the child standing there. You've heard the story, I'm sure. And Ashton Vaughan never even tried to find out who did it. Maybe because he knew the Backra woman he was married to was behind it. No, bo, that man was no father of mine.

"He got his in the end, though," she said, her mouth a cruel line. "With all the land and houses he owned he died without a soul he could call family at his side. Had not Carrington been there there wouldn't even have been anyone to close his eyes. But his sort never end good. Take that woman in England who ruled me for years. The last I heard, she was sick unto death. How the mighty have fallen, eh? But then God, as we say in Bournehills, don' love ugly."

There was a silence; then she was whispering between clenched teeth, "You would have thought the little idiot of a child would have at least remembered what the face behind the gun looked like."

"Oh, Merle, don't."

"No, she said, "I need to talk about it. It'll do me good to say it out loud for once in my life. She should have remembered," she repeated. "All right, she was only two, but my God, even a child of two has some sense and should've been able to point to the person. That face should have been imprinted forever on her mind. But nothing. Just a blank."

"You know, of course, you're asking the impossible," he said.

"No, I'm not!" she cried. "She should have remembered something, the little idiot. Why some children can talk plain as day at the age of two. Even a half-wit like Seifert up at the almshouse would be able to point to his mother's murderer, I bet. Not me, though! Not your friend Merle! People say I was just standing beside her body sucking my thumb like nothing had happened."

"But you were only a baby, for God's sake," he said. "How could you possibly have known what was going on? You're being unreasonable."

"I don't care," she said. "Something, some little thing, should have stuck in my mind. I've never told anyone this, but once when I was attending that high-priced Juju man in Harley Street I asked him to put me under hypnosis to see if I could remember anything about that day. He wasn't very keen about the idea but he finally agreed. But a lot of good it did! He said that as soon as he started questioning me I woke up. Again, nothing!"

"Forget it, Merle, forget it." Leaning across he placed a hand on her arm. "You can't hold yourself responsible for what happened to your mother. Because you know as well as I do that her death, as well as her life, the way she was forced to live, her relationship with your father, even the way he treated you when you were little, all go back to the same goddamn inhuman system that began before you were born, here in Bourne Island, in my country, all over the hemisphere. You know that. So how can you blame yourself for her death? That's like blaming yourself for the entire history that brought it about.

"Don't get me wrong," he said quickly as she started to pull her arm out from under his hand and rise, "I know you're trying to come to terms with some of the things that have happened in your life. To go back and understand. And it's a good thing. More of us should try it. It's usually so painful though, most people run from it. But sometimes it's necessary to go back before you can go forward, really forward.

"And that's not only true for people, but nations as well," he added after a reflective pause, his creased lids coming down over his eyes. Next to him, Merle followed their movement and was still. "Sometimes they need to stop and take a long hard look back. My country, for example. It's never honestly faced up to its past, never told the story straight, and I don't know as it ever will. The juggernaut's going too fast for that. It's not likely to make it though.

"But do you know something . . ." his eyelids rose abruptly and he was smiling. "Mis-Merle's going to make it. She's going to come through."

"You think so?" Her tone sought to disparage this, and thus herself.

"I know so."

And, slowly, under his steady gaze, she, too, finally smiled— a thin, unwilling but tentatively hopeful smile. "You're just trying to make me feel less hopeless about my damn self," she said.

"And why not? Even I've begun to feel less hopeless about myself since coming to Bournehills."

As they continued to sit there, a clock inside the house struck three, its gently whirring notes conveying a sense of the cool dim rooms inside with their polished wood floors and crocheted antimacassars. Shortly afterward they saw through the entrance to the veranda groups of students passing on their way home from the nearby girls' high school. All they could see of them above the fence were the tops of their regulation navy jumpers and white blouses and the wide-brimmed boaters of soft straw they wore jauntily on the back of their heads. Their girlish laughter carried easily across the yard.

"You used to turn in at this gate," he said.

Merle nodded. "And glad to get here." But she was smiling. It seemed that as a result of their talk, as brief, really, as it had been, something of the hurt she still felt because of the taunts of her schoolmates long ago had eased; she could even dismiss them with a smile for the first time.

Saul, leaning close to her chair, his hand passing lightly over her arm, was thinking as he watched the straw hats float by that if he were blind and knew her only by the feel of her skin he would imagine her to be no older than the girls passing. And there was something of the young girl in the uncertain, almost cautious way she opened to him when they were together, and in her insistence, at those times, on pretending that he was not who he was but one of the mixed Backra people on the island with their fair skin, light-colored eyes and reddish hair. But there was the woman also. The faint, self-absorbed, self-congratulatory smile he sometimes caught on her face at the height of their embrace said she knew her woman's power to move and delight. And there was a woman's unmistakable, almost frightening authority in the way she had once, to spell him and delay the end, taken his face between her hands and lightly joked with him.

"Three o'clock gone," she said, and started up.

"I'm not going yet if that's what you're hinting at." His hand on her arm, he was smiling up at her, but his eyes on hers were very still.

Reading their look, she laughed, "What, love in the middle of the day with children coming home from school! Never heard of it," she teased him. "No," she said as he tightened his hold. Then, softening somewhat, "But I like you a lot, you know. Even though I'm using you."

"Really?" he said, and dropped her arm. "How?"

She bent on him a fond, sad smile. "Why you're my new Juju man from Harley Street, don't you know that, love?"

"Oh, Christ, Merle," he said. "Let me stay."

Later, in the room in which she had slept as a girl, high under the pitched room of the house, she said, "You don't really mind, do you, my making use of you? People always do in one way or another, you know. . . ."

He didn't answer but, his face against hers on the pillow, his mouth opened against the lobe of her ear from which he had removed the earring she wore as a reminder of her long subjugation, he shook his head, saying no.

13

Early morning. Allen along with Merle—who had returned
to Bournehills some weeks ago—stood in the guesthouse yard
listening to the sound of Cane Vale's horn, which reached them
clearly despite the distance and the loud grieving of the sea.
They wore puzzled expressions, because the horn's sound was
not the usual hoarse foghorn blast that signaled the change in
shifts, but a deep plangent cry that had a note of finality to it,
of things having come full circle and a long cycle at an end.

"But I wonder what the devil's going on this morning?" Merle
cried as the horn continued to desecrate the dawn quiet. She
stood with her hands on her hips, the full sleeves of her worn
maroon kimono hanging down.

"Something must be up," Allen said. "It wouldn't go on like
this for nothing."

"But what could it be?" she said. "The only time they blow
the horn this way is at 'the blowing out' when they've finished
grinding all the canes for the season and are about to shut down
the machines. But how could that be when the smallholders
haven't had theirs done yet—" She broke off; a look of foreboding crossed her face like a shadow passing over the newly
risen sun out near the horizon. Her voice a frightened whisper,
she said, "Allen, make haste and go over there and see what's
up. Take the car."

When he returned later with a visibly upset Saul seated beside
him in the Bentley, she had dressed and was standing waiting
for them in the same spot in the yard.

She took no notice of the car or the two men as they drew
up. Her face, and her gaze were turned in the direction of the
village, and although the horn had ceased blowing, she appeared
to be hearing it still. Even when Saul came over and, taking her
arm, informed her that the main roller had broken down and
Cane Vale would be closing, she didn't appear to see or hear
him. But she said, her voice short, peremptory, "Let them fix
it."

"They say they can't. Not right away, at any rate," he said.
"They're sending what's left of the estate crop over to Brighton

factory all the way on the other side of Cleaver's. And they're
saying the small farmers will have to do the same. How the hell
they're supposed to get there without proper transportation I
don't know. No donkey cart will ever make it over these hills
with a load of canes. . ." He paused, his distressed eyes reflecting
the morning's tragedy. "I don't know what to say, Merle. There
doesn't seem to be anything we can do. Merle . . ."

She continued to stare beyond him. Then, abruptly, she
snatched her arm out of his light hold and without a word
walked over to the car and got in beside Allen, who had remained at the wheel.

They drove in silence over to Cane Vale, Saul in the back
seat, Allen driving and Merle at his side gazing stonily ahead.
They arrived to find the tall iron gates of the factory closed and
a notice up announcing the shutdown and barring all trespassers.
Inside the yard, the run-down mill and its outbuildings loomed
silent and empty, their doors yawning open. Nor was any smoke
to be seen rising from the great chimney, and the special silence
which reigned over Cane Vale during the off-season was already
in force.

Virtually the entire population of Bournehills stood outside
the gate. Silent, impassive, their arms folded loosely at their
waists, they were all, even the children, caught in that stillness
of body and gesture only they were capable of; which, at times,
made them resemble statues that had been placed on an abandoned landscape to give it the semblance of life.

Crowding back onto the shoulder of the road, they made
room for the Bentley to pass. As it moved through their ranks
and they glimpsed Merle, they quickly dropped their gaze—
embarrassed, knowing that as someone who lacked their re-
straint, she would surely do or say something rash. But their
downcast gaze also expressed solicitude and love: they knew the
toll that outburst would exact and would have spared her the
pain if possible.

From under their lowered lids, they watched her refuse, with
a curt wave of her hand, Saul's offer to accompany her; they
followed her every move as she pushed open the gate (it was
not locked) and ignoring the notice on it strode into the yard.

She went first to the weighing office, where Erskine Vaughan, a distant cousin of hers, who was the manager, could usually be found supervising the weighing of the loaded trucks on the scale outside. Finding this deserted, the door locked, she proceeded to his house, a large plain bungalow with scaling walls and louvered shutters at the windows and doors that stood within view of the gate.

It seemed a long walk to those watching, but she covered the distance quickly, her heels raising little flurries of dust and cane chaff each time they struck the ground. She vanished out of sight behind a large sandbox tree which hid the entrance of the house. But they soon heard her knock on the door—an imperious sound that carried easily in the silence; and then her voice, faint but very clear and ominously pleasant, addressing the servant: "Would you call Mr. Vaughan here for me please, Ilene."

It was a long wait before the servant—a young girl from her voice—returned to say through the shutters on the door that Erskine Vaughan was busy and couldn't come. Merle called him herself then, shouting his name repeatedly through the tightly closed shutters. She hurled it like rocks against the walls of the house. When he still did not answer, she cursed him—and as her rage erupted those at the gate further lowered their eyes. Not knowing anymore what she was saying, not caring, she called him a coward, a lackey and a conniver. She accused him of having broken the roller on orders from Kingsley. It had been purposely done, she cried. With the estate canes almost done, they had seen no point in keeping the mill running, and had ordered him to break the machine. She challenged him to deny this to her face. She disowned him, declaring he was no family to her. She cursed his mother for giving birth to him, his father, a distant cousin of her father's, for having sired him, and finally the long-dead planter Duncan Vaughan for having, she said, spread his seed like a disease from one end of the island to the other, contaminating them all.

But in the face of the unassailable silence of the house, the abuse she heaped on him sounded hollow, ineffectual, even pathetic. As quickly as the curses rose they fell. Those outside could almost see them falling like downed birds through the air.

She, too, must have realized the futility of her harangue because her voice soon began to lose its force and finally broke off altogether.

She reappeared after what seemed a long wait to the crowd outside and they could immediately see the change in her. The determined step that had borne her swiftly across the yard was gone and her feet dragged. The dress hung limp on her body. Pausing in the middle of the yard she slowly looked around her with a dazed expression. It was as if she didn't know where she was and had, moveover, forgotten what had brought her here. In their slow confused sweep round the mill her eyes encountered the silent faces beyond the gate and she still didn't see to remember. And then she spied the men who had arrived for the day shift just as the horn had sounded. They were crowded to the front of the others, directly behind the tall iron bars, and they were holding, as if they didn't quite know what to do with them, the chipped enamel kits containing their eleven o'clock breakfast of rice and saltfish. At sight of them she shivered once in the early morning heat; her head dropped and her body went as limp as her dress.

She remained like this for some time, a slack, bowed figure in the middle of the empty yard, under a sky that due to the dry season was also empty except for the single glowering eye of the sun. Then, as though she could not bring herself to confront the villagers and see in their faces the reflection of her own powerlessness, she turned and, catching sight of the opened door of the mill, she started toward it, walking slowly, the dust scarcely stirring at her heels this time, and disappeared inside.

She was gone for close to a half hour when Saul, realizing that no one in the crowd would dare venture past the notice posted on the gate and go to her, left where he was standing beside the Bentley, and stepping into the yard followed her same path across to the building.

He entered the factory to find her—once his eyes adjusted to the dimness—standing on the platform above the roller pit, staring down at the silent machines over the guard rail. He made his way toward her through the ship's-hold gloom of the mill, with its brown light and close, sickening sweet smell. The cane chaff which had whirled like a minor sandstorm around his head on his previous visits hung motionless in the air, and although the metal floor with its raised studs was warm underfoot, he knew the fires were out in the huge furnaces below. But strangest of all was the silence. Coming in the wake of the unrelieved drumming and pounding of the machines and the almost human shriek of the rollers, it was so absolute it seemed no amount of noise could ever fill it again.

Merle, standing with her back partly to him, gave no sign she heard him approach, and he paused midway up the short flight of steps to the platform. A hand on the railing, he studied her rigid back and what little could be seen of her face, trying to assess her mood. And part of him said it would be better for him to return as silently as he had come and wait at the door. Above all, it cautioned him not to speak. But he did, after holding back for a time. Bracing himself as he always did, almost instinctively, when he wasn't sure how she would receive him, he softly called her name. She didn't respond and he repeated it, somewhat louder this time, thinking she might not have heard him. He called her again and was about to take another step up when she slowly turned his way. And the sight of that face, which at times appeared to contain in ever-shifting and elusive forms all the faces in Bournehills, drove him back to the lower step.

She didn't speak. With her arms dangling at her sides, she simply stared at him with the utterly blasted and enraged eyes. Finally, in a deceptively calm voice, she said, "Is that all you can do, stand there and call my name?" She waited; then, in the same even tone: "Do you think maybe if you call it often enough this roller might start working again? Perhaps you've heard that my name is some magic word people say over broken machines and before you know it they're fixed. Is that it? Well, you heard wrong, bo. My name never fixed a thing. *Merle!*" She spat it at him, the bitterness, the cruelty even, which were never very far behind her smile, which had always from their first meeting held him and all like him accountable, rising swiftly to the surface of her voice to sweep aside the false calm.

"Is that all you can say or do, for that matter: stand there rehearsing my name, I ask you?" she cried, and the old decayed building, which the silent machine had turned into a huge echo

chamber, rang with the words. "Can't you maybe try to fix this
thing? You said you came to help, didn't you? That's the reason
you're in Bournehills, isn't it? All right, here's your chance. And
you don't have to do anything big. We're not asking for any
million-dollar schemes just now, no big projects. You don't have
to play God and transform the whole place into paradise overnight. All we're asking is that you fix one little machine. That'll
be enough for now. And that shouldn't be difficult for you.
After all, you're from a place where the machine's next to God,
where it even thinks for you, so I'm sure you know how to
repair something as simple as a roller. Machines come natural
to your kind. Well, then, show your stuff and fix this one.

"Go on, get down there"—a slashing hand ordered him over
to the ladder that led from the platform into the pit with the
rollers "and fix it so those people out at the gate can get their
few canes ground before the little juice in them turns to vinegar.
If you like them as you say you do, if they're your friends—
Stinger, Delly, Fergy and the rest—if you feel for them, fix it. If
you love me, fix it. That's the least you can do. Or is that asking
too much? Perhaps all you can do is walk about asking people
their business. Collecting data. And writing reports. Is that all
you're good for? And sitting around worrying about something
you say you can't understand about the place. Well, open your
eyes, damn you, and look. It's there for a blind man to see.
Look at those poor people standing out there like they've turned
to stone, afraid to set foot inside the gate when they should be
overrunning this place and burning it the hell down, or better
yet, taking it over and running it themselves. Talk about change?
That's the kind we need down here, bo. Look at this damn
roller which was broken on purpose. That's right, on purpose.
You couldn't tell me different. The estate canes were in and
they didn't see any point in bothering with those belonging to
the smallholders so they had their lackey break it. That's how
it was. It was purpose work. Look at me," she screamed, but
her face was so distorted by her rage she didn't resemble herself,
and Saul, stranded on the stairs, lowered his gaze, refusing to
look. "What more answer do you need? Does somebody have
to draw a picture for you, so you'll understand? You know what
your trouble is? Do you know?" She took a menacing step

toward him, but he held his ground. "You can't see for looking, that's what. Or maybe deep down you don't really want to see. But I don't give a blast, just fix this bloody roller or don't ever call my name again. Or, if you go down there and see it can't be fixed, then take some of the multimillions you're planning to spend on us when your big project gets underway and go buy a new one. Buy two so we'll have a spare. Order them today from England or America. The jet can have them here tomorrow. Do it, I say. Do something, but oh, Christ, don't just stand there with your head hanging down doing nothing. Oh, blast you. Blast all of you. You and Sir John and the Queen and that smooth high-toned bitch of a wife you've got and that other bitch who tried to turn me into a monkey for her amusement. Look, don't come near me, you hear. I don't want to see not a white face today. Not one! *Fix it!*"—and the scream shearing off the top of her voice set the cane chaff hanging motionless in the air moiling again. "You're a so-called scientist, aren't you? Well, what's the good of all that science and technology they teach you in that place you're from if you can't fix one little machine? Great is the magic of the white man? Well, then, let's see some of it. Get down in this pit and start this damn wheel turning. Come on. Form yourself here for me." Once again she ordered him over to the ladder, the gesture loud with the crash of her bracelets. When he again failed to respond, her scorn knew no bounds. "Look at him, yes. He's supposed to be a big-time scientist and can't fix a simple wheel. But I'm not surprised. Because I know what all that science they teach you people is really about. I've studied you all good and I know. Kill!" she cried, the word issuing out of the darkness that could be seen closing over her eyes, snuffing out the light and sanity there. "Destroy! That's all your science and big-time technology is good for. Don't think I don't see it for what it is. Everything and everbody blown to bits, the whole show up in flames because you couldn't have it your way anymore. Everything flat, flat, flat. No—wait!" She paused, seeing another image projected on the darkened screen of her gaze. "No, they'll use that other one I read about someplace that they call the neutron or some damn thing, that they say only kills off the people—the people, everybody, just vanish into thin air, but everything else, the

buildings and so are left standing right where they are. Yes!
That's the one the brutes will use. All the buildings will be there
but there'll be nobody inside them. Empty. The cars and buses
right where they were on the roads when it dropped but not a
driver in sight. No passengers. Not even a dead body to be seen
on the streets. The houses with the curtains at the windows like
people are living in them but not a soul inside. Every living
thing just gone from the face of the earth. Oh, God, the silence!
You can hear a pin drop the world over. Everybody gone. All
the poor half-hungry people who never had a chance. The little
children. The baby's gone. Everything in place but both of them
gone. Oh, how could he have done that to me? I see it, you
hear, I see it. The whole world up in smoke and not a fire to
be seen anywhere!"

Her eyes were so filled with that apocalyptic vision, her words,
echoing through the empty building, had made it so vivid, that
Saul, struck dumb on the steps, could almost see that flameless
fire raging between them on the platform. And just as it reached
up to consume her utterly, a faint light glimmered within the
darkness overtaking her and she saw him, and even as her eyes
went dead and the raving began again, she cried, screaming it
like one drowning, "Saul, oh, Saul, take me out of this terrible
place!"

When he led her distraught and crying out in the broken
voice, over to the door, he found the old woman, Leesy Walkes
and several women from the crowd at the gate standing waiting
in the drenching sunlight outside. They had heard her scream
and had come. Without a word, they drew her from him, and
forming a protective circle around her slowly guided her back
across the yard.

14

That night, Saul arrived at the guesthouse to find Carrington
seated on guard outside the door to Merle's room. Her face,
her tall figure, were indistinguishable from the shadows filling

the passageway and he would not have seen her but for the white bibbed apron and cap she wore at all times, even on her day off. She rose from her chair and stood towering and mute as he came down the hall, and for a moment he was afraid she meant to bar his way. But perhaps his determined step dissuaded her, because as he drew near she wordlessly moved aside to let him pass. He asked her how Merle was, and touching her temple she gave the little eloquent gesture that said "out": "the head's out," meaning Merle had sunk into one of her long, frightening, cataleptic states.

Opening the door he caught sight of her on the bed. His first thought was that she had fallen asleep while sitting propped up awkwardly against the headboard, and he almost started to withdraw. But crossing to the bed he found that her eyes were partly open, although there was no indication of life in them.

"Merle . . ." he said, bending over so that his face was in line with her vision. But nothing happened in her eyes. There was no sign of recognition. It chilled him and he quickly straightened up. It was as though she had fled the surface of herself for a place within where nothing could penetrate, leaving behind a numb spent body and the empty stare.

As he stood there gazing helplessly down at her, he was struck by a sense of déjà vu. He had stood feeling the same helplessness at this bedside before. He was positive he had. And then he remembered his first wife Sosha, who had died following a miscarriage while with him on a field trip in Honduras six years ago; the sight of her lying in the same comatose state during the brief lulls amid the delirium that had ended her life. In Merle's vacant gaze and lifeless form he suddenly saw that other woman he had loved, whose death he had brought about by delaying taking her to the hospital—the nearest one being miles over the mountains when she felt ill. He had been at a critical stage of his research and had been reluctant to leave. Once, at Aunt Tie's house, he had told Merle the whole story—of how he had failed that woman, and of the guilt and remorse that still plagued him. And now their faces had merged, becoming one as he stood there.

And hadn't he, now that he thought of it, sometimes glimpsed Sosha looking out at him from behind Merle's gaze? Hadn't he in fact, heard her screaming at him in Merle's voice this morning from the high platform? Behind Merle's angry demand that he fix the roller had been Sosha's anguished plea that he give her a reason for her suffering. In the abuse Merle had hurled at him for his ineffectualness had been contained the curses his wife had scourged him with at the end. And it fleetingly occurred to him, the thought merely glancing his dazed mind, that perhaps in Merle he was being offered a chance to make good that old failure. Perhaps this, more than anything else, was what bound him to her. What had she said that time at the old woman's house in town about the uses to which people put each other?

The faces separated, his dead wife's receding, Merle's coming into focus again, and he saw that her eyes had closed. But it was no different than when they had been open. Even though asleep, she was still huddled like a child in a dark corner of herself. He leaned over and very gently straightened out her body and then drew the sheet over her. This done, he sat down on the edge of the bed and taking her hand, which felt muscleless and cold, began chafing it between his.

It was then he became aware of the room, her room which he was seeing for the first time. Because although they had been together a few times at Aunt Tie's, they had never risked meeting anywhere in Bournehills.

Curious, he looked around him. The large room was filled with heavy old-fashioned furniture of little style or grace. Dominating was the bed, a massive antique with cherubs trailing garlands of flowers carved on the headboard. It might have been the bed in which old Duncan Vaughan had sired the forty-odd children before retiring for the night on his planter's chair.

A number of faded prints and drawings depicting life in Bournehills long ago, hung on the walls. Some of these offered beguiling scenes of the planters' wives and daughters out for an afternoon airing in their horse-drawn buggies and taking high tea and playing croquet on the lawn. One showed a plover shoot with the planters in knee gaiters imbibing coffee and rum while awaiting the birds. There were prints of the great feasts held back then, in which whole calves were consumed by the diners while their liveried slaves, some of them no more than children, stood in attendance behind each chair.

And there were other scenes as well, these mostly of black figures at work in the fields and filing in long columns up the ramps to the sugar mills bent double under the load of canes on their backs. Amid these hung a large drawing of a three-masted Bristol slaver, the kind famous in its day. It had been meticulously rendered in cross-section to show how the cargo of men, women and children had been stowed to take up the least room in the hold.

To all this Merle had added her personal belongings. Books on West Indian history were scattered everywhere. There was a sewing machine with a foot treadle, a gift from Ashton Vaughan to her mother long ago. Beside it lay remnants of the colorful cloth she used for making her dresses. A cluttered vanity table held a large tin of the talcum powder she used on her face and neck and the hot comb with which she straightened her hair. Several steamer trunks from her years in England stood open but half unpacked in a corner.

She had brought the memorabilia of her lifetime—of more than her lifetime—and dumped it in a confused heap in the room. The confusion was rampant, although there were, to her credit, a few signs that she had tried to impose some order on the chaos. Several books were neatly ranged on a shelf. She had created a small sitting area with a few of the armchairs. A photograph showing her, her husband, and a baby who gazed at the world with her eyes occupied a clear space on a table. But mostly the furniture and other effects had been left unarranged, so that the room resembled a warehouse, an antique shop, a museum.

It expressed her, all the things which brought on her rages and her frightening calms as well. As his gaze wandered over the room Saul felt he was wandering through the chambers of her mind. But the room also expressed something apart from Merle, it seemed to him. It roused in him feelings about Bourne-hills itself. He suddenly saw the district for what it was at its deepest level, the vague thoughts and impressions of months coming to focus at last. Like the room it, too, was a kind of museum, where the era recorded in the faded prints continued to exist intact beneath the present reality. One not only felt it, but saw it at every turn, often without realizing it. Bournehills, its shabby woebegone hills and spent land might have been selected as the repository of the history that included the hemisphere.

And it would remain as such. The surface might be jarred as it had been by the events today. People like himself would come seeking to change it, to improve it, to shake it from its centuries-old sleep and it might yield a little. But deep down, at a depth to which only few would penetrate, it would remain rooted in that other time, serving in this way as a testimony to all that had gone on then: those scenes on the walls, and as a reminder—painful but necessary—that it was not yet over, only the forms had changed, and the real work was still to be done; and finally, as a crude memorial to the figures packed in the airless hold of the ship in the drawing.

Only an act of the most sweeping proportions could redeem them. Only then would Bournehills, its mission fulfilled, forgo the wounding past and take on the present, the future. But it would hold out until then, resisting, defying all efforts, all the halfway measures, including his, to reclaim it.

As Saul groped his way out of the room, his eyes had the look of someone who had been struck blind temporarily so that he might see in another, deeper, way. Besieged by the vision that had come to him, he stumbled from the room, past Carrington at the door. But she didn't notice him, for she had dropped off to sleep, her chin fallen onto the great breasts that had been used, it seemed, to suckle the world.

15

In the weeks following there was a virtual pilgrimage each day out to the guesthouse to inquire about Merle. People from the village, from all over Bournehills brought gifts—a dozen cashews with the kidney-shaped nut attached to the fruit, a few specially selected mangoes, a chicken to be made into soup for her, a freshly baked loaf of coconut bread which they knew she liked. Coming up to the kitchen door, they would ask, "And how's she today, Mistress Carrington? Has she come to herself yet?" And the silent Carrington would give the sign that said she was unchanged.

Just beyond where the visitors would gather, the sea was undergoing its seasonal change. Every year at this time the water darkened and the cry of the breakers as they moved in over the reefs, that loud sob of outrage and grief, was taken to a new high. Moreover, each time the swollen waves hurled themselves onto the land they left behind great masses of seaweed dredged up from the bottom, dumping it like mounds of rotting refuse along the length of the beach. The sea, Bournehills people said, was cleaning itself, and they stayed away from it.

Saul was usually part of the crowd outside the kitchen door. Although he was busy helping the small farmers secure transportation for their canes, he nonetheless made a point of stopping by almost daily to check on her. He would have gone and sat with her sometimes, as on the first night, but Leesy Walkes had replaced Carrington outside the bedroom door and she refused to allow anyone in.

Soon, people meeting him on the road and knowing he was a regular visitor to the guesthouse began asking him for her. At first he somewhat apprehensively searched their faces, worried that in their shrewd way they had seen through to the larger feelings that prompted his concern: his love—the affection and friendship which shaped it. But though he probed their faces and eyes he could detect nothing. Indeed, something in their manner said it was only right that he should go there and wait humbly with the others out in the yard for Carrington's terse report. This, they seemed to feel, was an act of obeisance due her.

16

As Harriet had expected, Merle was on the veranda. While still some distance up the beach she made out the faded red of the kimono, the smoke rising from her inevitable cigarette and the dark feet propped on the lower rung of railing. Finally, closer up, there was the face, black and grave and spent-looking from her illness which had lasted over two months.

"I see you're up and around again," she called from below—
and she was surprised at how easily she managed the light tone
and the smile. "How are you feeling?"

"I'll live, they tell me."

Merle's answering smile over the railing made Harriet think
of a pocket mirror being flashed in the sun. It gave off the same
harsh splintered light. It seemed hard with the knowledge of
something. Perhaps, she told herself as she went around to the
side steps leading up to the veranda, the woman had known it
would eventually come to this. It didn't matter. It would make
what she had to say easier.

"Good Lord, you tend to forget how really noisy the sea is
living in the village," she said coming over and taking a seat one
away from Merle. "Just listen to it."

"I know," Merle said. "It's been lecturing me the whole
bloody day."

"And the beach has become an unsightly mess with all the
seaweed."

"Yes," Merle said. "And it's no use trying to clean it up
because as soon as you clear away one load of the damn stuff
the waves come along and dump another. But what to do, the
old sea's cleaning itself. It's worse this year than I've ever seen
it. The water's rougher and the noise is enough to deafen you.
But it'll be done soon, and then, ah, then, it's like a brand new
sea, the water as blue and clear as in those fancy swimming
pools in New Bristol, and not a shred of seaweed anywhere.
You get the sweetest sea bath in the world then. The beach is
always mobbed on Sunday mornings."

She had said all this looking straight ahead, but she turned
now to Harriet with the hard-edged, knowing smile.

"Care for a drink?"

"No, I won't be staying long," Harriet said, although she
didn't look to be in any hurry. Under her tan linen skirt her
legs were neatly crossed, and she had settled her slender, somewhat angular body comfortably into the lawn chair. "I still have
a few pages of the report left to do. I'd like to have the whole
thing done by this evening if possible so we can mail it off
tomorrow."

"And then it's 'off' for the three of you also, isn't it?" Merle said. "Back to America for a little holiday."

"Yes, if that impossible husband of mine doesn't change his mind again, which he's subject to do!" she said with a laugh that again surprised her with its effortlessness. "I'm learning that being married to a field anthropologist is as bad as being the wife of an old-fashioned country doctor. With one, somebody's always having a baby in the middle of night. In Saul's case, it's one crisis after another so that you can never plan.

"But if he does change his mind again and decides he had better stay and go immediately into the next phase of the research, then we stay. Because I know"—and here her voice slowed and the words became more pointed—"how much the project means to him. . . ." There was a slight pause: "I think you do, too," she added quietly.

Their eyes met across the empty chair—Harriet's with the gray overcast that had darkened them since carnival, Merle's reflecting the sharp light of her waiting half-smile.

"Not only," Harriet said, "is this the first real field work he's done in years, but this particular project is the kind he's always wanted to do but never had the opportunity. And it only came about because I was able to persuade certain friends of mine at the Research Center to choose him. So you see it means a great deal to him, almost too much I sometimes think. He's gotten so caught up in the work and in Bournehills he hates leaving here for a day. Anyway, he's very anxious naturally, and so am I, that nothing go wrong. I think you are, too."

Again there was no response.

After waiting a moment, Harriet calmly continued. "I'm not speaking so much about things going wrong with the project, but about situations apart from the work which might create problems. Not very serious problems perhaps, but problems nonetheless.

"I wouldn't want to see that happen," she said firmly. "I—" Suddenly without warning, the firmness gave way and she lost her voice. It lasted less than a fraction of a second. With an effort that caused the long smooth muscle at her jawline to tighten perceptibly, she rallied, and said—but in a voice that now contained almost an appeal, "I—I just don't want to see anything spoil this for him, that's all—nor would you, I'm sure, were you in my place."

They looked at each other much longer than before. And this time as Merle's gaze which had the power, some claimed, to read a person's life at a glance, read deep into Harriet, a change came over her also. The little hard-edged smile died and was replaced by something close to compassion. She knew, the look said, what it meant for her—Harriet!—to have to come and plead for him like this. The love, desperation and need that had driven her to it. And because of this she, Merle, regretted her part in it, that softened expression said. Perhaps if she were not someone with nothing to show for the years but a white ele-phant of a house and a room filled with the miscellany of a broken life and history, none of it would have happened. Or she would have seen to it that it went no further than the one night. But she had been impelled by a need as complex and enormous as the one she glimpsed in Harriet. So that in spite of the fact they sat drawn up like two enemy camps on either side of the chair between them, they were essentially the same, the look declared: two women who had long been assailed by a sense of their uselessness, who had never found anything truly their own to do, no work that could have defined them, and so had had to look to the person of the lover for definition and for the chance through him, in helping to shape his life, to exercise some small measure of power.

Seeing that look, understanding its meaning, Harriet was afraid the woman would do something foolish, such as reach across and place a hand on hers to seal what she saw as the bond between them; and offended beyond words, she braced herself to spring back from that touch.

"I'm thinking of going away, Harriet." It was a compliant, sympathetic Merle who spoke.

"Yes, so I understand," she said. "In fact that's what I came to talk to you about. I was wondering just when you were planning to leave and where you were going."

"Well, I've pretty much decided on Trinidad," Merle said in the mild, conciliatory tone. "And I'll be leaving soon as the one or two guests I have besides Allen pack up and go."

"I see." She appeared dissatisfied. There was the suggestion of a frown. She said, "I'm a little surprised you've decided on Trinidad. It's so close, right around the corner, really. It's hardly like going away."

"I've friends there," Merle explained, "and a good chance of a job, which is important since I intend staying for awhile, for good perhaps if things work out."

"Oh, well, of course, it makes sense then," she said, but the slight frown remained. "Somehow I always had the impression from the way you talked that you were eager to leave the West Indies altogether. I could be mistaken but it seems you always indicated as much—and frankly, I think that would be best."

Merle gazed at her for a long moment, seeing not the face so much with its surface show of calm, but the angry hurt behind it. And compliant still, she said, "Yes, that would probably be best, but you know as well as I do, Harriet, that I don't have the wherewithal to be making any big moves right now. I'll be lucky if I can scrape together the plane fare to Trinidad."

"Yes, I know that," Harriet said. "That's why I thought that if you really wanted to go someplace far from here, you might consider letting me advance you enough money, not only for your fare, but to tide you over until you found a job. You could set the amount."

If she was at all aware that Merle had grown very still she took no notice of it.

"And there wouldn't be any need to repay it," she said. "You could consider it a gift or, if you like, a token of appreciation on our part. After all, you were very helpful in the beginning in getting us settled. So that it's only right we should return the favor. Anyway, I hope you can see your way to accepting it. Because then . . . "

"Harriet." Her hand had come up in a warning gesture and something in her voice almost pleaded with the other woman to stop.

"Because then," Harriet repeated, "you'll be able to go wherever you'd like and not have to settle for just any place. There's Canada, for instance."

"Harriet."

"I understand quite a number of West Indians have gone there

to live. And there's the whole of Europe, of course. And I hear
you have a husband and child somewhere in Africa. I don't
know what the situation is with your marriage but you might
like to live somewhere near your child . . ."

"Harriet!"

"Or if you wanted, you could return to England."

"England?" It was barely a whisper.

"Yes," she said. "I understand you have very close friends
there which means you'd have a much easier time getting settled.

"So," she said with finality, looking at Merle but ignoring
her stricken face, "if you'll let me know the amount you think
you'll need, I'll get it to you. And I'll see to it personally. No
one else need be involved. I'm sure you understand that. And
it might be best if you could arrange to be gone by the time we
return from our trip home."

She had no sooner finished than Merle's feet slid from the
railing to the floor, and turning around in her seat she stared at
Harriet.

It was the look which dated back to the first night at Lyle
Hutson's, when during their converstaion on his veranda she
had repeatedly leaned close, and openly, brazenly, peered into
Harriet's face as though she spied someone else lurking there.
She was looking at her now in the same way. And she had
grown very quiet again, her entire self given over to the search.
Only the saints on her earrings moved, shivering a little as though
the mild wind off the sea had turned cold.

Across the way Harriet disregarded the look. She simply sat
waiting for her offer to be accepted and the amount named so
that she could leave.

And then abruptly Merle swung back in her chair, placed her
feet back up on the railing, and throwing her head back she
laughed.

It was an ugly anguished scream torn from the top of her
voice. And she let it come. Her head flung back, her throat
arched, she forced it out, sounding like a woman in labor with
a stillborn child, who screams to rid herself of that dead weight.

Harriet ignored the laugh, just as she had the disconcerting
look. Her skirt draped over her knees, her instep arched, she

patiently waited it out. Her gaze wandered idly over to the feet
on the railing. They were blacker than the woman's face, with
childish toes that curled in and with ludicrous bisque-colored
heels and soles. (As a child, looking at the maid Alberta's pale
palms she had wondered how this had come about; why had
this part of them been spared?) Harriet's gaze drifted up to the
throat bent all the way back, and came to rest there. She could
almost see the screaming laugh rushing up through it. She saw
the creases and in them traces of the talcum powder the woman
was forever dusting on herself. And gazing as if transfixed at
that short, black, totally unaesthetic throat, she wondered—the
thought causing sudden chaos in her—whether when the two
of them were together he actually touched, caressed and kissed
that throat, and reaching down even did the same to those
feet . . .

She quickly looked away, and as if to spare her the full brunt
of the feelings that swept her, a numbness the same dense gray
as her eyes closed over her mind.

And the numbness remained so that she wasn't aware when
Merle, still convulsed by the laugh that was more a scream of
pain, struggled up from her chair and came to stand over her.
She couldn't have said just when the laugh finally ceased and
the woman started shouting. Only gradually did her mind rouse
to the sound of that voice.

". . .England now! Did you hear her? Does she have any idea
of the hell I saw in England? Why, that's the last place in this
world I want to see again. Canada. Africa. My passage paid to
the ends of the earth. Get thee gone, Satan, and here's enough
money to stay gone. Oh, God, this woman must be trying to
set out my head again coming over here this afternoon talking
about money.

"Money! Always money! But that's the way they are, you
know," she cried, her voice at a scathing pitch, informing the
sea, the long sloping veranda, the house with its ancient ghosts,
of the fact. "They feel they can buy the world and its wife with
a few raw-mouth dollars. But lemme tell you something,
m'lady"—her face, streaked white from the tears brought on by
her laugh, dropped close—"I can't be bought. Or bribed. And

I don't accept handouts. Not anymore at least. I used to. You
don't know about that, but I did. And for the longest time.
And because of it lost the two people who meant life itself to
me. But not anymore. I've grown wise in my old age. And
proud. Poor as the devil, but proud."

She raised up, trembling with her rage, unable to go on for
the moment. But slowly the trembling ceased as a thought took
hold of her, and her tears, those left over from her laugh, slowly
hardened to emit a cold light.

"And lemme tell you something else, m'lady," she said "I
don't think I'm going anyplace. I've changed my mind. Because
you're right, you know, it doesn't make a bit of sense for me
to go dashing off to some island that's right next door and pretty
much the same as here. That wouldn't be any real change. And,
although you didn't say as much, it wouldn't solve anything.
I'd still be too close for comfort. All anybody who wanted to
see me would have to do is catch a plane and he'd be there in
no time flat.

"No, I had best stay put until I can see my way to make a
really big move. Besides"—the derisive note dropped out of her
voice, leaving only the hard anger—"I don't like people ordering
me about like I'm still the little colonial. I've had too much of
that. So when they say gee now, I haw. When they say go, I
stay. And stay I will. Right here in Bournehills where I belong.
My mind's made up. And it'll be just between the two of us
why I suddenly changed plans. You don't have to worry I'll tell
a soul. Yes, m'lady, you'll be able to find me sitting up big as
life on this veranda anytime you like. And when you and Saul
take your little trip home and come back I'll be right here,
waiting for you. *England!*"

With that her head went back and the earsplitting laugh
erupted again. This time it was more a laugh and less the anguished scream that had sought to free her of the dead weight.
She might have been delivered. Turning, she started toward the
door, staggering a little under the force of the laugh, stopping
to hold onto a chair each time it seized her afresh. She entered
the house and the free ringing laugh set off echoes inside which
found their way out to the veranda and the seemingly composed
figure seated there.

17

As Merle had said it would be, it was like a brand new sea. The water, a clear, deep-toned blue that absorbed the sunlight to a depth far below its surface, looked as though it had been filtered to remove every impurity. And all trace was gone of the unsightly seaweed it had sloughed off like so much dead skin over the weeks. Most of this had been gathered up and buried under the dunes, but some was being used as fertilizer and a small portion had been carefully washed and boiled into bush tea to be drunk as a tonic. Even the sand appeared to have been passed through a giant sieve that had sifted out the coarser grains.

And a marked change had taken place in the several voices of the Bournehills sea now that the yearly cleansing was over. The outraged roar of the huge breakers as they flung themselves on the outer reefs had lost some of its fury, and the high-pitched ritual keening of the lesser waves had been taken to a lower register. And though the sea continued to hurl itself in an excess of grief and mourning onto the shore, sending up the spume-like tears, it did so with something less than its usual hysteria. Above all, the powerful undertow that had been worse than ever for weeks, and which everyone assumed had swept Harriet out to sea when she went for her usual early morning swim, had subsided.

Up at the guesthouse, a silent Merle sat in her familiar place on the veranda, her feet up and her head resting against the back of the chair. She was gazing out at the bright scales of afternoon sunlight adrift on the waves.

Beside her sat an equally silent Saul.

It was their first meeting in the three weeks since the drowning. After the futile search for Harriet's body Saul had gone to stay in New Bristol. And he would not have returned to Bournehills as yet if Allen—who had visited him from time to time—hadn't told him this morning that Merle would be leaving the island shortly, going to Uganda at last to see her child. He had driven back with Allen to say good-bye.

No mention had been made yet of her leaving, although they had been on the veranda for some time. But by way of confirming the news, Merle had gone in the house and brought out her plane ticket. It lay between them on the broad arm of her chair.

As if to avoid looking at it, Saul sat hunched forward, his elbows on his knees and his head bowed. It was the way he had remained for days on end, seated on the edge of the bed in his hotel room in town. He had gone over repeatedly in his mind all that had happened after Harriet had secretly written to her powerful friends at the Research Center and had had him replaced as head of the Bournehills Project, and the project itself suspended indefinitely. His rage the night he found out. He had told her they were through. And she had known that he meant it . . .

Still in the hunched-over position, he reached for the ticket. He held it in his hands without opening it.

"My traveling papers," Merle said quietly, both pride and sadness in her voice. "I had to sell practically everything I owned to raise the money to pay for it. You should see my room. It's bare as a bone. Everything gone—all that old furniture and junk I had cluttering up the place. I sold the whole lot week before last to an antique dealer in town. He'll make a fortune reselling it to these rich expatriates in New Bristol who love collecting stuff from the old estate houses. I even sold the very bed from under me and I'm sleeping on a cot these nights. I haven't slept better in years. And the wreck of a car is gone. Some millionaire American Lyle knows was only too happy to buy it when he heard it had belonged to the last English governor we had here. And the earrings I've worn all these years? Gone! A jeweler in town paid good money for them. Haven't you noticed how different I look without them?"

And he saw then, really looking at her for the first time since his arrival, that the earrings in the shape of the medieval saints were gone, and that without them she looked as she had those times when they made love and he would remove both the earrings and her heavy bracelets: unburdened, restored to herself. He saw too, that there was no talcum powder on her face and throat, and that her hair was unstraightened and stood in a small rough forest around her face, framing it. She looked younger, less scarred, with it that way.

"Yes," she said, "I've been busy these past three weeks. Nearly everything gone, sold, and my ticket bought. What do you think of that? I'm not so hopeless after all, am I?"

He didn't answer. Instead, replacing the ticket which he still hadn't opened, he said, "When are you leaving?"

"Saturday week."

His gaze dropped, and Merle, after waiting a few moments, said, "I thought you'd be pleased to hear I'd finally gotten up the courage to go."

"I am, Merle, I am," he said but kept his eyes down.

"It's as both of us have said any number of times," she began. "I'll never get around to doing anything with what's left of my life until I go and look for my child. You know that—" he nodded—"I'll just go on as I am," she said. "Doing nothing but sitting out on this veranda all day and inside that cave of a bedroom feeling sorry for myself and blaming everyone and everything for the botch I've made of things. And talking. Oh, God, going on like some mad woman all the time but doing nothing. And letting the least little thing set out my head, but doing nothing. Finish with that!" she cried strongly.

"Have you written to let them know you're coming?"

"No," she said, and she was suddenly worried. "You think I should have?"

"That might have been best," he said. He was looking at her now.

"Oh, I thought of it," she said. "But I was afraid he wouldn't answer the letter. He's never answered any of the others I've written. Or that if he did answer it might be just to say no. So I thought the best thing would be simply to go. And I'm not going there to make trouble," she added hastily. "You wouldn't recognize me I'll be so calm and reasonable. No raving. All I want is for him to agree to some arrangement that will allow me to see her from time to time. Maybe she could come and spend part of her long school holiday with me. He might agree to that. After all, it's been a long time and he's older now and maybe a little more understanding. Anyway, I'm going to take my chances and see." Then: "I'm being selfish."

"No, you're not."

"Yes, I am. Interfering in the child's life after all these years. That's what some people would say . "

"To hell with what they say. She's your child, too."

"Oh, she is!" She gave him a grateful look. "And that gives me some rights, doesn't it! Why, for all you know she thinks about me sometimes, wonders what I look like, what kind of person I am. She might even be happy to see me. That's if her father hasn't turned her against me."

"He won't have done that, Merle," he said. "Anyway, no matter what, she'll be glad that you've come to see her."

She looked at him, wanting to believe him but full of doubt. "Well, let's hope you're right," she said. "But even if she doesn't take to me, I'll try not to mind. I'll understand. After all, you can't very well expect a child of nine to welcome with open arms some woman who suddenly appears out of the blue claiming to be her mother. It'll take her a little time to get used to the idea. But even if things don't work out, it will be enough for me just to have seen her . . .

"And what of you, Saul Amron?" she asked gently, after a long silence. She placed a hand on his arm. "What of you? What will you do now that this"—she searched for a way to say it—"this terrible thing's happened?"

Slipping his arm out from under her hand he leaned forward again, his elbows on his knees supporting a body that was sodden with the tears that had accumulated over the three weeks. It felt waterlogged. Part of him might also have drowned, part of him might have died with Harriet. And in a way, this was how he had come to see his death, as a series of deaths taking place over the course of his life and leading finally to the main event, which would be so anticlimactic, so undramatic (a sudden violent seizure in his long-abused heart, a quick massive flooding of the brain) it would go unnoticed. It was the deaths occurring over an entire lifetime that took the greater toll.

"It's no use saying, I know, that you mustn't hold yourself entirely to blame." Her hushed voice scarcely intruded upon the silence. "Because you're going to, anyway. It's hard not to in a case like this where you don't know how it happened and never will. Even I feel in some way responsible. I never told you, but we had words the last time she came over here. It doesn't matter about what anymore, but we did.

"Oh, I still can't believe it," she cried. "I keep expecting to see her strolling along the cliff in the afternoon picking the little mangy flowers, or out at the crack of dawn swimming in that cold sea. Harriet. She wasn't an easy person to know."

He slowly nodded. "Not even for me, Merle," he said. "I'm ashamed to say I never got to know the real Harriet. Maybe it's that I didn't try hard enough. Or that all I wanted from her was that calm composed surface of hers. I don't know. Anyway, I never got through. I never found the way . . ."

And in the face of that mystery which had been Harriet, which he had been unable to penetrate even with his love—that awed, somewhat uneasy love he had borne her—his hands dangling lifelessly between his knees opened in a gesture of despair.

Nothing was said for some time. Seated there, their chairs close together, they appeared close, intimate, of a mind. But their separate thoughts—his of Harriet, hers of the journey ahead—had already taken them far from each other.

"But you haven't answered my question."

He raised his head.

"About what you're going to do?"

He slid back in the lawn chair. "I haven't thought about it," he said. "But I'll manage. There's always teaching. And there was some talk, I remember, at the place I taught before coming to Bournehills, about setting up a program to recruit and train young people in my specialty from overseas to work in their own countries. I'd like to be part of something like that. I'm more than ever convinced that's the best way: to have people from the country itself carry out their own research and development programs whenever possible. Outsiders just complicate the picture—as you and I know only too well . . .

"But whatever I do, one thing is certain: I'll be staying put this time. And I mean that. No more field work. And it's not a matter of giving up. It's that somehow, in a way I can't explain, after Bournehills there aren't any places left for me to go. Don't ask me why I feel this, but it's something I've come to understand these past three weeks.'

"You'll get over it," she said with the gentleness in her voice. "And be up and about this part of the world again."

"No," he said, "not after Bournehills."

His gaze dropped to the plane ticket on the chair arm. "I suppose," he began "you might be staying over there if things work out . . ."

"And what would Africa want with me?" she said with a sad laugh. "A slightly daft, middle-aged woman with history on the brain."

"Perhaps your husband will have had a change of heart."

"Ha!" it was her familiar hoot. "I wouldn't bet on it," she said. "If he just doesn't look at me as he used to toward the end as if I was contaminated, or worse, if he doesn't chase me from his door, I'll be more than content.

"But you're right," she went on. "I might stay over there for awhile, travel about, see the place. I've borrowed some money from Lyle and I can always get more from him if I need it. It's odd, but I have the feeling that just being there will be a big help to me, that in some way it will give me the strength I need to get moving again. Not that I'm going expecting to find perfection, I know they have more than their share of problems, or to find myself or any nonsense like that. It's more what you once said: that sometimes a person has to go back, really back— to have a sense, an understanding of all that's gone into making them—before they can go forward. I believe that, too.

"But I'll be coming back to Bournehills. This is home. Whatever little I can do that will matter for something must be done here. A person can run for years but sooner or later he has to take a stand in the place which, for better or worse, he calls home, do what he can to change things there."

She had fixed him with her clear, see-through gaze, and he said, "You mean me." She didn't answer and he continued with the weariest of sighs, "Yes, I suppose you're right. I'll have to get involved in some way once I'm back there for good, do something toward shaking up that system, although God knows I've little heart for the fight. I once had, but no more. But that's the only way I'll be able to take living there permanently. Despair," he said, "is too easy an out. Anyway, we'll see. And

what about you? Have you thought about what you might do
when you get back?"

"A little," she said. "I might try to get a government loan to
fix up the guesthouse and see if I can't make a go of the hotel
business. But that's not certain. Or, I might try teaching again.
Or, don't laugh, I might go into politics. Start a political party
of one, strictly radical. How's that?"

"I'd vote for you."

"Then I couldn't help but win," she declared with a laugh.
"And so would Bournehills people. They'd give me a vote.
Lord, I can just hear all those high and mighty folks in New
Bristol: 'Oh, God, have you heard the latest? Mad-Merle's in
politics!' " Her laugh rose, only to fall abruptly. "Not that I'd
be able to do all that much as things stand. But I bet that if I
was in Legco we would at least get the gabions and asphalt for
Westminster Low Road so it wouldn't wash away at the least
drop of rain. Because by the time I let loose a . . . a . . . ." She
turned to him. "What do you call it again in your country
when those Congressmen from the South try to talk to death
any bill that's to help the black people?"

"A filibuster."

"Yes, that's it. Well, by the time I let loose a filibuster on
those rascals in Legco they'd be only too happy to put some
asphalt on the road, if only to stop my mouth."

Then, with a thin threadbare smile she leaned close to say,
"And when I get to be a big shot and your government invites
me on a good-will tour, I'll come look you up. How's that? I'll
drop in for a visit."

"I look forward to it."

But his tone was too serious and she backed off. "No," she
said, "I doubt I'll ever come to America. Too many terrible
things go on in that place. And somebody seeing the two of us
together might make some nasty remark. We'd see the ugly
thoughts in their eyes. I know what these white people give,
you know. I got to know them only too well those years in
England. No, we wouldn't do there.

"Maybe," she mused aloud to herself, "it's only in a place
like Bournehills, someplace the world has turned its back on

and even God's forgotten, that we could have met and gotten on so well together, been such good friends.

"But not in that damn place you're from!" she broke out, anger splintering the sunlight in her eyes. "Where they treat the black people so badly, the very ones who made the bloody country rich in the first place; a place where, oh, God," she cried softly, "you read in the newspaper sometime back how they bombed a church killing four little girls the age of my daughter; and where, every time you look around, they're warring against some poor, half-hungry country somewhere in the world . . ."

"Merle," he said. "Merle."

"Yes, I know." She nodded wearily. "There's no use my upsetting myself. Such thoughts, as Lear said, lead only to madness. Oh!" She again uttered the soft cry, but differently this time as she was caught by a memory. "I loved that old king nobody wanted around anymore. I used to read that play over and over again as a girl. He was an almshouse child like myself.

"You're to promise me something," she said with sudden urgency.

"Of course."

"Not to leave here till I do," she said. "Because if you go before me I just might not make it on the plane. With all my guff I'm really a coward, you know. Scared. Why I might never have gotten around to buying this ticket had not for you. I wonder if you realize that?"

"And have you any idea what you've been for me? Done for me?"

"Yes," she said promptly. "I've let you know you don't fail everyone."

"Oh, Merle." And in that gesture of obeisance he had seen others pay her, he brought his lips to rest briefly on her cheek, and then down on the dark hand lying on the chair arm.

"You don't know it," she said over his bowed head, "but I started to come and see you any number of times these past three weeks. I just wanted to come and sit quietly with you, the way you did with me that time I took in so badly over Cane Vale. One night I even drove as far as Cleaver's, but lost my nerve and turned back. I was afraid you didn't want to see anybody."

"How I wish you had come," he said, lifting his head. "Or I had come to you. I wanted to. It was all I could do some days not to get in the car and drive down. In the midst of everything I was feeling about Harriet I wanted to see you. . . ." He numbly shook his head, remembering how he had sat in the hotel room mourning Harriet and wanting Merle, his grief and desire one.

"How much are they charging you at the place you're staying in town?" she asked abruptly, with a hint of a smile that was both playful and sad.

"Why do you ask?"

"Just tell me."

He told her.

"Those thieves!"

"You think it's too much?"

"Too much! It's far too much! Why you could have all this"— her wave took in the decaying guesthouse behind her, the listing veranda upon which they were sitting, the perennially sorrowing sea out front—"for half that amount."

"But they have lights and hot water," he said, entering into the joke.

"Yes, but they don't have Merle."

He smiled wanly for the first time. "You have a point."

"We have," she said very quietly, "these few days before I leave." And as quietly he nodded.

She left a week from that Saturday. And with the exception of Saul, whom she asked at the last minute not to come, it seemed the whole of Spiretown accompanied her to the airport. Dressed in their town clothes, the women with their faces powdered near-white, the childrens' arms and legs shiny with Vaseline, they crowded into the Bournehills bus and into the few trucks and vans in the village. Some even pooled their money and hired taxis from town. Merle was in Saul's small English Ford, seated in front between Allen, who was driving, and Leesy Walkes in her austere white dress, her hand clutching the window ledge in profound distrust of the car. Carrington and two other older women rode in back.

The cavalcade set off down the main road, the car with Merle in the lead. Saul, standing to one side, caught a final glimpse of her as the Ford passed. Silent, painfully tense, she was staring straight ahead. Her gaze was trained so intently on the road, she failed to notice the hands raise to her in the traditional salute along the way. She had, it was clear, already left Bournehills—at least for the time being, and her eyes, her mind were fixed on other scenes, other faces, on all that awaited her.

And she was not taking the usual route to Africa, first flying north to London and then down. Instead, she was going south to Trinidad, then on to Recife in Brazil. And from Recife, where the great arm of the hemisphere reaches out toward the massive shoulder of Africa as though yearning to be joined to it again, as it had been in the beginning, she would fly to Dakar and, from there across the continent to Kampala.

BIBLIOGRAPHIC NOTE

"The Making of a Writer: From the Poets in the Kitchen." *New York Times Book Review*, 9 January 1983.

"The Valley Between." *The Contemporary Reader*, August 1954.

"Brooklyn." *Soul Clap Hands and Sing.* New York: Atheneum Publishers, 1961; Chatham, N.J.: The Chatham Bookseller, 1971.

"Barbados." *Soul Clap Hands and Sing.* New York: Atheneum Publishers, 1961; Chatham, N.J.: The Chatham Bookseller, 1971.

"Reena." *Harper's Magazine*, October 1962.

"To Da-duh, In Memoriam." *New World Magazine*, 1967.

"Merle." Adapted from *The Chosen Place, The Timeless People.* New York: Harcourt Brace Jovanovich, Inc., 1969; London: Longman Group Ltd., 1970; New York: Avon, 1976.

The Feminist Press offers alternatives in education and in literature. Founded in 1970, this non-profit, tax-exempt educational and publishing organization works to eliminate sexual stereotypes in books and schools and to provide literature with a broad vision of human potential. The publishing program includes reprints of important works by women, feminist biographies of women, and nonsexist children's books. Curricular materials, bibliographies, directories, and a quarterly journal provide information and support for students and teachers of women's studies. In-service projects help to transform teaching methods and curricula. Through publications and projects, The Feminist Press contributes to the rediscovery of the history of women and the emergence of a more humane society.

FEMINIST CLASSICS FROM
THE FEMINIST PRESS

Antoinette Brown Blackwell: A Biography by Elizabeth Cazden. $9.95
paper.

Between Mothers and Daughters: Stories Across a Generation. Edited
by Susan Koppelman $8.95 paper.

Brown Girl, Brownstones, a novel by Paule Marshall. Afterword by
Mary Helen Washington. $7.95 paper.

Cassandra, by Florence Nightingale. Introduction by Myra Stark.
Epilogue by Cynthia Macdonald. $3.50 paper.

The Convert, a novel by Elizabeth Robins. Introduction by Jane Marcus.
$6.95 paper.

Daughter of Earth, a novel by Agnes Smedley. Afterword by Paul
Lauter. $6.95 paper.

The Female Spectator, Edited by Mary R. Mahl and Helen Koon. $8.95
paper.

Guardian Angel and Other Stories, by Margery Latimer. Afterwords by
Louis Kampf, Meridel Le Sueur, and Nancy Loughridge. $7.95
paper.

*I Love Myself When I Am Laughing . . . And then Again When I Am
Looking Mean and Impressive,* by Zora Neale Hurston. Edited
by Alice Walker with an introduction by Mary Helen
Washington. $9.95 paper.

Käthe Kollwitz. Woman and Artist, by Martha Kearns. $7.95 paper.

Life in the Iron Mills, by Rebecca Harding Davis. Biographical
interpretation by Tillie Olsen. $4.95 paper.

The Living Is Easy, a novel by Dorothy West. Afterword by Adelaide M.
Cromwell. $6.95 paper.

The Maimie Papers. Edited by Ruth Rosen and Sue Davidson.
Introduction by Ruth Rosen. $11.95 paper.

The Other Women: Stories of Two Women and a Man. Edited by Susan Koppelman. $8.95 paper.

Portraits of Chinese Women in Revolution, by Agnes Smedley. Edited with an introduction by Jan MacKinnon and Steve MacKinnon and an afterword by Florence Howe. $5.95 paper.

Reena and Other Stories by Paule Marshall. $8.95 paper.

Ripening: Selected Work, 1927–1980, by Meridel Le Sueur. Edited with an introduction by Elaine Hedges. $8.95 paper.

The Silent Partner, a novel by Elizabeth Stuart Phelps. Afterword by Mari Jo Buhle and Florence Howe. $6.95 paper.

These Modern Women: Autobiographical Essays from the Twenties. Edited with an introduction by Elaine Showalter. $4.95 paper.

The Unpossessed, a novel of the thirties, by Tess Slesinger. Introduction by Alice Kessler-Harris and Paul Lauter and afterword by Janet Sharistanian. $7.95 paper.

Weeds, a novel by Edith Summers Kelley. Afterword by Charlotte Goodman. $6.95 paper.

The Woman and the Myth: Margaret Fuller's Life and Writings, by Bell Gale Chevigny. $8.95 paper.

The Yellow Wallpaper, by Charlotte Perkins Gilman. Afterword by Elaine Hedges. $2.95 paper.

OTHER TITLES FROM
THE FEMINIST PRESS

Black Foremothers: Three Lives, by Dorothy Sterling. $6.95 paper.
But Some of Us Are Brave: Black Women's Studies. Edited by Gloria T.
   Hull, Patricia Bell Scott, and Barbara Smith. $9.95 paper.
Complaints and Disorders: The Sexual Politics of Sickness, by Barbara
   Ehrenreich and Deirdre English. $3.95 paper.
The Cross-Cultural Study of Women. Edited by Mary I. Edwards and
   Margot Duley Morrow. $8.95 paper.
Dialogue on Difference. Edited by Florence Howe. $8.95 paper.
Everywoman's Guide to Colleges and Universities. Edited by Florence
   Howe, Suzanne Howard, and Mary Jo Boehm Strauss. $12.95
   paper.
Household and Kin: Families in Flux, by Amy Swerdlow *et al.* $6.95
   paper.
How to Get Money for Research, by Mary Rubin and the Business and
   Professional Women's Foundation. Forward by Mariam
   Chamberlain. $5.95 paper.
In Her Own Image: Women Working in the Arts. Edited with an
   introduction by Elaine Hedges and Ingrid Wendt. $8.95 paper.
Las Mujeres: Conversations from a Hispanic Community, by Nan
   Elsasser, Kyle MacKenzie, and Yvonne Tixier y Vigil. $6.95
   paper.
Lesbian Studies: Present and Future. Edited by Margaret Cruikshank.
   $8.95 paper.
Moving the Mountain: Women Working for Social Change, by Ellen
   Cantarow with Susan Gushee O'Malley and Sharon Hartman
   Strom. $6.95 paper.
Out of the Bleachers: Writings on Women and Sport. Edited with an
   introduction by Stephanie L. Twin. $7.95 paper.
Reconstructing American Literature: Courses, Syllabi, Issues. Edited
   by Paul Lauter. $10.95 paper.

Salt of the Earth, screenplay by Michael Wilson with historical
     commentary by Deborah Silverton Rosenfelt. $5.95 paper.
The Sex-Role Cycle: Socialization from Infancy to Old Age, by Nancy
     Romer. $6.95 paper.
Witches, Midwives, and Nurses: A History of Women Healers, by
     Barbara Ehrenreich and Deirdre English. $3.95 paper.
With These Hands: Women Working on the Land. Edited with an
     introduction by Joan M. Jenson. $8.95 paper.
Woman's "True" Profession: Voices from the History of Teaching.
     Edited with an introduction by Nancy Hoffman. $8.95 paper.
Women Have Always Worked: A Historical Overview, by Alice Kessler-
     Harris. $6.95 paper.
Women Working: An Anthology of Stories and Poems. Edited with an
     introduction by Nancy Hoffman and Florence Howe. $7.95
     paper.
Women's Studies in Italy, by Laura Balbo and Yasmine Ergas. A
     Women's Studies International Monograph. $5.95 paper.

For free catalog, write to: The Feminist Press, Box 334, Old Westbury,
NY 11568.

Individual book orders: Include $1.50 postage and handling for one
book and 50¢ for each additional book. Send orders to The Feminist
Press, P.O. Box 1654, Hagerstown, MD 21741.
To order using MasterCard or Visa call: (800) 638-3030.

Library, school, and trade book orders: Call (800) 242-7737 or write
to Harper & Row Publishers, Inc., % Order Services Department,
Keystone Industrial Park, Scranton, PA 18512.